PRAISE FOR
LILITH SAINTCROW

"Simply put, Saintcrow doesn't f*** around."

— CHUCK WENDIG, AUTHOR
OF *WANDERERS,* ON *AFTERWAR*

"Incredibly timely, well written and important.... A testament to Saintcrow's skill."

— *LOS ANGELES TIMES* ON *AFTERWAR*

"A true faery story, creepy and heroic by turns. Love and hope and a touch of *Midsummer Night's Dream.* I could not put it down."

— PATRICIA BRIGGS, AUTHOR OF THE MERCY
THOMPSON SERIES ON *TRAILER PARK FAE*

"Painfully honest, beautifully strange, and absolutely worth your time. Lilith Saintcrow is at the top of her game. Don't miss this."

— SEANAN MCGUIRE, AUTHOR OF THE
WAYWARD CHILDREN SERIES ON *TRAILER
PARK FAE*

"Lilith Saintcrow spins an incredibly imaginative and delicious tale with vivid language and a story you will not be able to put down. I loved every minute!"—

— DARYNDA JONES ON TRAILER PARK FAE

"Honestly, I wish I'd written it."

— CHUCK WENDIG ON TRAILER PARK FAE

"Unique, twisted, lovely, and raw. Just fabulous."

— FAITH HUNTER ON TRAILER PARK FAE

DAYWALKER'S LEMAN

DAYWALKER'S LEMAN
TALES OF THE SANGUINANT
BOOK I

LILITH SAINTCROW

For M. S., who gets all the jokes.

CHAPTER 1

Everything went according to plan until Bea actually drove the stake into the monster's heart.

Sneaking in with the catering crew was smooth as warm butter, using the right bathroom on the fifth floor to change was no problem. Even fixing her hair to cover the top end of the stake and touching up her makeup was no hassle, though it caused a moment of mourning when she dumped the supplies. A necessary pang, since she couldn't be weighed down, but it was *such* a nice color kit.

The red dress—low neckline, cap sleeves, tailored to hide the stake down her spine, strings of red crystals hanging in rows to match the Roaring Twenties costume theme—did its job, and the monster had zeroed in on her just exactly as Beatrice Dunlevy had hoped.

Even getting the monster alone was almost revoltingly easy. Bea had been so doggedly unobtrusive for over four long years, it was a relief to slip into something pretty and the resultant self-confidence had a near-magical effect.

Maybe it wasn't precisely 'near'. After all, the world held Mothmen, little green men, and bloodsucking monsters like the one collapsed under her in a mirrored elevator. Why not magic as well?

"That was for Jared," she whispered, just as she had in so many dreams. No feeling of vengeful triumph, just simple nausea because the stake had gone in with the firm, crunching sound of biting a very crisp apple. All her practice in the meat-packing plant paid off, though she did have to brace both feet against the elevator wall, cracking one of the mirrors.

The monster—all six-foot-something of lean, sandy-haired fiendishness masquerading as a reclusive businessman—obligingly collapsed, and truth be told she hadn't been entirely ready for complete success.

Bea had expected a blood fountain, a baring of fangs, a screaming hiss or puff of dust like in the movies or the stories circulating on tightly controlled dark-web forums. Something, *anything* other than the monster just...sprawled akimbo, reflected endlessly on polished glass. A soft mechanical chime sounded, the doors finished closing, and she had to reach the panel in time because getting caught in a box with a dead body was *not* in the plan.

Despite all the evidence her brother and Don had collected, Beatrice was suddenly, terribly unsure if she'd killed an actual monster. Which would mean she'd murdered a human being, an entirely different ethical dilemma.

Don't panic. Stick to the goddamn plan. A cold, calm voice spoke up inside her head, and as usual, it sounded like so much like Jare she flinched. The motion rolled her off the monster's body, her hip hitting blue industrial carpet hard enough to bruise; she was scattering red crystal beads everywhere.

Cop forensics were going to have a field day with that.

Come on, Bebe. You had a good plan and executed the biggest chunk. Freeze now and it's all over.

Her shoulder hit mirrored wall just under the buttons, another impact hard enough to hurt through a fluffy cotton padding of shock, and she used it as leverage to get numb feet underneath her. For a moment she'd been certain the monster was going to shake off the stake and bite her, drain her like a juice box, and her extremities weren't entirely sure how that had *not* happened.

"Right kind of wood after all," she heard someone whisper. The cracked, singsong little voice was her own, and she would be able to laugh about that later, how all the arguing over what the stake should be made out of had landed on the proper choice. Considering it had only happened after Bea literally threw up her hands and told Don to just flip a fucking coin, get whatever, she wasn't the one with the fucking folklore fetish.

Besides, I'm stronger than I look. She blindly muscled her way to standing, peered at the panel, and punched the roof access button. A private box, going all the way up to the top floor where she suspected 'Chris Everly' had a penthouse, given how the blueprints they'd been able to get their hands on were arranged.

So much research was useless until it came time for one tiny, critical detail to save your ass. The elevator began to rise.

Bea gingerly braced one red Saratrava stiletto heel between the monster's legs; he'd really fallen in the best way possible, and his arm had somehow ended up underneath her stupid head so she didn't get a concussion from banging the floor. All in all, she was luckier than she had ever thought possible, and maybe all the bad stuff before was so this particular moment would pay off? That was an interesting philosophical—

Ohshit did he twitch?

"Jesus!" Her shoulder hit the wall again, *hard*; she slid down, landing on one knee with a fresh deep crimson-purple flare of ignored pain. Her heart wouldn't stop pounding. She finally decided he wasn't moving, it was only the elevator's motion and her eyes playing tricks.

Criminals got jumpy after a murder; she could now confirm monster hunters did as well.

Another pleasant mechanical ding, the elevator just doing its job, and the doors opened with a businesslike whoosh. Bending over to tug the monster's legs straight was unpleasant since it made the rest of the body rock slightly, but the limbs were still supple and the longer she could put this box out of commission, the better. Lead time to escape was a priority—were there cameras up here? Didn't matter, she was undoubtedly captured on a few, getting *into* the elevator with 'Chris Everly'. Still, so far as she and Don could tell there weren't any electronic eyes in the private lift, and that was a bonus.

Now she had to get out of the building with a minimum of evidence. Bea staggered from the square of golden light spilling onto the roof, Saratravas making soft sweet sounds, bead-strings swaying. Frigid October wind moaned between HVAC hoods and other hunched metal shapes; this high up the rush of air was probably constant even on calm days.

At least it wasn't raining. Yet.

If 'Chris Everly' wasn't a monster, what kind of guy would bring what he thought was a completely drunk stranger all the way up to his penthouse? Sure, she'd flirted him into it, but that wasn't an excuse. Bea was well within her rights even if he was just a date-raping piece of shit. When they arrested her, she could claim both insanity *and* self-defense, especially if a defense lawyer would use the footage from Jared's house. *Your Honor, my client had reason to believe the victim was a vampire.*

A brand-new legal precedent; she'd go down in history.

You know he's not human. The evidence was incontrovertible— the property records, the pictures, the yellowing newsprint Don and Jared had pulled up when researching 'Everly', the records from the monster's previous lives—always rich, always strange, the whole Chicago thing, disappearing after a bloody mass murder—and to top it all off, the security footage from just outside the stable.

After Jared's death Don was more than convinced, though Bea was pretty sure he never thought she'd actually go through with this part of the plan.

The wind was a wall of knives. Teeth chattering, she groped along concrete facing, her dyed-black hair doing its level best to cover her face. The two silver clips were long gone—had she dropped them in the elevator?

Don't care. Keep moving. Bea's fingertips found a vertical metal handle. She yanked with terrific strength, absurdly afraid that this next-to-last part of the plan had somehow gone wrong, and nearly went flat on her ass when the fire door opened easily.

Unlocked after all, because monthly inspections were due any day now. Another case of Beatrice paying attention to minutiae other people considered boring, though there was nobody nearby to be amazed at her halfass criminal prowess.

The learning curves for supervillains and monster hunters were no doubt steeply parallel. Bea choked on a small, forlorn laugh. No matter what else, she'd accomplished this much. Her brother was avenged and she'd removed a great evil from the world.

Hadn't she?

The stairwell was dark as the grave and cold as fuck, though she was distinctly relieved to get out of the wind. Bea's palms slipped on chilly metal banister as she felt her way down, so feverish the thought of crouching to rest her forehead against it sounded wonderful.

"Keep moving," she mumbled, echoing Jared's voice in her head. "Just keep moving, that's the thing."

The stake had gone in cleanly. All the way through, though? Or could you just wiggle it into the pericardium and that was good enough? The ribs were the bitch, really. She could make a little song about that—a blues number, a lone guitar giving a chop or two behind her while she wailed about practice sending big sharpened dowels into sides of half-frozen beef.

You must have done it right. Maybe he'll poof once the sun rises—does that door face east? Worry about that later.

Descent took far longer than she ever could have imagined, the lightless well full of murmuring echoes. Bea counted stairs and landings as best she could, feeling along the wall side of every turn with her right foot. Eventually she nearly tripped over the backpack, and the thought that she might break her own fool neck falling in the darkness was so grimly hilarious she crouched, clinging to the banister, and broke into a fit of sobbing laughter which did not echo only because she buried her mouth in the crook of her elbow, muffling the sound.

She'd practiced changing with her eyes closed, but it was a different thing entirely to perform while shivering, listening to the wind rattling a fire door several flights above, and expecting at any moment the blare of alarms—or worse.

You're half-naked in a stairwell after murdering something that looks like a man, dare I ask what could be worse?

"Easy, you smug sonofabitch," Bea whispered. "That door opening."

The trouble was having to know stinking little green men in loincloths and centuries-old bloodsuckers with dark eyes, sandy hair, and a penchant for three-piece suits existed. Once those became facts, all sorts of other things started to sound plausible, from Sasquatch to aliens, Hookhand to staircases in the woods. Bea buttoned her jeans and let out a shaky sigh of relief. Her knee stung—she'd scraped it somehow, either in landing on the elevator floor or tripping over a monster's legs.

Really, the way the guy dressed was painful. Too young to be so retro, though if you didn't know he was a bloodsucking monster she supposed it would have been kind of charming *except* for that haircut. Even the conversation had been nearly flawless—he was a helluva flirt, though with a laughably East Coast prep-boy accent, and Bea had been surprised at her own wisecracks, the lingering eye contact.

Her college friends would be proud; Sami and Felicia had given her endless lessons in how attractive self-confidence could be, how she didn't have to shoot herself in the foot by assuming no guy would ever want Jared Dunlevy's silly little sister. She'd done both her former besties proud, catching a monster's eye, pretending to be fascinated, reeling him in.

All while the cold iron of hatred burned her chest and her heart triphammered, seeing that unmistakable profile again. Even if she hadn't glimpsed him crouching over Jared's body in person, she'd gone over the footage from the camera mounted on that post outside the old deteriorating stable so often his face was burned into memory. He was a little different in living color, but that just made it easier to pretend, to play the game.

Girl, you're one hell of an actress. He bought it...a little too well, but he bought it.

That was the problem. It had gone without a hitch, almost as if he understood the plan. Every conversational turn, every shy smile, every half-simulated gulp of domestic white wine served because the pre-Halloween party was for business networking instead of real fun, all had been perfectly answered. Like a well-rehearsed dance number, as a matter of fact.

She tied the hightop black sneakers by touch, stuffed the Saratravas into the backpack atop the crumpled dress, and followed them with the bra. If she was going to be arrested or chased down the stairs by an angry bloodsucking thing, she would at least die unconstrained.

Get moving. She closed her eyes, breathed a quick *Hail Mary fulla grace* like Don was always doing, and stood, settling backpack straps over her shoulders. Her thumb found a black plastic switch; she pressed it, heard the click loud and clear. When she opened one eye, cautiously, she found the flashlight worked.

The single small beam of light did wonders for her nerves. Even the far-above fire door's rattling was somehow muted, driven back by the fact that she could now see painted concrete, the rough antislip strips on the stairs, the dimensions of the landing she had thankfully not fallen off.

You've got this far, you're doing great. Let's go.

"Get this circus rolling," she whispered, and set off down the stairs. Only forty more floors to go, then she could slip along a short corridor to another set of elevators—for internal business-tenant travel, and bound to be far less luxurious than the one she'd allowed herself to be 'persuaded' into when the monster said, *Would you like to see something special?*

Well, she had. In that the night was an unqualified success, *amen and yes ma'am*, as Jared might say.

Bea gasped in great jagged gulps, black rubber waterproof flashlight in one aching fist, her other hand wanting to convulsively squeeze the banister every few steps. She forced her fingertips to glide, counted to twenty over and over inside her head, and struggled to get her lungs under control so she wouldn't be wheezing in the next elevator she had to endure. She felt a *lot* like throwing up.

But it was done.

CHAPTER 2

It had been many a mortal year since Lukas had felt even mildly...interested. The hawthorn stake was a thing of beauty, and she had applied it with no little force. He eased the sharpened, oiled point free, inhaling softly as ageless flesh reknit, and hoped he had done well.

It would have been churlish to laugh, either at the quaintness of the method or the obvious enthusiasm with which she deployed it. The lady wished him dead; very well, he would temporarily play along. A gift only he could grant, the first of many.

He had almost lost control as her body slithered free of his, almost moved to protest the separation. Had listened to her fumbling passage, held himself perfectly still and unbreathing, body and mind both in abeyance. A hunter's trick, waiting until certain of prey's temporary escape.

Anticipating a reunion was bittersweet, for she would be startled at his reappearance—possibly enough to do herself some harm. Yet it had to happen soon, for he was uneasy at letting her wander. She had achieved her goal, very well.

But why? And with such an intriguing weapon as well.

The lift's floor was scattered with red crystal beads fallen from her dress. Lukas brushed at his suit—what little claret escaped him had been reabsorbed, but the damage to his shirt was highly visible. Good thing it was a costume fête; he wondered if he should return. The mortals would be drunk enough not to question his reappearance and he could feed very nearly at will.

His true teeth stirred vaguely at the thought, but the scent of her still filled his nose. He found he did not wish to drink, save from a certain perfumed chalice bearing that marvelous bouquet.

Why on earth do you want to kill me, beautiful girl? He had been enjoying himself far too much, Lukas supposed. Such purity of purpose was rare, no matter the era. More than that, he was very nearly drunk with joy.

A leman, walking fearlessly up to him as if she knew her own impossibility, her own absolute pricelessness. He had never thought to find such a creature before calcification took him; he had settled for staving off the numbing with single-minded determination.

Lukas let the elevator doors close, touched the button for his private floor, and patted at his pockets. There was his main phone, in its rubbery shockproof casing. Such ingenious toys they had these days.

"Sir?" Wrenfeldt's dry, careful voice through the ear-speaker, very welcome indeed.

"The lady in the red dress does not appear to be a journalist. She's somewhere in the building—see that her exit is unob-structed, step up surveillance." Lukas considered the beads, decided to simply leave them be. He could track her, certainly, but it was sometimes best to allow hounds a bit of hunt as well. "I want to know where she goes, what she does. Half-hourly reports."

"Yes, sir." Naturally this was well within a dogsbody's capa-bilities, especially with a well-oiled edifice of money and safety to aid the operation.

One wasn't supposed to call them *dogsbody* anymore; to

Lukas's mind the currently fashionable term was far more insulting, so he chose to use neither aloud. "Protection is the first priority, invisibility is only slightly behind." He paused. On the other end of the line, Wrenfeldt waited, perhaps mystified but ready to obey. "I am going by the suite for a spare suit."

"Shall I…?"

"No, simply watch the lovely little rabbit run, my friend." He really should have personally investigated her, instead of accepting Wrenfeldt's assumption that a pesky mortal journalist was suspicious enough to believe something about the demimonde. A capital error—how many others had he committed? For the first time in centuries, Lukas was entirely, wholly awake. "And take some nourishment, if you have not in the past few hours."

"Yes, sir." A smothered chuckle—so, Wrenfeldt was in a droll mood tonight.

Well, there were worse things. "Have the guest quarters in the penthouse cleared by dawn. Leave only the bedstead." It was hardly a saferoom—the windows, for one thing—but could hold a mortal prize for a few days while Lukas made other arrangements. He considered further playing at absent-mindedness; it was often part of good rule, and served a double purpose. Underlings were not allowed to know of the ossification, though no doubt many dogsbodies had suspicions.

Any ageless creature tended to become hidebound.

"Yes, sir. Of course." Wrenfeldt now sounded very nearly startled.

"And make certain the linens are clean." *Because she is coming home.* He allowed himself a single moment of reeling, impossible emotion at the thought, staring at tiny red glitters caught in blue carpet. Even deadened sanguinant senses were far, far more acute than mortal, but he had been peering through a thickening grey veil for quite some time now. His fangs still longed to burst free—had she harmed herself in the fall? No, he had cushioned her from the worst of it; still, she might be stiff and scraped. "That will be all, Wren."

"Very good, sir." Still an amused edge to the words.

Lukas quelled the urge to fidget, another rarity. Of course one had to move like mortals while in their company, only lapsing into uncanny stillness when entirely safe of witness, but he was almost…

No. It was official, he was *eager* for the next event. Truly this was a time of miracles, and him still alive to feel wonder. The shackles were falling from his senses, and a thin thread of delicious scent stayed with him. There was only the faintest hint from a single carmine drop swelling upon her wounded knee, but it was more than enough.

He had a blood trail, now.

CHAPTER 3

As soon as Bea got inside the warehouse, she realized Don had been pacing. He'd also put coffee on, as if he expected to wait until dawn.

Her knees went gooshy as she flicked the deadbolts, and the shivers wouldn't go away even though it was perfectly warm due to the living quarters' space heaters. A double row of crucifixes arranged along the wall stared agonizingly at her; even if walking past a wall of Roman tortures gave her the willies it was still necessary to believe in *something*.

Besides, Don put those up, and he'd been at occult and conspiracy theorizing for a lot longer than her—almost longer than Jared. A little bit of Catholic couldn't hurt, might even help, why not? Maybe that was the only reason she'd gotten this far. She redid the salt line just inside the door, carefully pouring a little extra from the blue Morton's canister set on the otherwise empty shoe rack.

"Jesus *Christ*." A shadow swelled in the archway to the kitchenette, birthing a lanky man with chestnut hair sticking up anyhow since he'd no doubt run his hands through it several times since returning to the warehouse after dropoff. "You okay? You weren't at the rendezvous, I thought...shit. How...what..."

"Will you relax?" Suddenly Bea's knees were fine again, the consciousness of having to pull herself together for another person grabbing like a big friendly python squeeze. "It went great, by the way."

Don Bertram looked like a teenager again when he cocked his head like that. "Define *great*."

"Can I at least pee and have some of the coffee I'm smelling?" Bea's kidneys had been working overtime, probably due to adrenaline and other happy bloodstream chemicals. "In that order?"

"Were you followed?"

"*Please*, Don." She was clear of tails, or at least she should be—why would anyone follow a skinny, unassuming woman in jeans, a pale pink baseball hat, and a shapeless green fatigue jacket? She'd looped around between two different trains and several short bus jaunts, hopping aimlessly, watching her own backwash with every trick she'd read about and practiced for four years.

Nothing out of the ordinary. She felt invisible gazes on her all the time, sure, but that was just overactive imagination, which she was prone to in any case and besides, had to happen when you started hunting down monsters. There were enough problems in the world without her getting paranoid.

"Well?" Don hopped from one loosely laced combat boot to the other; he really did look like an excited stork. "I'd ask how exactly it went down, but..."

"That's a dress I'll never wear again, let's put it that way." She'd gotten rid of the gown, bra, and the poor beautiful shoes separately in different dumpsters; her backpack was empty save for the flashlight, a protein bar wrapper, and a few lonely red beads. Bea hobbled for the kitchenette, deciding her bladder, though complaining, could continue its service for a few more minutes. "And the world is now down exactly one bloodsucker."

"You..." He stopped halfway to the coffeepot, turning on his heels with faint rubbery squeaks. "No shit. You actually staked Christopher Everly?"

"The thing calling itself Everly, yeah." Her knees and bruised shoulder all throbbed, her kidneys ached, and the gurgle of Don's coffeepot alternated between the most comforting sound in the world and a reminder of the worst day of her life.

She'd been doing the bills when Jared took the dog out, and he'd groused about wanting to wait for a pot of java to finish brewing.

Don's fidgeting stilled. "What happened?"

"Uh." Bea stripped black knit gloves, rubbed her hands together. An excessively casual glance—she couldn't see any blood, but she'd love to wash anyway. With *very* hot water. "Well, he fell down."

"What? He didn't *poof*?"

"There was no *poof*-ing. Unless he turns to dust at daybreak now that he's dead." She would have to check the blueprints to figure out if that elevator faced east. If it didn't, hopefully everyone would assume it was out of service or that the 'businessman' didn't want guests after taking a girl upstairs, and the body wouldn't be discovered for a while.

"Will he?" Now Don stared at her, expectantly, eyebrows up and mouth slightly open. "They're supposed to poof, even the ones who stroll around in daylight."

"*You're* the expert, Donny. I've only just killed my first one and I'm not feeling too good about it, all right?" Bea shouldered him aside and stopped at the sink, twisting the water on savagely. Liquid handsoap claimed to be chamomile-scented; she'd picked it up two weeks ago on a grocery run, turning over the map of the Everly building inside her head, thinking about contingencies, wondering if crashing the costume party was an inspired good idea or the rumblings of insanity. "I staked him, he fell right down. *Boom*." A splatter of swiftly warming water; she grabbed the nail brush and went to work lathering up.

"Shit." Don had gone the color of old cheese. "Wow. So…"

"So now you go back to chopping cars and doing your podcast, I hit the road." She might have to hide for the rest of her life, especially if they were both utterly crazy and she'd murdered a human being. "That was always the plan."

"Yeah." Was it relief, crossing his lean, beaky face? He'd stubbled up quite a bit in the past few days, and the look suited him, though Callie might not like getting scraped. "It was. But, Bebe…"

That was Jared's name for me, not yours. At least he didn't mispronounce it—*Bee-tris* instead of *Bay-ah-tris*—like strangers and spam calls did. Not that she'd had a phone for years, now. "Look, if you're ever linked to the whole thing, a good defense lawyer will get you an insanity plea, or mild conspiracy-to-commit at most. You didn't do anything really legally actionable, I made sure that was all me."

"Jesus." He stared like she'd grown another head. "You…you really fucking…goddammit, Bea. You are the craziest bitch I ever came across."

"Not like it's a surprise, you've known me since grade school." She was scrubbing hard enough to hurt, Bea realized, and put the foaming nail brush down with an effort. Rinsing her hands only made them sting more, and she couldn't be sure she'd gotten every bit of blood off.

Though 'Everly' hadn't leaked much at all. Just dropped, like a switched-off toy. The crunching sound when the stake went in, so different than a side of beef.

At least I don't have to work in meatpacking ever again. Though she might get desperate, who knew? The smell was awful, the cleanup worse. Still, it was comparatively decent money, long hours, and men generally left you alone when you were swinging one of those knives. Especially if you gave them a long, silent look every once in a while.

She'd hated every minute, even if it turned her into a vegetarian and gave her perfect practice. Maybe she should've cut the monster up afterward, scattered the pieces?

What, like you're gonna revisit the scene of the crime? No use in dwelling on the past, Bebe. Jare had always said that last bit, usually when she had to come up with a practical plan to get them both out of trouble.

"Things are different now," Don said, giving her one of those looks she knew so well, and oh God but she had been hoping to avoid this.

Be a bitch. It's not hard. "Why? You've suddenly developed feelings for your dead best friend's kid sister? Come on, Donny-boy. You and Callie are a better couple anyway, she at least feeds you." *Waters you and turns you towards the sun, too. All with that long-suffering look, but she never leaves.*

Sometimes Bea caught herself wishing Callie would find a less passive boyfriend just to teach Don a lesson. But it wasn't any of her business. She'd been here to use his contacts and knowledge, ruthlessly trading on the fact that he'd been her brother's bestie. She could vanish now, and he would be safe—*if* he could refrain from telling the world about this entire endeavor on his goddamn podcast.

His listeners numbered only in the single dozen; the man was an encyclopedia of weird folklore and urban legend, sure, but with the on-air personality of a potato. He funded the whole affair with a variety of slightly criminal enterprises, most of which were logistical support for mid-level mobsters.

All in all he and Bea hadn't done too badly, and he'd come through with the catering job like a champ.

He deserved at least some gratitude. Bea twisted the water off, grabbed for the already-damp sunflower towel hanging from a suction cup hook on the side of the fridge. Looked like Don had been doing a little Lady Macbeth action of his own tonight.

Doing 'favors' for the local syndicates was a dirty business. So was monster-hunting. She was hoping 'Everly's' connections with higher-echelon criminal elements didn't mean they would dig very hard into his demise—or disappearance, if sunlight took care of that surprisingly muscle-dense body.

"Will you at least have a cup of coffee with me?" Bless his heart, Don sounded nearly wistful. "It's not like I'm stupid. The car's gassed up and ready, like you asked for."

Bea turned, leaning on the counter, and tried a smile. It felt strange, as if her face would crack, but after a moment the sensation passed and the grin became genuine. "Clean plates and a full tank?"

"If I go to prison it'll be for something like that, I guess. Instead of accessory to vampire murder."

Bea almost winced. She didn't like the V-word, it sounded hokey. *Monster* was much better, and universally applicable to anything going bump in the night. "Only if you keep doing it. Let it be like that one summer at band camp."

"Did Jare ever tell you..." He visibly decided to leave a hilarious story untold, for once. "Anyway, cup of coffee and you should have a protein bar too. You'll adrenaline crash soon."

"Yeah." She'd already scarfed one on the bus, despite a dry mouth and shaking hands. It sat uneasily in her stomach, congealed to rock, but the ballast was useful. "Maybe I'll hit up a drive-thru on the way out of town, get some fries." *Not a burger. I know how those are made.* "I'm gonna go get changed, and I suggest you burn what I'm wearing now."

"Just not with you standing up in it." His Adam's-apple bobbed as he swallowed, rapidly. "Right?"

"Your comic timing needs work," Bea told him, straight-faced, and headed for the bathroom.

Four hours later a strengthless yellow winter sun rose over the city, filling her rearview mirror with wavering gold as wet, heavily patched freeway hummed under the tires. The Nissan was a piece-of-shit sedan, paid for with the last cash remaining from her inheritance, but its innards were good, its wheels were new, and there was a whole American continent to lose herself in.

She could work retail or under the table, she could stay off the radar...and any big city had to have a monster or two in its depths. Her first one was dealt with, so she had a notch on her belt. Now she knew how to slip around after dark, the proper questions to ask in headshops, grungy dive bars, and occult stores. She knew the difference between the marks of wannabe satanists, garden-variety obscene graffiti, and other weird bull-shit; she knew how to find the one librarian in every system who holds the key to shelves where certain books are kept, and how to prove bona fides to a closed online forum of monster hunters.

God, how Jared would have loved this shit. Growing up, he and Don bonded over Art Bell, alien abduction stories, and creepy films, going on Sasquatch hikes and exchanging weird comic books. The property on Noll Mountain, paid for with Jare's half of their parents' bequest plus the advance for his first book, was supposed to be part of his growing literary mystique. *A writer has to have a good setting, little sis.*

Honestly Bea wasn't sure what kind of setting living out in the Vermont sticks was, but Jared was the smart sibling. Her own niche was in practicality, getting the bills paid on time, dishes washed, laundry done. There was no need to really shine with ol' Jare around, and after her first year of college she'd been grateful for that one eternal fact.

She could do without the pressure. Just look at the way her hands were shaking.

"The place was dirt-cheap," she muttered, and cast around for sunglasses. No dice, so she flipped the rearview mirror; dawn was a goddamn headache. *That was why he bought it, you think you can get that kind of acreage for a good price without something wrong? Something in those hills, there were stories going back at least thirty years. He walked right into his goddamn research material.*

Bea reached for the radio, hoping for some classic rock; she shouldn't be mulling these things in the morning. They were nighttime thoughts, and she was running short on sleep and patience both. Gordon Lightfoot crackled softly through terrible, staticky speakers, and that was good enough. Just over the state line, she could stop in a slightly above-fleabag motel and get some rest.

It was the last part of the plan. After that she had to sit down with a notebook and do some thinking. *Plotting*, Jare would call it, waggling his blond eyebrows. *Gotta have a plot, Bebe.*

Well, she'd plotted her way into murdering a monster. You could even view it as having done some good in the world, so now she'd probably be run over by a bus on her way to fleeing the country. Or get into an embarrassingly short car chase, ending with a fiery crash and go figure, she wasn't wearing clean panties.

Laundry had become far less of a priority, the last few weeks.

At least the news would probably not bother covering a police-assisted vehicular fatality, and might not even mention the disappearance of a reclusive businessman, even if he was a big wheel in behind-the-scenes money. When Don got going about how the government and corporations didn't want anyone to know about the monsters, she had to admit he was unquestionably correct. *He* thought it was a conspiracy; Bea was of the opinion that people simply didn't want to think or hear about unpleasant things.

Not that anyone ever asked her opinion, except sometimes Jared.

That was the thing she missed most, being able to *talk* to someone. Jare thought she was a plodding pedestrian thinker at best, sure, but her brother also couldn't find his own socks in the morning and had gotten himself killed by a bloodsucking monster after months of daily torment by said monster's little green henchmen.

It was a day for helplessly going over things she didn't want to admit had happened, apparently. Revenge was supposed to feel better than this. She was supposed to feel triumphant, goddammit, but it was just like losing her virginity during senior year of high school—minus the damp embarrassment of having to deal with the condom, at least. A big fat pile of disappointment.

Ghosts had better be real, Jare. You'd better be watching this, and reconsidering some of your life choices.

Not like it mattered anymore.

Twenty miles over the state line she spotted a likely motel. Shortly afterward a woman with ID proclaiming her Sarah Monroe checked in, closed and locked the door to room 23, and headed straight for the bathroom to test the shower.

The pressure wasn't good but the soap was fresh and water unequivocally hot, so that was when Beatrice finally cried. Snot and tears both disappeared down the drain—when she was little she used to wonder if poo felt sad after it was flushed, bobbing up and down in stinking darkness—so she could be the tough bitch again tomorrow.

She even tried a bit of singing, since Jared always swore it showed courage and confidence. It was going great until her voice broke and she realized she was warbling about wasting away in Margaritaville, one of Jare's particular favorites.

Which shut her up but good.

A puff of steam as she opened the door to the room, attempting to fasten an incredibly flimsy towel around her chest, and Bea's body froze before she realized both the bedside lamp and the slightly more anemic version wired to the dresser were burning brightly at max.

I just turned the bedside one on, didn't I?

"Hello." The monster she'd killed sat on the double bed, wearing a grey three-piece suit and leaning forward, elbows on his knees, a familiar wooden stake dangling loosely in his right hand.

CHAPTER 4

OF ALL THE THINGS HE COULD HAVE SAID, IT WAS BY FAR THE MOST banal, and an unfamiliar urge to explain rose in Lukas's throat. "Might I ask why you stabbed me?"

Now he sounded prim, not at all how he had intended this meeting to begin or proceed. Small talk had become increasingly difficult as he fought calcification, but Lukas had thought himself still possessed of more suavity than *this*.

Still, one did not find a leman every day. Or every century, or every millennia; the exceeding value was commensurate with their rarity.

The girl stared at him, her lush mouth slightly open. He remembered the green eyes, but not exactly how their irises were threaded with gold; he remembered the black dye on her hair but not the exact shape of her much-paler eyebrows. Each new discovery was a padded hammer striking his own pulse. Droplets gemmed her shoulders, the beautiful arch of her throat, her bare, shimmerpale legs. She'd twisted her freshly washed hair into one thin, too-small towel and wore another; he could only be grateful for whatever cost-cutting had decreed these precise dimensions to the cloth clinging upon such pleasing curves.

As if he needed any confirmation, an unaccustomed light-headedness swallowed Lukas whole. The scent was heavy, carried on steam, and a sharp wave of desire rose from the base of his spine, tingling all through arms and legs, sinking a claw into his lower belly.

He was actually, painfully erect. When had *that* last happened? Wonderment hit him once more—a real, living, unbonded leman in close proximity. He was careful to stay very still.

It wouldn't do to startle her. And he did not wish the first time to be in this dispirited little lodging-house room, even if she were entirely tantalizing.

Especially as the towel began to slip.

That is...very distracting. Water clinging to fresh, damp mortal skin, those lips quivering slightly, the instant leap of a sweet-singing heartbeat, and that fascinating, mouthwatering, absolutely addictive aroma. The totality, the gestalt was overwhelming in the extreme.

Just how calcified had he been? It crept up upon one, certainly, and—

"*FUCK!*" the lady screamed, whipping the towel free of her splendid litheness as the cloth upon her hair tumbled free, since she also rather violently lunged aside. Lukas watched, curious and appreciative, as her hands flickered, twisting sodden fabric, and her shoulder clipped a corner of the closet obtruding rather awfully next to the bathroom door.

He was tempted to use the whispering speed, an initiating twitch denied. The movement was instinctive, a precursor to blinking across empty air and thrusting his hand between mortal flesh and the unforgiving wall. But that might...alarm her. Even dogsbodies sometimes had difficulty witnessing sanguinant reflexes, requiring a moment of calm attention to soothe atavistic prey-response.

She didn't appear to notice the impact, and the vivid scrape on her knee was another taunting reminder. Spotting her across the event space—Wrenfeldt had alerted him the moment she intruded with the catering staff—Lukas had planned on simply beguiling the journalist who was so interested in his business; according to Wren, her surveillance was very nearly professional enough to escape the notice of overlapping security details.

He had thought her a new variety of paparazzi, but once Lukas caught her scent the entire configuration of the universe had shifted a few crucial degrees. Now he must consider her perhaps impelled by a variety of instinct, as some leman were rumored to have actively sought out pairing.

It was a lovely thought. Was she as fascinated as her suitor?

In any case, she had tried to ram a stake through his heart. He could appreciate that manner of feral affection, Lukas supposed; leman were so very uncommon, even a crazed specimen too precious to disregard or let wander.

She froze, her throat working convulsively. Rosy nipples, an enchanting freckle high on her left breast begging for attention, glistening water-jewels caught in her secret curls, her adorable knees trembling, dainty bare toes incongruous against cheap dun carpet—Lukas enjoyed the view a great deal, but all the same it would be easier if she…

He was in the thrall now, sanguinant responding to that maddening, wonderful fragrance, and his control rendered somewhat imperfect. He very much wanted the first time to be rather more comfortable, not to mention aesthetically pleasing, than this.

"Come on." A small, defiant whisper. She lifted the twisted, sodden towel in what could perhaps be considered a threatening manner.

Was she actually inviting him? The pleasure of that prospect was overwhelming. "You would like me to approach you, then? I though I was doing passably well before…" He lifted the stake slightly, watched her gaze flicker to touch it, veer away. A brief light flared in those stunning eyes before fading, a shiver passing through her lovely frame.

Perhaps she was cold? It was winter, and she mortal for at least a short while longer.

"Creep." The lady was breathing rather rapidly now, which caused her to shudder even more fetchingly. "Who takes a drunk date upstairs like that, huh?"

"I thought you might not like others to hear our conversation. You've been watching me for some time, after all." *What do you want, hm? Tell me quickly.*

It was quite something to feel impatience again. To feel at all, really—now he was aware how agonizingly close he had brushed to numb, suffocating true-death.

Her pupils swelled. She was alarmingly pale, really, and her marvelous warm musk held a tantalizing edge of raw yellow fear. The contrast only underscored its unrelenting deliciousness.

"You killed my brother." Did she think she was screaming? Her throat must be terribly constricted, and even this soft, strangled whisper was charming. "I'll bet you don't even remember, do you."

What? He had to halt and replay the last few moments inside his head, just to be certain he had heard correctly. Another rarity —to be so distracted, his control fraying as it had not since he was new in the Blood, a mere fledgling upon the steppe. *I haven't drained anyone to death in at least a century. Is it business, someone who lost a company? I would have remembered her face, if it were.*

Not to mention that scent.

"Your...brother?" Calm puzzlement was best, he decided. "What was his name, then? Perhaps we may start there."

Apparently she did not wish to do so. Instead, the sublime creature who had staked him let out a rusty scream and lurched into motion, moving with a great deal of swift efficiency for a mortal. It was like seeing a colt astagger in a spring meadow; Lukas lost himself in further appreciation for a moment before rising, catching her wrist, and spinning her slight weight on its axis. Locking his other arm about her naked waist was perfectly wonderful, though the warm living weight clasped tightly to his own much more durable frame strained his control again.

The stake hit the carpet.

She was so *soft*. Pitching back and forth, kicking, hissing like a maddened cat, his new leman also loosed a torrent of surprisingly foul modern obscenities, delivered in a husky, enraged contralto which slid a pleasant rasp down Lukas's back.

If she did not cease moving so beautifully against his entire front, he was going to do something truly regrettable. He wanted the initial encounter performed correctly; a leman could indeed be broken, but that was hardly ideal. They were traditionally given the Gift immediately upon meeting, and perhaps he should do so.

Ruthlessness was generally best. His arms tightened, his mouth next to her perfect, shell-like ear, and a whisper left him as the psychic pressure of *quietus* clamped upon a helpless mortal.

"Shh, kitten." He waited as her struggles slowed, inhaling deeply. Filling his lungs with the fragrance of an unbonded leman was contradictory, both powerfully soothing and tightening his every bloodstring. His groin throbbed painfully. "I am an animal, yes. But a considerate one; do not make this difficult for yourself."

She held out far longer than other, physically stronger mortals; the stubbornness was charming. Finally, though, his prize went limp, breathing deep, her eyelids fluttering dreamily.

So, so tempting. Yet she was also so very thin, ribs and the high sweet curves of her hipbones clearly visible; fresh bruises lingered on fine, tender skin so pale the blue map of her veins begged for tracing with reverent fingertips.

He had to move very carefully to lay her upon the bed, and could not take more than small furtive glances at the *tableau* while dressing her. He should have brought something of more quality, but the time constraint of chasing down the most valuable prey of his entire existence precluded any such nicety.

A cursory search found her only luggage, a backpack, contained a change of clothes—no red dress, just denim trousers, T-shirt, a cheap dark-blue jumper. Indigo, a fitting color for such a prize, though no longer so expensive. He could not bother with the underclothes, since his hands were shaking imperceptibly and the thrall-throes mounting with each moment spent breathing her in.

Yet he did pause while working a battered trainer onto her perfect, sock-clad left foot. Lukas's head cocked, a faint brush at the edge of sensitive hearing not quite breaking the spell of his new, somnolent leman.

How very odd. The attention was certainly malignant, but was it coincidence? This was a far too urban an area for such things. Had someone nearby angered the little excrescences? Lukas slipped the phone from his jacket's breast pocket; at least he had changed his cloth and possibly made a good first impression.

Wearing the same blood-spattered suit she had attempted to murder him in might have given the wrong idea.

Wrenfeldt answered on the second ring, perhaps a little nervous at his master's uncharacteristic behavior. "Yes, sir?"

"Bring the car around." Lukas had to enunciate carefully, for his fangs were achingly sensitive. "You have a bit of cold iron upon your person, yes?" Any dogsbody was taught such elementary self-defense against no few of the demimonde's weaker annoyances.

"Nail in my pocket, sir. As usual."

"Good." Lukas found himself staring at her hand, laid gently against cheap pink counterpane. Her pretty fingers were slack, delicate knuckles wounded perhaps in the elevator; he would have to exercise far more care with this most enthusiastic play-mate. The slight sound of invisible interest remained, a watchful, lingering bane.

No matter. She was removed from the mortal world now; very few even in the demimonde's higher reaches would interfere with a daywalker's leman. He scooped up the stake, since perhaps it held some sentimental value. Had she attempted this with others of his kind?

No, for she would have been taken. Even a fledgling, rendered drunk by the scent, would seek to hold such a gift.

A few minutes later Room 23 was empty, outer door firmly closed, the light in the bathroom burning. Steam still hung in the air, slowly settle-swirling.

CHAPTER 5

After the jolt of terror and strange swimming delirium, there was soft cloudy nothingness. Bea was vaguely aware of low voices, of movement, but it was all very far away. Nothing mattered.

Am I dead?

It wasn't entirely out of the question. You heard all sorts of hideous things while attempting to break into the monster-hunting scene. Sasquatch, bloodsuckers, werewolves, the little green men with their shark-teeth and clinging fog, the staircases in the woods, Mothman, phantom hitchhikers, alien abductions all had their places in folklore or urban legend, but nobody wanted to see the autopsy reports or wobbly, staticky recordings. Nobody cared to think about the missing-persons statistics, or hear the truly goosebump-inducing proof of *anything* truly weird.

Most people simply liked to leave a movie theater after a good scare, the itch scratched and catharsis achieved. Anything truly wiggy tended to make sane human beings run in the opposite direction, plus most folks refused to testify about really inexplicable happenings. Ignoring was safer, consigning the events to neat little mental boxes only unlocked by booze or late-night AM radio ravings.

It was very bright. Bea blinked several times, waiting for the glare to resolve into shapes and colors. Or maybe she was in heaven?

That's really unlikely.

No, her eyes were just fucked up. A few moments of further blinking and rubbing revealed, of all things, a bedroom.

At least, the room *had* a bed. A real gollywhopping four-poster number, spires of lovingly polished hardwood carved into tall, skinny winged figures. The sheets were pale blue and felt high threadcount, aquamarine and navy cotton blankets, a vast indigo velvet comforter that had to be filled with down. And she could tell the sheets were good because her legs were bare, along with her shoulders.

Jesus Christ. Bea was, in fact, wearing a white silken spaghetti-strap slip which fit, sure, but was *definitely* not hers.

A matching nightstand of the same heavy dark wood, though thankfully not carved with...were they angels? Cherubs were different, fat little flying babies; these figures seemed vaguely female. The floor was lighter hardwood, also polished, and the rest of the very large room was empty, nothing but space and light. One wall was made of glass, and that plus two skylights explained the glare. A grey winter afternoon lingered just outside, and at first the glitters were pretty until she realized it was a view of downtown laid underneath a middle-grade skyscraper. Not the shortest, not the tallest, but situated nicely for a good view.

What the hell?

Her legs were a bit unsteady, the floor cool but not quite cold. Bea crept to the window cautiously, and when she realized she was looking at familiar terrain her heart leapt into her throat before embarking on a wild can-can beat through all the rest of her.

Okay, think. You came out of the shower and the monster was sitting on the bed. Or was this a very intense nightmare? The slippery feeling of being unmoored in reality was familiar, and she hated it.

She'd thought Jared was just being dramatic, or at worst getting up his own ass like he used to when they were kids, always swearing he *saw* things. Well, so did she, but didn't advertise it; that was a surefire way to make people notice an overactive imagination and mock you into the ground.

Or they'd call the men in the white coats, and she loved her brother too much to consider him fully insane. Or so she thought now, after the fact. At the time she'd been super annoyed at having to drop everything in her own life, *again*, because Jared was having a crisis.

Bea raised her right hand, stared at her fingers for a moment. Then she reached to pinch her left arm with a savage twist, hissing as her eyelids chopped bright, directionless winter light into manageable strobe-chunks.

Okay. Not dreaming. Maybe dead, we'll see.

The city sprawled lazily under her perch. There was the Loop in the distance, there the main eastern freeway—yes, looking over downtown from the west. There were the four park blocks, trees both leafless and evergreen crowding walkways and water features turned off for the winter.

Oh, shit. Is this…

It was the Everly building. Had to be. There was the bar across the multiple one-way lanes of Third Street, at the corner where it joined Kinski Avenue. She'd sat near the window watching the facade of this granite-sheathed heap, off and on, for at least three months. Different hours, different conditions, she'd pored over any available blueprints of the place as well, and scoured social media for inside views.

She had to be on a super high floor. Maybe…maybe even the penthouse?

Oh, crap. Not good.

Two doors, one to a bathroom. *Hold that thought.* She tried the second—a double, looked like solid oak, and locked, of course. So the bathroom got its own inspection. Plain white tile, an antique cast-iron tub, a safety-glass mirror over a pedestal sink, no cabinet. The towels were white as well, big and fluffy, stacked on a thick glass shelf instead of hanging on a metal bar.

And an actual bidet. Wow. It didn't do her any goddamn good, since there wasn't a toothbrush or anything resembling personal care items. A shell-shaped bar of soap the exact color of a robin's egg sat in a sculpted sink-divot. There was no cup, but she gingerly tried a few palmfuls of cold water and decided that was okay.

She might starve to death locked in here, but at least she'd be hydrated.

The quiet was eerie. Bea found warm air issuing from recessed, disguised ceiling vents—too far up for any monkey business, even if she could drag the heavy nightstand over to stand on. Skylights did say top floor, unless there was some kind of architectural wizardry going on. Bea squeezed her eyes shut, calling up the blueprints—why hadn't she done a more thorough internal study? She'd been so focused on escape routes after the staking.

Clearly you didn't get it all the way through. So you're back to square one, or maybe even further back since now he knows you're gunning for him. How in God's name had the monster found her? Did he sniff her out like a bloodhound, ha ha, very funny, or had she been followed despite using every trick in the book to clear her backtrail?

Was Don all right?

"Oh, God," she whispered, creeping to crouch next to the bed, hands sealed over her ears to shut out the deep, soft quiet. Breaking a window would be useless—even with all those blankets, she couldn't hope to climb down more than a floor or so.

If she managed to crack high-altitude glass and tossed a nightstand out, would that attract some attention? Maybe she could use it as a diversion, and escape in a silk slip?

The skirt was far too short, for God's sake, though the material was heavy, soft, and clearly expensive. "Should've had a gun," she mumbled, and leaned against the bed's flank. At least the piece of furniture was solid and reassuring, complete in its own weirdness.

There was plenty of space underneath, antiseptically clean as the rest of this prison. Not a single dust bunny, which was weird as fuck but that was where she lived now, for however much longer. Should she hide? The only other place possible was in the bathtub, and that was just asking to be...what? Trapped like a fish in a barrel? She already was, for Chrissake.

Why hadn't he simply killed her? That would have been preferable, but maybe she'd pissed him off and the monster was going to watch while his short, swollen-headed green henchmen drove another Dunlevy insane? Peering through the filthy dust-lensed window at her brother's mangled body in the ancient, falling-down stable, the huge sopping-wet patch of blood, the screams swelling in her throat but unable to break free because of the bastard crouching over what used to be Jare, her Jare...

A click, a slight brushing, both loud in the stillness. Bea was almost too busy hyperventilating to hear, but her body sensed something—a breath of movement, a flickering shadow—and she scrambled under the bed, barking her knees painfully, whapping both elbows for good measure, plus hitting her head on something structural.

Ow. Ow, ow, ow. She got to the middle of the bed's shadow, its entire bulk crouching protectively over a single very scared mouse, and her nose was full because her eyes had started leaking. The nips and gnawing of small aches had tuned up; her body was an orchestra of ignored pain.

She was glad she'd used the toilet. Maybe running water alerted him the prisoner was up and moving around? She should've looked for camera lenses in the ceiling, goddammit.

Black wingtips, polished to a mirror sheen. The soles were funny, thicker than ordinary dress shoes. Almost tactical; Bea's left hand clamped over her mouth, though her nose was too stuffed to breathe through.

Be vewy vewy quiet, Jared whispered inside her head. *He's hunting Bebes.*

The shoes waited, neither tapping nor shifting with boredom. Finally they moved again, separating and turning, before a knee clad in grey Italian wool touched the floor.

The monster stretched out alongside the bed, peering into the cavern of her precarious safety. If he could shake off a stake to the chest and find her almost eight hours later, maybe he could pick the bed up and throw it, too? Everyone agreed bloodsuckers were hella strong to begin with, accumulating force with age.

He smiled, propping his cheek on a bent arm. His eyes were just as dark as they had been last night, and the rest of him was the same as well. Sandy-dark hair, over-conservative cut, long nose, a thin mouth, wide cheekbones. Only the suit had changed —now he wore vest and trousers, two out of three pieces, and his dress shirt's crisp white sleeves were rolled up, exposing forearms corded with muscle. A silver watch gleamed on his left wrist, winking cheerfully at her.

They regarded each other for a few heartbeats. Bea cowered under the bed and tried to think of something, *anything* practical or useful.

And coming up completely empty.

"Good afternoon," the monster said. The same pleasant tone as yesterday night—or this morning. Had she been knocked out overnight? What day was it? "Would you like a drink? Alcohol, or fruit juice perhaps?" A small pause, his expression turning grave. "Ah. That might give the wrong impression. Are you hungry? You must be."

The shudders fused, locking Bea in place. Don swore you could hypnotize chickens, and that's what she felt like—a bird staring at the cat about to eat it, a rabbit just before the hawk's claws punctured furry hide and something small was swept, dying, into the sky.

The smile returned, a natural, easy expression. The human camouflage was exceptional, but when he stilled again it was like being slapped in the face. An essential *difference* was visible in that unmoving, and every fear-soaked nerve Bea possessed knew a predator when it sensed one.

"Your identification says Sarah Monroe, but that is clearly false." Did he sound *cajoling*, of all things? "Will you at least grant me your name?"

Why? You don't remember killing Jare, we humans must all blur together for you bloodsuckers. Bea kept her hand over her mouth. The urge to scream rose to a sharp peak, and she wasn't sure she could contain it.

"Very well." The monster's smile didn't diminish, but his eyelids went to half-mast. "I do apologize, I had a meeting and thought you would sleep until nightfall. Stubborn, very stubborn. I will wait until you feel like speaking."

He settled back into that uncanny stillness. Bea tried once more to come up with a response to this turn of events, settled for being grateful she hadn't peed herself with terror.

Yet.

No clock in this big bare room, no tick-tocks to measure out time's subjective flow. Only the silence, the faint whooshing of warmed air. Was he breathing? Even with his eyes mostly closed he was clearly watching her, an unblinking catlike gaze tangling with her own.

No sir, this chicken won't be hypnotized. She hurriedly looked away, but that was a mistake too because the thought that he might suddenly slither under the bed and she would miss the initial warning motion was almost as horrifying as ditty-bopping through a bathroom door to find a monster in her motel room.

It took work to peel her hand away from her mouth. Her vision blurred; why did she fucking *cry* every time she was scared?

Her teeth wanted to chatter. It took two tries to form recognizable words. "Just kill me," she croaked. "I staked you, fair enough. Just get it over with."

His eyes closed fully, then slowly opened. "Why would I do that?"

Bea might have thought he was honestly baffled. His little green henchman had played with her brother for months, though, slowly breaking down Jare's sanity. So she wasn't fooled one bit. "You want to torture me? Nothing could be worse than what you've already done. Just *kill* me."

"I have...wronged you, somehow." Thoughtfully, as if this was the first he'd heard of a distressing factory accident. He probably used that expression a lot in meetings; 'Chris Everly' was known to be exceptionally low-key. *Reclusive* was the word they used—even the local tabloids had better subjects to lie breathlessly about. "Tell me, so I may make amends."

Oh, you sonofabitch. Cats played with their food, bloodsuckers were probably the same way. It might even be natural behavior in the ecology of the weird. Sasquatches were sometimes thought to be Neanderthals or ape-related, too; there were some questions whether the aliens abducting folks were extraterrestrial or extradimensional. Her brain kept leaping from question to question, all of life's imponderables now likely to remain unsolved.

Because she would be dead soon, that much was certain. The plan had completely, utterly, undeniably failed. The worst thing was feeling ridiculous, hiding half-naked under a bed. She couldn't decide if this was an occupational hazard she should have been aware of, or just a sign of her own ineptitude.

Beatrice Dunlevy did not mind being frightened so much, but humiliation was another thing entirely.

Another long silence. She glared at him, though her heart hammered so hard his shadow swelled and wavered, blocking winter daylight on that side of the bed. Through it all he regarded her somberly, and even had the gall to look expectant.

Fine. Jare swore I could irritate anyone to murder, I'm about to do my level best. "You'd rather hand me over to your little green henchmen, right? Let them dissect me alive. Do you watch, and record it for later? Snuff films—is that how you get your kicks? The internet must be a playground for guys like you."

His teeth were very white; the smile was broad and apparently genuine. The shape of his jaw had shifted slightly, and the fangs were no cheap special effect or magic dentistry. They looked completely natural, as if blunt human chompers were the deviation.

Oh god, they were true. All the stories are true. She was completely numb, Bea realized, too worn out to be more afraid. Maybe her fear gauge had busted.

"You're very frightened." Calm and even, as if discussing the weather, enunciating carefully because those multiple fangs looked *extremely* sharp. "I do not want to use the *quietus* again, but I will if I must. Would you prefer that?"

Maybe he's more into psychological torture? She was probably going completely cuckoo; Bea wouldn't rule it out. "Am I supposed to know what that means? Why don't you give me my stake back and we can go for round two, huh? Or maybe you should call a few of your little green baldies to make it even."

It sounded like whiny, terrified bravado instead of a movie-star prisoner of war daring his captors, not at all what she'd intended.

"Sorry." A slight shake of his head, as the fangs retracted, morphing into regular, very white human teeth. "My control is not quite what it could be, and your attempt at aggressiveness is adorable. Or, no, they say *cute* now, don't they? Cute."

"Yeah, well, your Ivy League accent sucks and you're too young to dress the way you do." *What the fuck am I really saying?* It was both exhilarating and unnerving to have all her brain-mouth filters removed. Why had she ever watered down what she thought? What was the goddamn point?

If she'd been more aggressive, as the monster called it, she might have saved Jare. Bullied him out of that house, off that stinking mountain, and back into the sane, rational world she wished very badly she had never left.

"I know." Gravely, as if in serious agreement. "Fortunately, you will teach me better."

"What the fuck?" For a moment Bea was unsure if she'd said or just thought the words, but yes, it was official, she was past caring and everything was spilling right out of her mouth, willy-nilly. "Look, either kill me or let me go. I'm really tired of all this."

"Ah. Well, neither of those choices are acceptable, little leman."

What the fuck do lemons have to do with anything? "This is the part where you tell me how you're going to torture me, right? Fine, if it gets you excited. Go ahead and talk."

"This is extremely interesting, but your knee is bleeding."

Bea froze. Was it true? She couldn't tell, she was literally numb from the neck down, and who knew the cliché had a core of absolute truth? All the same, it was not the sort of thing you wanted to hear a bloodsucking fangmonster say. "God, ohGod," she whispered, unable to even glance at her own body because if she looked away he might wriggle under the bed and get her. The sudden mental images were hi-def Technicolor, and she knew, with miserable certainty, that she was about to start screaming and never stop.

The monster moved.

Things went blank for a moment—like a glitch while streaming music, a sudden cessation. The next thing Bea knew she was flat on her back, propped on a mound of blue pillows, blankets tucked tight as mummy bandages. The sense of constriction forced her into panicked motion; she scrambled into a crouch, the mattress giving a faint whisper as it shifted. The bed was a soft cavern, the wall of windows bright with orangeish citylight.

Nighttime. And she was...oh, Christ, she was in the Everly building.

Wrapped around the knee she'd scraped in the elevator was a bright white bandage, gauze packed solicitously against something that hurt like rugburn. It was a nice job, but looking at the pale blot caused a rush of nausea so intense she choked.

So the level beyond 'crying scared' is 'vomit scared'. Good to know.

A soft warm breeze ruffled her hair, thrilled along the slip's hem. Something loomed next to her in the darkness.

CHAPTER 6

HE HAD MOVED SLOWLY, YET MORTAL NIGHT-VISION WAS POOR indeed. His leman screamed, a rending sound of utter terror, and scrambled away with surprising speed, falling off the bed in her haste. A flurry of tender, delectable limbs, and she was on her feet.

Lukas had often witnessed mortal bodies knowing they could not fight, therefore choosing flight. The trouble was, she headed straight for the windows. She could not break the glass even with hysterical strength, but might well snap a bone or two battering against it. A small, colorful bird, driven to panic.

Another dismal beginning. He was in motion almost before realizing it, his arms closing around her once more. Her legs kept going, thrashing blindly.

If not for the soft broken sounds of distress, it would have been extremely pleasant. She sounded lost, miserable, and truly hopeless; a strange sensation filled his chest, as if she had sought to stab him again.

Heartbreak. Oh, that's lovely. Also uncomfortable, yet the sheer gorgeousness of emotion again after so long was perilously akin to a drug's swimming disorientation. Some substances could affect the claret, of course, but by and large any fledgling surviving past their first century was proof against any toxin. How much more an elder, then, and by the time one reached daywalker status, all fear of poison was long gone.

The effects were marvelous, jolts of sensation where only the slow creeping numbness of age had rested, new context and interest filling the world. Many of the old traditions around leman had become starkly clear to him in the past day or so; the protective instincts outstripped even mating urges, and both paled beside sheer wonder.

But what did you do with a mortal in such terror? Normal methods—a cervical snap, draining them with a few quick gulps while the *quietus* squeezed, or panic-herding them into a river— did not apply. The back of her head bumped his chin, and she could very well cause herself injury against his greater durability as well.

Nothing for it, then. He had tried, but as so often, ruthlessness was best. His true teeth were already out, throb-aching, a burst of change agents filling his mouth with hot liquid sugar.

He had to wait for a breath as she wriggled, but the moment she flung her head back again he struck, burying primary, secondary, and lower fangs deep. She froze, sucking in a shocked gasp, and the tiny sound fused a deep, heretofore unknown circuit inside his ageless skull.

His mouth was full of nectar. The first swallow erased any previous vintage; now even the most vital of mortals held only silty sludge in their veins—nutritious enough, to be sure, and he would be hunting for two. Without a leman, the only temporary relief from calcification was an old-fashioned feast, with all the danger that implied. Yet now the risk of bloodcraze was gone, the glut-urge with it, and though the control necessary to drink without killing was a reflex burned below conscious thought, he would never be tempted again.

Not in that direction, at least. Now the only thing he craved shuddered in his arms, attempting to fight the *quietus* with surprising strength. He was also tempted to bite a little harder, but there was a line between lesson and cruelty. The first was necessary for fledglings or dogsbodies; the second unthinkable for a leman.

Sweet. So sweet. They were to be prized, these succulent bulwarks against calcification. Pampered, indulged—and held, with any and every strength a sanguinant could muster. He also found he lacked even the passing, reflexive desire for savagery.

So he took a last shallow, lingering swallow, enjoying the deep honeyed burn, and let his teeth shift back to bluntness. Licked along the punctures, cleaning throughly, and the healing substances from different glands turned his lips numb for a moment. Traces of her spread through his veins, a maze of firefly lights.

Now her fragrance held a hint of burning. No doubt the largest component was pure surpassing fear, but another note was his own scent, spreading in thin tendrils from the bite until the message was unmistakable.

Do not touch. Or, even more starkly, *Mine.*

"Be still," he murmured in her ear. Her blood lingered on his tongue, and with it a rush of chaotic emotion. Raw, untinctured terror, defiance, a concentrated sorrow too large for words, all bursting like a pierced artery. "It is done. A little sting, and all is well. Everything else will be much more pleasant, I promise."

She coughed weakly, hanging in his grasp. Had he taken too much? Barely a taste...but she was so thin, and mortal besides.

"At least tell me your name," he continued, soft, so softly. Sooner or later, she would—or the searches already deployed, electronic and otherwise, would turn something up. She had covered her tracks rather thoroughly, though he was keeping in reserve the questioning of a certain petty criminal she had apparently purchased services from. Tracking her from the fellow's warehouse-hideout had been enjoyable but not, in the end, very complex.

Still, if she kept to the fiction of Sarah Monroe, unraveling the lie would be an interesting game. Lukas allowed his arms to loosen, bent to place her gingerly upon dainty feet. The nightdress was far too long, though its clinging—like the towel—left very little to be imagined.

He did not straighten, did not let go entirely. A delicate situation, requiring concentration and care; it was a joy to have something so deliciously complicated to absorb.

"You...bit me?" Dazed, slightly slurred, the words blurring together beautifully. She did have a lovely voice, even roughened from terrified cries. "Oh my fucking god you *bit* me."

"I will do much more than that." A heady promise, indeed. "Be reasonable, little leman. I can and will explain whatever you like, but you must help me."

"Help you? Help *you*?" At least she was hissing instead of screaming; she sounded positively incensed. If this were her anger, he could not wait to see other states of excitement. "You murdering vampire *fuck*, you think I'm going to help you do anything, I swear to God—"

"Do not," he interrupted sharply, "make an oath you do not intend to keep." For a dogsbody, the command would be more than enough; it was an effort to think of what else to add, what a leman might require. "Please."

The single taste of her did not entirely satisfy. As distracting as her physical closeness now was the mounting, blurring buzz of desire, and her shivering infected him as well.

She had slept in this room; the bed was saturated with that intoxicating fragrance. He was in the thrall very badly now, and hoped she would not move.

At least, some fading restraint in him hoped that. The rest was longing for her to take a single step, attempt escape. Any move would break the stasis, and he would give in.

"If you're going to kill me, do it now." Brittle defiance, at what had to be the extreme edge of her courage. Were all leman so determined? "Because I'm going to avenge my brother, even if you do turn me into a bloodbag slave."

I never did that, not even in Venizia. There was no need, and besides, at that point he had already been rather jaded. "I have no desire to break you, little leman."

She was silent for a few ragged breaths, shaking, safely caged. "So, what?" A forlorn question, expecting nothing good. "What are you going to do?"

"Take you to bed," he heard himself say, in a soft, musing tone. "Unless you would prefer to discuss matters without moving, so I may regain some control. Whatever you choose."

"Oh, now the monster wants to *discuss*. Why not pop my head off like a Pez dispenser? Did I not stake you hard enough?"

"The blow would not have entered without help." He was doing rather well, Lukas thought. His shaking was nearly imperceptible, and though the end was assured he could postpone true fulfillment some short while. "I thought it polite to let you try, in order to discern what precisely you desired." The blur-buzzing intensified pleasantly, a hum settled in reinforced, thicker sanguinant bones.

The Gift would render her far stronger and more robust, but she would never match an elder's strength or speed, let alone his. An edge to be thankful for, since he suspected this leman would swiftly learn how to use his absolute craving to gain anything she wished.

Another wonderful prospect.

"I want you dead." Fierce and clear. "You murdered my brother, you bastard, and *I want you dead*."

And of course, since it was clearly not in her nature to be reasonable, she attempted to elbow him rather viciously, twisting in his arms and scraping her bare heel down his shin as well. She had trained in some manner of self-defense; had he been mortal she might have had a chance.

Finally. The leash snapped, and Lukas found himself momentarily free.

CHAPTER 7

Her wrists were trapped, stretched overhead and crushed against pillows. The bed was suddenly *there*, sinking underneath her, without any intervening time or movement. A yelp of surprise was effectively smothered by a feverish, insistent mouth fastening on her own, and not only was she flat on her back again but he had somehow settled between her legs. He still had his clothes on; wool burned against her inner thighs and Bea panicked afresh, her jaw cramping as she bit savagely. The monster made a muffled noise, not precisely of pain, and a metallic taste coated her tongue.

Oh, Christ, no. Maybe it was adrenaline, or some kind of alcohol lingering on his breath? But it was hot, and smeared on her lips; after a moment the taste shifted. She tried her best not to swallow but an odd, unfamiliar sweetness trickled down the back of her throat—and he kept going, pressing into the bite.

Then he stilled.

Her jaw loosened; he eased away, his cheek resting against hers, hatefully intimate. The shadow over her exhaled, a long shuddering sigh.

Did he…

A very respectable hard-on was still jammed against her,

straining at a few thin layers of cloth. She couldn't tell if he'd fired early, and devoutly hoped so. He had her wrists in one hand, and despite carefully bracing his weight the difference between this monster and a human male was more than apparent. Either that or he just seemed a lot heavier, since she couldn't goddamn *move.*

"My intentions must be clear enough," the monster purred. "One last time, kitten, would you prefer calm discussion or shall I free myself of all restraint? I have no objection to this being our first."

What. In the hell. "Get off me." As if she had any hope of making him do so. It wasn't so much the terrible, inhuman strength as the control—she was now absolutely certain this guy could wrestle Superman to a draw. But so far, he had avoided hurting her, and that was almost more frightening than being beaten up.

No. That was wrong. It was *exponentially* more terrifying.

"I don't think I can," he said, thoughtfully. "Not yet. Keep talking, if you prefer. You could at least tell me your name."

"Why? You're not Christopher Everly, even if you somehow bribed someone into giving you a birth certificate. But that was easy, I bet. You've got enough to pay for anything you want, right? I swear, I could forgive you for being an actual blood-sucker but it turns out you're a business leech. It's disgusting." If she could just get him so angry he killed her, rather than...anything else, that would be best, right?

Normally, Bea would say she wanted to live. But being held down like this was enough to make her reconsider. Was whatever he had planned worse than letting those bald, gleaming, nearly naked green things slice her to bits? How could she decide?

"You have some small knowledge of the demimonde." The monster shuddered, fractionally heavier as he sank onto her. "How exactly did I kill your brother?"

The position was horribly exposed; nothing but the silk slip to save her, and that was useless. "You tried to run him off the mountain. When he wouldn't sell, you sent your nasty little green men. They nearly drove both of us insane and then you killed him." The lump in her throat would not go away, and it tasted syrup-sweet. It couldn't be blood, *his* blood, could it? "I saw you over his body. You disappeared, but there was a security camera outside the stable—" She was babbling, she didn't tell this story, she *never* told the whole thing, even to Don.

A dark, hideous relief filled her for a few heart-pounding beats. Saying things out loud made them real, but also let the terrible weight slide free of her shoulders for a single moment. "You even killed Snowball," she finished. "Who does that? Who kills *dogs*, you fucking monster? And why did you have to do that, to her...to her body? She was just a little..." *A mophead with legs,* Jare said, but he also snuck her treats and bits of cheese all the time.

"Little green..." The monster's breath warmed her hair, caressed her ear. "Ah. Wait, let me think. This was in Vermont, yes?"

It was downright insulting, how little he remembered of the worst day of her entire fucking life. He probably did this shit all the time, it was just another ho-hum Tuesday for him.

Was today Tuesday? Weeks blurred together; a monster hunter lived on her own schedule. The party was Friday night, a week before Halloween. How long had she been unconscious? Bea's knees ached. Her back arched slightly, attempting to ease the strain in her hips, and the monster actually *growled,* long and low in his throat.

Just like a big cat. The deep thrum resolved into words. "I recall more now. The house, south side of the mountain, wasn't it? Which was strange, they usually prefer the northern."

What? "So you do remember something."

"Another journalist, was he not? The young man."

Novelist, you asshole. "His name was Jared. Jared Dunlevy." *God, if I had the stake right now...*But she didn't. She'd failed at killing the monster, and now he was playing with her. Had Jare ever felt this helpless? It could drive a person right off the deep end.

"Yes, that's right. You...were there, that evening? Impossible. Unless..." He moved again, a supple wavelike motion passing down heavy muscles, before burying his nose in her tangled hair and continuing, a little muffled but easily audible. "No, I am mistaken. Quite possible, since the reek of *greiben* was strong and they are noisy in withdrawal. How strange."

"How strange." She put all the mockery she could into the words, despite the little voice in her head tentatively broaching the idea that maybe he'd just let her go, tell her not to fuck around with monsters anymore, and what would she do then? Slink away knowing she'd been too much of a coward to do what she promised at her brother's grave? Both Bea and Jare's agent Nanci had insisted he get a will drawn up, the funeral arrangements an unpleasant discussion she was squirmingly grateful for since in the end she'd been too terrified even to call the cops. "Next you're going to tell me it wasn't you, that the one-armed man did it."

"The *greiben* had only one arm? That's odd as well."

Oh, my God. "No, that's from a movie. You are just unreal, you know that?"

"I have forgotten more than most mortals ever know, Miss Dunlevy."

She almost flinched, almost asked *how did you figure out my last name,* then realized she'd said Jared's out loud. Dumbest move of the week, and she'd been doing so well up until the actual murder. Had she and Don cleared away enough traces? She'd disappeared the night her brother died; Beatrice Dunlevy didn't exist anymore. Sarah Monroe was born a few weeks later, Don getting her a fake Social Security number and enough ID to get a job, at least. "Is that enough discussion? Are you going to kill me, or have your little green bastards do it? Hurry up, I've got places to be."

The steel grip on her wrists eased, bit by bit. "Slowly," the monster said. "I am going to move very slowly, and I would suggest you stay still as possible. If you attempt self-harm or escape, I will have you immediately. Do you understand?"

Which was more chilling, the 'Chris Everly' who had flirted, chatted, and joked with her for hours at a dull-as-doornails business costume party, or this lightning-fast, overpowering being who held her down so easily? Some varieties of bloodsucker were supposed to have rules, like compulsively counting knots or flax seeds. Was that part of folklore true?

If he had rules, maybe she could survive. Somehow.

"Please." It sounded a lot like begging; Bea was past caring. The bed creaked, though neither of them had shifted. "Why don't you just kill me?"

"I did not harm your brother, I was trying to save him." The monster's shadow vanished, reappearing next to her as the mattress suddenly gave under redistributed weight.

Bea knew she wasn't supposed to move, but she couldn't help it. Her knees flew up; she spilled onto her side, curling into a tight, protective ball. She didn't even care that the monster was behind her. Her entire body had decided *nope, not doing this, peace out*.

A featherlight brush against her bare shoulder, hard fever-warm fingertips settling a thin silk strap more comfortably. Bea twitched, an undignified squeak boiling in her throat. The monster's hand drew away, and she waited for whatever would happen next.

Finally, his voice came again—very close to her ear, a maddening tickle. "When you wake, I shall have answers." Another long, slow inhale; he was sniffing her hair again, like a total creep. "But for now, little leman, I did not harm your brother. Rest."

Not fucking likely. She huddled on tangled blankets, listening intently for footsteps, for the sound of the locked door opening or closing.

Nothing. Was he still playing with her, cat at the mousehole? The instant she moved, he'd bite her again.

Or worse. Her neck didn't hurt, simply felt swollen and warm, as if wrapped in a smooth thick scarf. The trembling came in waves, and each high tide pressed more tears between her tightly closed eyelids. She lay, cramps gripping her leg or the arm under her head, and prayed for dawn.

Which was ridiculous, she'd seen 'Chris Everly' walking around in daylight with her own two eyes. Fucking confusing, except for the number of serious occult weirdos—not to mention monster hunters on the dark-web forums—who swore some bloodsuckers could do that. Plenty of the old folklore said so as well, in as close to original sources as she or Don could get.

She had unequivocal proof about a lot of things now. Fat lot of good it did her. Her breath came in short hard chuffs as she shook, hoping against hope to be ignored for as long as possible, and when she finally passed out it was a blessing.

It wasn't the first time she'd awakened in a bathtub—there had been a couple really wild college parties, back when Bea thought she was actually going to make something of herself. Best time of her life, really, out from under Jare's shadow and feeling halfway pretty.

It was, however, the first time she'd achieved consciousness in a huge cast-iron number, clutching a pillow and two blankets dragged from a giant four-poster bed.

At some point last night she had apparently headed for what her subconscious considered safer ground. Under the bed clearly hadn't worked, but that was beside the point. The slip was twisted all around, she had to rub her eyes twice before she believed anything they were telling her, and there were still no toiletries, just that pristine shell-shaped cake of blue soap.

Hollow-eyed, lank-haired, she examined the six marks on her

neck. Pale at the edges, the punctures each bore a single bright crimson dot in the middle. The upper arc was made of four holes, larger to the outside and smaller nestling inward; the remaining two had to be from the lower jaw, clamping to provide leverage.

So that's a real vampire bite. I know what one looks like now, yippee for me. When she gingerly brushed the marks with bruised fingertips a strange sensation poured down her back, causing a shiver, goosebumps, and a rollercoaster flutter in her belly.

A frosted skylight beamed gently down at the bathroom, filling the mirror with pale winter sunshine. One floor below the roof, most likely? Almost definitely the penthouse—if she found the elevator, could she get out the same way she had before? What about fire stairs?

The past few days had taken on a shimmering underwater unreality. Stress, lack of food? Or had she gone really and truly around the bend?

The soap was blueberry-scented. She washed her hands, waiting for the water to warm up; it turned close to scalding while she lathered. No nail brush, but she made it work, and it gave her a perverse satisfaction to drop a blue hand towel from the glass shelf into the sink afterward.

In any case, her hands no longer felt bloody. She'd have to take the notch off her monster hunting belt; he was definitely alive and kicking. Which was great for her conscience but now she was wondering just how badly the immediate future was going to go.

First she had to look for tools—something, *anything* she could break or splinter.

Then she'd see about that big oak double door.

CHAPTER 8

His daylight office had taken on new interest, each edge sharply delineated, the desk glowing secretively and the shelves of decorative trash alive with murmuring meaning. Walnut barrister files stood stolid sentinel, though any information in their grasp was also safely contained within his own mental halls; the faded, antique Persian rug worked with geometric designs was vivid enough to fall into.

Just how ossified had he been? Very close to the edge indeed, and the truly embarrassing thing was how he had not guessed. The muffling of physical senses and mental acuity, settling into the rigidity of a too-old beast in a modern world, had hunted him with skill and patience.

All burned away, now. No wonder leman were so prized. An eternity with these sharp sensations would barely scratch the surface of their beauty; even the painful acuity of fledgling sensation when new to the Gift paled into insignificance.

And his servants had been busily collecting what knowledge they could. "Jared Michael Dunlevy." Wrenfeldt laid the file on the desk blotter, retreating with quick mincing steps. A dogs-body knew to be cautious, especially when their master or mistress appeared thoughtful; like many very large mortals, he was surprisingly light on his feet. "Writer, two books of historical fiction. First one garnered some critical acclaim, second posthumously published. Dead four years ago, just before May Eve."

Four years. Such a short while, though nearly endless for some mortals. Lukas nodded, opening the file. A black-and-white headshot, probably taken for the lad's book covers. Yes, there was a distinct resemblance to his leman; the pale eyes, thickly lashed, the shape of the underlip, the cheekbones, the exact proportion of wave in light hair. A handsome boy, though he had not shared his sister's sheer incandescent sensitivity. "Vermont. We made more than one offer for the property, yes?"

"Several, escalating to far more than it was worth. He and one other holdout refused to sell, and I recall you said something personal was needed."

"Yes." Sometimes the *quietus* could be used to gain longer-term mortal compliance, if applied with a skilled touch. Lukas's memories were returning, hazy but distinct, as he leafed through papers—property records, a *vitae* done by a private investigator's firm, copies of the publishing contract, death certificate, a few coroner's pictures showing the immense damage wrought upon a mortal body.

And she had witnessed...what? Now Lukas remembered following the stench of *greiben* and mortal death to a ramshackle building which had once indeed been a stable, to judge by the faint tang of horse hiding in its depths. He had seen the young mortal lying in pieces upon dirt studded with ancient hay, and now that he thought of it there had indeed been another lump of white-furred flesh nearby.

Who kills dogs, you fucking monster? "Nothing about a sister here, Wren."

"That's the original file." Wrenfeldt held up another manila folder. His suit jacket flapped briefly, giving a glimpse of the shoulder holster. Mortal weaponry, useless against dangers a sanguinant could easily overpower, but camouflage and dealing with mortal authorities were by far a dogsbody's more important duties. "I went back, did some other digging. Dunlevy did have a sister, best guess is two or three years younger. She vanished that night."

Now *that* was interesting. "How thoroughly?"

"Nothing remains online, not even old social media profiles. A search in the physicals of the hospital where the brother was born turned up a birth certificate plus a few more Dunlevys, mother and father. The patriarch succumbed to liver failure when Jared was fifteen or so, dear mother to leukemia when he was twenty-four. None of the others seem viable connections."

Alone in the world, little kitten? No wonder you are so fierce. Perhaps she had removed herself from the gaze of mortal authorities before setting out for vengeance? Purity of purpose, indeed; of course leman were exceptional, but the reality was somewhat startling to behold. "Did we pay off the coroner for the young lord? It says *accidental.*"

"There was no need; it was an odd death, and they always like to bury those. The only records I could find of our lady are here." Wrenfeldt approached again, laying the second offering upon the blotter. His shoes made small pleasant leather-noises, and though he was observing proper caution there was little enough fear in his scent. "A single secondary-school yearbook, the girl and her brother both listed. Managed to find some uni transcripts as well. She attended a different establishment than young master Dunlevy—smaller, and left three credits short of her bachelor's of art in January of that year. He died late April."

Lukas used a single fingertip to open the new file. The photo was blurry from magnification, but it was unquestionably a younger version of his prize, her shoulders hunched defensively as she regarded the camera, a slight, apologetic smile caught just before it faded. Her hair was much lighter than the current black dye, her eyes wide and guileless, and he glanced over the extended college transcript.

Did very well in the humanities. Chemistry, that's an interesting choice. Dropped the same philosophy class twice, I wonder why? The sheer luxury of interest swamped him. Lukas had to pause, strangling the urge to simply rise, dismiss Wrenfeldt, and glide for the guest room. The thrall lingered behind his slow, unhurried pulse, digging into his vitals, and the texture of his clothing was unbearably irritating.

"Sir?" Wrenfeldt, tentative, rubbing at the blue shadow of stubble on one leathery cheek. Even a sanguinant's warding off of time from their trusted servants was imperfect; age sat upon poor Thomas with increasing heaviness lately. "If she's an actual hunter, there's probably a cell behind her we ought to keep an eye on. I can bring that Bertram fellow in for questioning; he went to school with the brother. They were close, it seems."

Discovering the criminal had a podcast devoted to strange occurrences and occult happenings had been highly amusing. "She may have some emotional tie to him. We'll keep that in reserve." A gift of restraint, even if it was traditionally best to free leman of all mortal encumbrances immediately. Enough room for escalation was perhaps best; a certain pressure could be deployed later, threatening a mortal she must care for.

Her possible entanglements were a difficult, unnerving thought, scraping hard against the possessive instincts. His next interaction with her had to be carefully planned.

"Yes, sir." Wrenfeldt did not bother to disguise polite disagreement. Naturally mortals did not often prevail against sanguinant—though messy fledglings and ossified elders were sometimes caught and disposed of by enraged peasants or the occasional knight.

Mortal cooperation was a powerful weapon both for and against his kind.

"No hunter's cell," he murmured. "This is highly personal. And you needn't worry for my temper, my friend. I have not felt this amused since the night we met." A good year, not least in his luck finding a dogsbody of such wit and competence.

It was a shame Wren was so temperamentally unfit for the

Gift, not to mention deeply duplicitous. No matter, his cunning served Lukas well.

"Coronation Day." Wrenfeldt's smile was faint but definitely fond. "God bless the Queen, for the devil will have his due. I do worry a bit, sir; they're beginning to call you *eccentric*."

Which meant Lukas's camouflage had been slipping. It was a wonder he'd been able to bespell her during the party—but perhaps she had been seducing *him*, planning to isolate and dispose of the creature she considered her brother's murderer.

Most puzzling. Normally the *greiben* did not do such things. His kind often hunted them for sport, and by long tradition the scurrying annoyances were barred from taking mortals, since sanguinant were rather jealous in the matter of prey. Eliminating a few clan elders and leaving certain invisible markings upon the south side of that very green, reasonably remote mountain had been sufficient to express Lukas's displeasure with what appeared a simple mistake by mindless half-fungal goblins. The mining companies had found nothing of interest and left after sinking a few shafts; now the entire mountain belonged to a maze of holding companies, safely buffered from further mortal involvement while cold iron and the deep gashes served to bind and engage *greiben* interest.

His very own holding companies, to be specific. Was that how she found him? He really should have investigated Wrenfeldt's report of a pesky journalist more thoroughly, but it was his own incompetence and in any case that particular rarity: a forgiving mistake which in the end did not matter.

How entrancing. Now he knew the *how*, but not the *why*. Little green henchmen, indeed—she assumed he controlled them, as one did mortal businesses?

Disabusing her of that notion might require proof. He was still more exercised with how, in the name of his mortal tribe's gods, he had not smelled a leman through the reek of *greiben* and mortal death. Where had she been hiding?

And what a pretty name, it suited her well. Lukas found

himself tracing the line of her chin in the yearbook picture, tasting her again. Musk and sweetness, salt and syrup, she was in his veins now.

"*Greiben* simply do not act thus without reason." It bothered him a great deal, Lukas realized. The feeling was glorious, save for its rasp against protective instincts. It would have been very easy indeed for both Dunlevys to die in that decrepit stable; now he remembered the house as well—sprawling, almost-colonial, with a wraparound porch. "But perhaps the lady knows more than she thinks. Have breakfast sent up, she must be very hungry by now."

He could attempt taming with food. It was time for another dose of change agents as well; he almost salivated at the thought. Next came another bite, and another, and at some point the actual claiming.

Anticipation, a luxurious torment.

"Yes, sir." Wrenfeldt did not quite hesitate, though his pace gave plenty of time to add another command. He sloped from the office, consigning this mystery to his master's tender attentions.

Lukas stared at the yearbook picture. Grainy, printed at a size guaranteed to lose a great deal of definition, it was still unquestionably his prize. A leisurely meal, a few explanations, and—

His ears tingled. His hearing had been dulling fraction by fraction over centuries; for a moment he thought he was simply imagining the pleasure of her company. No, there was the heartbeat he was always listening for now, the soundless song of ragged breathing he recognized almost as deeply as his own. The succulent little padding noises were her bare feet, creeping delicately doelike down the hall.

So she had tried the door, left unlocked since he was in residence. Did she think it an oversight? Still, far braver than many mortals, or she was frightened enough to risk any hazard.

How lovely. Simply keep moving, lady mine, you are almost within range. Did she recognize the dance she was inviting? He had granted fair warning, though she did not seem disposed to listen.

Pleasant anticipation halted, broken cleanly as a snapped bone. Lukas's nostrils flared slightly, and his fangs gave a hard, distinct crackle as the reek reached him.

Wet rat-rot, fungal decay, and metal.

Greiben.

CHAPTER 9

OF COURSE IT WAS A TRAP. BEA CLUTCHED THE NAVY-BLUE COTTON blanket tighter, pushed the heavy oak door open another few inches.

Outside, a softly lit hallway carpeted with thick blue pile ended at what looked like a quasi-familiar, brightly polished elevator. Was it the one she'd been in last night? Possible, but she couldn't be sure yet, since staking the monster had occupied her entire attention.

Two recesses halfway down the hall held matching floral arrangements, just imperfect enough to be real instead of artificial; also, two doors on the left, one on the right.

Not only that, but on a row of decorative iron hooks mounted to the left-hand wall hung a black blot, her backpack looking very small and shabby indeed. Bea's heart thundered, a strange light sensation filling her skull.

Oh, what the hell. Might as well go down fighting. She tried not to open the door any further than absolutely necessary for a skinny monster-hunting bitch to slip through, almost catching the blanket on an inside knob. If she could get down to the lobby, even the sheer outlandishness of wearing a makeshift toga might not matter. And she would absolutely take hypothermia outside over a monster holding her down on a bed and biting her.

If he thought she'd sit still and wait to become Lady Dracula, he had another think coming. Bea grabbed her backpack, unzipping it as her legs trembled and she sank into a crouch.

No clothes, no ID, that figured. The rolls of emergency cash were still tucked under the patented false bottom-flap, though. A few thousand in good old greenbacks, plus the switchblade with silvered flats she'd ordered from a gun shop in Pittsburgh where the bespectacled, suspenders-wearing proprietor kept a back room stocked with things like experimental ammo, crucifixes blessed by a local priest, ampoules of holy water, and other stuff guaran-goddamn-teed to work.

Beatrice had her doubts, but the knife was a comfort. And there was the rosewood box, too, opening with a click.

Silver herringbone chain, an ornate setting of curlicued metal too light to be sterling—Jare had thought titanium—holding a thumb-sized rectangular-cut emerald, alive with its own inner light against a pad of grey watered silk.

Happy birthday, Bebe.

A gaudy antique piece, all she had left. The family photo albums were probably moldering in a landfill somewhere, she'd hunted down and erased her own digital footprints, done what she could to make sure no trace of Beatrice Dunlevy ever surfaced again. Even visiting family graves was out of the question, since each time she got close to where Jared was buried the high piercing whine began, inaudible to others. Then, inevitably, the little bulbous-eyed henchmen showed up to rattle doors or peer through windows in the dead of night.

Her ears were ringing like hell at the moment, though that could just be stress. Bea fumbled with the chain's catch—if she was going to die, she'd do so wearing Jare's last gift. If she escaped, well, she could call it a lucky piece and probably get mugged for its gleam in some city far away from here.

That's a great thought, actually. Hold onto it.

She dropped the emerald down the front of her halfass blanket toga, settled the backpack straps on tense aching shoulders, and pressed the switchblade's button. The knife sprang free, and she definitely wasn't imagining it—the drilling, piercing noise going straight through both temples and eardrums was what happened right before the henchmen showed up.

Maybe that was the reason for the unlocked door—why bother keeping it fastened when any prisoner desperate enough to try leaving would be torn to pieces by the childlike, darting things with their bulbous black eyes and malformed paws? It had a certain efficiency, Bea could admit.

"All right, assholes," she whispered, and used the wall to drag herself fully upright. "Let's tango."

She padded down the hall, moving quietly as possible. Of course, she was barefoot and the carpet was thick; the closer she got to the elevator the more her heart rose, pounding with hope as well as terror.

No keycard access, just a regular old up-and-down button pad. It did look a little familiar.

Awesome. Doing really great, Bebe. Don't fuck it up.

It wasn't her blinking, the hallway lights were actually stuttering. Bea snapped a glance over her shoulder and swallowed, hard.

Mist. Greasy yellow fog, rising in tendrils. Knee-high near the double oak doors, spreading with tiny rasping sounds, little tongues dragged across carpet fibers.

Stairs might be better, even if they're not the ones I want. To her right, a recessed doorway with a small set of lights overhead. Did she want to be trapped in a stairwell or a metal box when the little green men came for her? She could pull a fire alarm, though it would be better to set off the sprinklers—Jare swore the things didn't like running water, maybe that would be enough? If she had a cigarette lighter…

She'd play it by ear. The elevator might distract them while she ran for the stairs, that was a good plan. Bea punched both elevator buttons, exhaling shakily when their margins lit. A soft sliding sound of displaced air moved behind blank, shining metal.

A mellow chime. She had never been so glad to hear an elevator ding in her *life*. Bea rose onto bare toes, bouncing slightly in preparation, and snapped another glance back at the fog.

As if it had waited for her attention, the clinging vapor shot down the hall. Electric bulbs in heavy brass Art Deco sconces died as the mist slithered past, and Bea bolted for the stairs even though the elevator was opening, burnished metal drawing aside with majestic slowness.

The fire door shuddered as something outside banged against it, hard; she skidded to a stop, bringing the knife up. *Oh hell, they're down there too. Crap, what do I—*

A skittering, the high babylike chuckles behind her, hatefully familiar as the mist.

Bea threw herself aside, her back meeting the wall with a heavy thump that didn't matter because they were boiling out of the fog, chittering and champing small, sharklike yellow teeth. Their big black eyes held neither iris nor pupil, but she sensed the wet, nasty gazes focusing on her. The knife jittered in her hand, backpack pressed hard against the wall.

Crunch. A snap, a pop, a spattering sound like sand dislodged from high crevices. The mist cringed, flushing crimson instead of vile greasy yellow, and the things halted, piling against each other Looney-Tunes style, ones in front nearly going down under the weight of crowding as they backpedaled. More than a dozen had scurried out of the mist, however-many were still in the fog, plus reinforcements on the other side of the fire door.

The visible henchmen reversed, crawling over each other in skinnyshamble haste, several with loincloths askew and small gleaming-green buttocks working as they scrambled.

Jesus Christ. Is it the knife? Bea tried an experimental jab, heard a low thrumming growl from the mist. Fresh scarlet spread through its confused billows, and she decided sticking around for whatever was making that noise was an even worse idea than diving into the stairwell.

The elevator's door began to close. Bea peeled herself from the wall, carpet burning bare feet, and bolted into a brightly lit, mirror-walled box carpeted with familiar, shorter blue nylon. She fumbled for the door-close button, managed to press at least four different floors at once, hit the lobby too for good measure, and leaned against the brass rail—it *did* look like the elevator from last night, but she couldn't see a single red bead or bit of cracked glass.

Maybe it had been cleaned and repaired? Rich people could do that, make evidence vanish. She grabbed the brass handrail—now she remembered bracing herself against it last night, driving the stake in, her entire body a solid bar of muscular intent.

It seemed to take forever before descent began; she could barely tell the difference between movement and the deep unsteady fearful flip-flopping of her stomach. *Oh thank God. Thank you, God. You are a monster too, but you just might exist.*

At least, so she thought before the lights flickered and the whine mounted once more. Bea wedged herself in a back corner, knife clasped tight in one sweaty, smarting palm, and bit back a scream when the elevator jolted to a definitely unscheduled stop.

No Muzak. Nothing but the thumping of her heart, a faraway screeching, the drill-whine fading before it, too, abruptly stopped. Were there cameras in here; was the monster watching? Would she just be driven into smaller and smaller boxes before he let the little green child-things tear her to bitty pieces?

Jared, if we meet in hell I'm just gonna kill *you.* She gripped the knife, tried to slow her heaving lungs.

The elevator shuddered. Machinery whirred, a series of

chimes sounded. When the movement began, she at first couldn't tell in what direction she was going.

Then it became clear, judged by stomach-flips, ear-tubes, and the subtle shift of gravity.

Up. She was being taken back up.

Could be good. Or very, very bad.

She could do nothing but wait and see.

The door slid aside, calm and quiet, *just doing my job, ma'am*. Bea stared, blinking, one bare arm extended, the blanket's hem quivering a few inches from the floor and the switchblade's point making a wavering shape in the air.

The monster stood, toes placed precisely at the metal threshold; he must've had his nose nearly pressed against the outer shell. If she was watching this situation from comfortably outside, Bea might have felt like laughing.

His gaze fastened on her, and she could swear there were little red pinpricks in his pupils.

Oh, God. No need to swear, in fact. The crimson dots were indubitably real, waxing and waning as he regarded her.

The monster turned his head slightly, dropping his chin. He wore yet another grey suit, but this jacket was torn to ribbons and his trousers soaked to the knee with something viscous-dark.

"Sir?" A voice from behind him, a pleasant tenor. Bea's heart leapt with sudden, frantic hope—another human, maybe capable of helping—but the yell died in her dry, scraped-raw throat. There might not be any point; this stranger sounded like the big mustachio'd bodyguard who ran some part of 'Everly's' security apparatus, the one who liked to wear bowler hats. "I believe they're gone."

"Clear the building and leave." The monster did not deign to truly look at whoever it was, simply continued issuing orders.

"Wind down the business concerns, torch the Everly and Jamison identities, make sure Comptain is also thoroughly gone, since I am rather uneasy about current events. Ready Andranov and Caine for use, prepare a matching set of alternates for my lady. Use whatever bolthole seems best for tonight; I shall meet you tomorrow at the lair upon the north hills."

Everly. Jamison. Comptain. She knew about Everly, and Comptain was the name she and Don guessed the monster had used as late as 1905, still occasionally mentioned about on podcasts and niche radio shows dedicated to the unsolved mysteries of Chicago.

Hearing it was like being pinched in a sensitive spot, and she couldn't even feel good about their theories being correct. *Jamison* must be similar. How many names did he have?

Another little detail: *lair on the north hills.* If she escaped this, maybe digging through more public records would—but that was stupid. There was nowhere to go, she was even more fish-in-a-barrel than under the bed.

Still, she had the knife.

"Yes, sir." Nothing else, just a dead silence and a shadow passing behind him before the faint whoosh of a fire door's controlled closing, a final deadly click.

Oh, sure, that *guy can use the stairs. He's a henchman too, I bet, or five of them stacked under a bowler hat.*

The monster stared at her, his sandy head cocked, and his hands—broad, capable, with blunt square nails—hanging at his sides. The goo on his shins dripped from trouser hems; his shoes weren't shiny any longer. His lower lip relaxed, showing two tiny divots where the longest fangs just touched the skin, almost worse than the red pinpricks.

Almost.

Do it fast, Bebe. Jare's voice in her head sounded tired. Auditory hallucination or actual ghost, she'd find out in a few minutes at most.

Her arm bent. The knife's sharp, cold tip pressed cold against her own throat. The monster tensed, his shoulders swelling under strips of grey wool. He leaned forward, his toes still just at the elevator's verge.

Does he need an invitation to come in? That would be hilarious. "I'll do it," Bea said, amazed at how normal she sounded. Husky, as if coming down with a cold...but matter-of-fact, determined. "Believe me, I *will* do it."

"I cannot fault you for attempting escape, with the *greiben* so insistent." Every word edged, the monster enunciating carefully. Maybe because of the fangs, they had to be sharp. "But I warned you about self-harm, Beatrice."

Hearing her first name was a nasty shock even if he accented it all weird, *bay-ah-tree-cheh*, very Italian. Had he been pretending not to know? She flinched, and the knifepoint jabbed hard against her pulse.

One little push. It wasn't so difficult, all she had to do was make up her mind.

A thin hot fingernail traced down her neck. *See? Just rip the bandaid off, Bebe.* Her arm tightened.

The monster might even go for the blood like Snowball after a piece of dropped Havarti, and wouldn't that be laughable as well?

Hilarious. You're a very funny girl. "See you in hell," she said, and stabbed.

Or tried to, because there was another of those skipping timestream-stutters, this time followed by a metallic clatter as the knife went flying. Her blanket-toga was ripped clean away, cloth shearing neatly. The monster hissed, a sharp indrawn breath, and her head lolled drunkenly as fangs pierced, driving deep.

Go ahead. Juicebox me, I don't care.

Her shoulder rubbed hard against slick cold mirror, metal dragging briefly past her hip—the brass rail, useless because she was lifted, pressed against the wall. The elevator rocked; Bea let out a surprised little cry as her knees were pushed apart. Heavy warmth spread from her throat; for a moment she thought it was arterial spray and all her problems were over.

The monster growled again, biting down. It hadn't hurt the first time; now the sensation was doubly odd, spreading warmth, the rest of her body just plain refusing to work. Her arms were stretched overhead again—*he has a real thing for that,* she thought, with slow, dazed amazement.

Rough, scorching fingertips slid up the inside of her left thigh. She realized he wasn't going to stop just as they found what they sought, tender flesh parting.

Her lungs wouldn't work. Tiny helpless sounds echoed against glass, mixing with a low insistent noise—the stop-elevator alarm, she realized, amazed her ears were still on the job. She was floating just outside herself, hearing a series of strengthless moans, and figured out it was her own voice just before he shifted, fingers withdrawing. Another faint sound, a tiny *shhhip* of zipper, and dear God, he was working on his pants with one hand while holding her against the elevator wall, pinning her wrists more firmly.

The pressure at her throat retreated, sharp intrusions sliding free of yielding flesh. Fire spread as his tongue moved, caressing the wounds, flicking a sweat-damp hollow. An insistent, scorching probe between her numb legs; her back arched, a last useless resistance.

Hot, hard, undeniable, the monster thrust into her. Bea tried to scream again, but his mouth was over hers, a narcotic sweetness filling tongue and throat. He growled again, a low chest-rattling sound, and surged forward a second time, then a third.

CHAPTER 10

afresh in his veins; he was hilt-deep before the snap of his control breaking registered. It was not what he had hoped for in a first time, certainly.

Yet mortals often took such pleasure after combat or disaster, affirming survival. Fear was simply another arousal, and she was soaked in it, nerves primed, so slick and wet he had no trouble imagining her willing or at least compliant. She writhed, instinctive protest against invasion merely seating him deeper, and exquisite glassy pleasure roared through every nerve, muscle, artery, and winding vein he possessed.

Something had sought to take her away; the animal crouching at the very floor of consciousness was enraged, restrained only by the sweet slack mouth he plundered with his own, only by the fact that he was *in* her, all the fragrant promise and thick honeyed musk drawn strangling-tight. It was like lingering at the threshold of mortal death, the heart stuttering with strain, a few final syrup-drops wrung from aching thunder —yet it was his own oblivion he pursued, driving hard enough to print himself upon her fragile, lovely skeleton.

First the bite, then the claiming. So many layers to the proverb, whether in making fledglings or taking a leman.

Now he knew what true-death felt like for his kind, an insect struggling as tree-sap petrified slowly into amber, suffocating by centimeters. Calcification's bony, rigid grinning jaws had almost closed in his vitals, but a lamp in the night had saved him and he was fully, gratefully immolated. Invisible flame obliterated every remembered sensation—even the strongest, like the stinging moment he found himself first capable of walking in cloud-weakened sunlight, or the still-raw thought of his mortal passing.

Objectively, it did not take long to please her—a mere short eternity, her mortal body snatching release after agonizing terror. Her fascinating, trapped writhing stilled on the cusp; Lukas tensed, burying himself deeply as possible a bare moment before the crisis took her, concentric pulses shattering every universe so poor as to lack such a beautiful linchpin.

The temptation to allow his own release was undeniable, but that would be greedy. Not to mention dangerous; he could not afford the resultant temporary vulnerability.

Soon. He promised as much with a last lingering kiss, though she was far too mazed to respond. The noise was irritating—ah, the alarm for the elevator, hit almost as an afterthought. *This is awkward.*

Also, satisfying. His entire body protested another withdrawal, but it was done. She was claimed, the addiction holding his calcification at bay sealed. Her transition into the Gift could be accomplished in safe stages, bite by luscious, heated bite.

She was whole and relatively undamaged though trembling hard, fresh bruises rising on her shoulder and smooth, lovely thighs. The change and healing agents would be busy repairing and beginning alteration; she was in little danger. Still, his chest twinged internally once more as he set his clothing to what rights were possible, that wonderful if unpleasant sensation tugging at his old, obdurate heart.

All those centuries he had thought poets merely pretty liars; what they described, however imperfectly, was only stark truth. Lukas licked his lips, hungry for any remaining drop, and checked her slim, pretty neck.

Fresh but properly healing, bright as a brand, the fang-marks were pleasing indeed. He hadn't even noticed the necklace, though the chain's scintillation spoke of true silver.

He was no fledgling to flinch from that gleaming. Still, the emerald and its setting caused him a single long pause, its sly green gleam peering over the nightgown's silken, plunging neckline. Naturally gems suited her, though the setting had pressed hard between her breasts, marking tender skin with pale divots he longed to kiss. And that enchanting little freckle, as well.

"I see," he breathed. *A greisoul. No wonder they are so insistent.*

She could stand, though only barely, and when he spoke she swayed as if about to swoon. The *quietus* was not necessary; she seemed stunned, Danaë after a luminous visit or the Deer Girl waking to find the Sunwolf in her tent.

He had not thought of either tale in a very long while. Lukas stroked her hair, smoothing tendrils from sweat-silken forehead; she neither flinched nor accepted the movement, just gazed slightly past him at the elevator's frozen-open door, pursing the lush mouth he also longed to sample once more. Soft and wavy, dyed black, the roots pale giveaways with a coppery tinge. Strawberry blonde, was that the term? He also examined the *greisoul* closely, faintly envious of the gem enjoying such close living warmth.

Which led to another consideration. The nightgown was not nearly enough to keep a mortal from the elements, and he had torn the blanket—she was a resourceful lass, indeed—to shreds. His jacket was likewise in tatters, so he stripped it free.

The fungal excrescences were no friends to good tailoring. He hadn't gone through laundry like this since the incursion of a fellow sanguinant onto his Chicago territory, at the turn of...yes, the previous century. At least the brief burst of maneuvering and paroxysm of final combat had sharpened him for a short while, staving off slow creeping numbness.

Yet he could now trace how ossification had returned, fogging both mind and body by infinitesimal increments. She had arrived in the very nick of time.

His leman staggered sideways when he moved to drop the ruined jacket; Lukas's hand blurred before closing gently, firmly on her upper arm. "Steady, now." He found American words in his mental storehouse; he could teach any tongue she wished later, at leisure. "All is well, Beatrice."

Such a lovely phrase, tasting pleasingly of her spice, musk, and gorgeous scorching presence.

She shook her head, as if denying her own name. Lukas bent, his arm sweeping behind her knees; she fit very neatly, cradled against him. In fact, her head drooped, mortal-feverish cheek resting against his shoulder, and he pressed his lips to her temple as he turned.

Her scent was dyed with his; he was ringed with the feel of her. The Everly cover had reached the end of its usefulness, and in any case he had very little time or desire for playing business games at the moment. Even the next few covers would have to neglect such things, though not entirely.

"We both need better cloth." A calm tone would soothe, comfort—and, Lukas realized, he did wish to console, or at least pacify this fascinating creature. "And then we shall take a short ride."

His driving might be a bit rusty, but all things considered, the afternoon had gone very well indeed.

CHAPTER 11

Of all the weird shit on her internal bingo card, Bea had never expected to find squares labeled *fucked in an elevator by a monster*, or *dressed like a doll and put in a BMW*. It didn't seem to matter very much—nothing did, she had sailed clean out of sanity and found being crazy was actually kind of peaceful.

Bloodsucking monsters and little green men were not normal, therefore, she had to be insane. It was a relief to have that decided for good. Her throat felt hot and her mouth was dry as the Sahara, but the rest of her floated in a clear, warm haze, treacherous postcoital glow.

She literally could not decide how to feel. Every silver lining had a huge black cloud. She'd lost her knife, but there were no little green men or greasy yellow fog around. The monster had bitten her again, but she wasn't in any real pain at the moment. He'd taken her backpack, tucking it behind her seat—it wasn't absolutely gone, but that could be a temporary state of affairs.

Her legs shook, but the fear was hiding somewhere else as a low hum of purely physical relief settled in its wake. Did *'crazy'* just mean *'not scared anymore'*? Someone should've told her before now.

She still didn't quite know how he'd ended up in yet another three-piece suit. He had a very nice dark-grey London Fog as well, which was tucked around her at the moment. He'd even put socks on her, lifting each foot in turn while she sat on a padded bench inside a mirrored walk-in closet the size of a neighborhood coffee shop. Looked like the empty bedroom wasn't his, since there was a far more comfortable mini-apartment through one of the hall doors, the view from its glass wall-windows completely different, looking south instead of east.

Black cotton socks snuggled solicitously past her ankles to go with a pair of slate-colored yoga pants in her size, a white T-shirt and feather-soft grey plaid flannel button-up—all that and the coat, but no goddamn shoes.

Maybe he doesn't want me able to run away? She stared at the windshield, wipers moving in silent synch. It was a nice car, leather seats and a cushioned ride barely swaying even on the pothole-ridden mess of Old Meadow Street before the Causeway. *No, probably just doesn't have anything in my size. Does he do this a lot, kidnap women who stab him?*

Glaring rubies in winter dusk—brake lights, like paired bloodclots. Traffic was oddly sparse, but then again she didn't really know what day it was.

And he'd bitten her again.

That isn't all he did. For a walk of shame this is pretty good, don't you think? And let's not even talk about what...how I...

Nope, she really didn't want to think about her own body's response. Even Jare's voice in her head was gone; maybe he was disgusted. She couldn't tell—should she be disgusted with herself?

"Your pulse is rising," the monster said, as the sedan finished turning on the Causeway. The rain intensified, but the passenger seat was heated.

The very lap of luxury. How did he have pants in my size, even Spandex? Buzzing, grimly inconsequential thoughts simply wouldn't stop. "You bit me." Bea counted the wiper-swings.

One, two, three, four. The rain had ice in its heart, crystal spatters stacking in rows as they were shoved aside. "Again."

"Not what I had intended for the first, but what's done is done." How could he be so *calm*? Of course, he was at least a hundred and fifty years old, if Don's guesses were right. "I wondered why they were after you."

What. The fuck? "They're after me because you told them to be." She sounded weary, like a teacher at the end of a long school day. The dashboard glowed, a marvel of modern engineering driven by a monster out of creepypasta camping stories.

"No. They're after what you hold, little leman."

What does he have against lemons? Especially with that accent. She wasn't thinking straight, Bea knew, but none of this made any goddamn sense. It never had. "What, my knife? I got it after—"

"Your brother gave you the necklace." The car accelerated.

Gravity pressed her into cushiony leather, her entire body reduced to pudding. She could handle pain, no big deal. Having the agony taken away meant there was no reason to be brave, or to really care much about anything.

Was she really a coward at heart? "For my birthday. Was...is that why you wanted the house? The property?" Had Jared been sitting on an emerald mine in fucking *Vermont*?

That's fucking silly, Bea. Come on.

"I was concerned about the irruption of *greiben* on the southern side of that mountain. I held the northern ostensibly for mining concerns, but mostly to keep the infection from interacting too much with mortals. I hadn't had time yet to start operations—the cold iron in the machines would keep them weak and after a few years they would have empty mineshafts to hold their interest." The monster checked the mirrors, his hands settled precisely at ten and two o'clock on the wheel. "My companies made offers to buy out everyone on the south slopes. Your brother and one other refused to sell, then the evening I set aside to visit your brother personally, I found him dead. A great shame; I should have been earlier to meet you."

"Hold on." Bea lifted strengthless hands, fingers quivering like dry branches on a windy day. Watching her own trembling was vaguely interesting. "They began harassing him when he turned down the first offer. To drive him out."

"Did he have a habit of hiking, your Jared?" Testing the name. The monster sounded so fucking *human*, now, though the Ivy League accent was gone. He wasn't the target she'd researched so thoroughly, a red dress's beaded strings swaying as she sauntered into the party, everyone assuming she belonged because she *made* them think that, putting on a confident show.

And now look at her. "He went on walks," she mumbled, and dropped her arms, hugging herself. *Are we just not going to talk about the elevator? Maybe he's already forgotten it.*

Just like a man, but also a distinct relief. So much else was going on, she could ignore that incident. It would be fine shoved in a box and locked away. If she survived, she'd think about it then.

The monster glanced at her; thankfully, the red pinpricks in his pupils were gone. "Was he ever trapped underground on the mountain? Did he ever return late from a camping trip, dazed or incoherent?"

"He went on *walks*," she repeated, stubbornly, but it bothered her. There had been that strangeness two weeks before her birthday, when nobody had been able to get hold of Jared from Thursday until late Monday morning. He'd missed a local library event plus a scheduled call with his agent Nanci, who had been worried enough to call Bea during midterms.

It's probably nothing, he's holed up out in the sticks playing Thoreau, but...

He'd been apologetic and distantly affectionate afterward, smoothing the waters, promising never to worry her or Nanci like that ever again. At the time Bea had just rolled her eyes and filed it under *Instance of Jared being a weirdo, number infinity.*

Honestly, if he'd eventually turned into another backcountry Unabomber or something, she wouldn't have been at all surprised.

Just after that he'd refused an offer from the mining conglomerate owned by Everly, then the really weird shit began.

The necklace was warm against her chest; the monster had tucked it neatly under the T-shirt. How in the *hell* did he have clothes that fit her?

Before she could ask, the monster piped up again, in a low, musing tone. "I would guess he was gone for a day or two. And he would not mention it afterward, though he gave you a very pretty thing. It speaks well of him that he did not keep the gem."

You have got to be kidding me. "It's antique. Bought it with some of the money from his first book." Bea was foggily surprised at her own daring. Especially since she also pressed her knees together and a certain deep twinge reminded her of the here-and-now instead of years-ago. Could she tell herself the elevator thing was just a hallucination? "Because I was doing really well at school."

And a peace offering, sort of. *Sorry for taking up all the air in the room, Bebe.*

"A *greisoul* jewel is a gift bearing thorns, Beatrice. Unless given with love, it consumes the recipient." The monster settled in his seat, visibly relaxing. "When stolen from the warrens, it draws the *greiben*. They will not cease pursuit."

A sharp, bright flare of anger filled Bea for a few welcome seconds, drained away into dragging, numb hopelessness. "You're lying."

"Why would I?" Either he was honestly baffled or a world-class actor pretending to be. "I spent that night hunting down their clan-heads, since they had taken improper prey. I drove them deep into their tunnels; no doubt that allowed your escape. They have been tracking you since, I should guess. And you thought..." A slight shake of his head, a strand of sandy hair falling over his forehead. He tossed it aside with a quick flicker of motion, a very human movement though just a little too catlike-graceful.

"You're *lying*." She was repeating herself a lot right now. How much could a person be expected to take? And he...in the elevator, he had..."Why did you do that?"

"These days, buyouts are more efficient than simply relocating settlements, or putting them to the sword. I thought to visit your brother and the other holdout, gain compliance, make it worth their while to move. Simple, easy. But the *greiben* enmeshed him that evening—your dog was a deterrent, though a minor one. The little excrescences are dangerous in packs, and in their hunting mist as well." Another glance in her direction. "You must have sensed their pursuit. Is that why you disappeared from mortal authorities?"

"If I can find information on the internet, you can return the favor. Plus, you're rich." Why did she feel like she was being graded on her monster-stalking? "Money can dig people up, so I broke all the shovels I could."

"All the shovels you could," he echoed, quietly. "A good phrase, very apt. You are teaching me already."

What the hell? "So you're not going to kill me, just bite me and turn me into Lady Dracula? Is that the plan?" It wasn't unexpected—after all, he was a monster—but if what he said was true…

He was still a bloodsucking fiend, but if he wasn't in charge of the little green henchmen, she had fucked up bigtime.

Well, really, she was fucked either way. And in an elevator, too. Maybe that was all he wanted, and he'd ditch her out in the boonies, sockfeet and yoga pants notwithstanding.

Just as she began to entertain that fond hope, he had to go and crash it. "The plan is a short drive to a safer location, where I will tend to you."

Is that some kind of euphemism? "Like, turn me into Elsa Lanchester, or what?" *I don't believe it. He was right on the footage —first Snowball running in circles and yelling like she did when there were bad things in the backyard and we'd find the marks in the morning. She heads into the stable, then Jared follows like he's looking for something. And then, ten minutes later, the monster strolls in.*

While Bea had been paying bills and smelling fresh-brewed coffee, losing track of time since a few moments' worth of peace were hard to come by even while Jare was in his den finishing the goddamn second book.

She didn't want to think about that. The footage was clear; nothing else had entered the building. The rest of the stable had been locked up tight.

Bea wasn't shown at all, because she'd come from the house's side door instead of the front, momentarily confused at the one wan electric bulb high over stable stalls shining through the opening, illuminating a faint slice of weed-starred gravel. If not for a chance configuration of farm junk at the one miraculously unbroken and hence unboarded window providing a hole to peer through, she might not have seen the monster crouched over her brother's broken body, head slightly tilted as it was now.

He contemplated the traffic before the silver BMW just as he had her brother's corpse, with the same politely interested expression. "I don't understand the reference."

The camera near the stable kept rolling for two days after that, but nothing showed up, not even raccoons. And by then Bea had been long gone, barely daring to sign in, download the footage, and never touching a scrap of her previous identity again. No phone, no log-ins, no calls to anyone saying she was still alive, showing up on Don's doorstep shivering and barely coherent…

How did he get out of the stable? If he left without going past you, could the henchmen get in without you seeing?

In other words, was this 'Everly' guy actually telling the truth? Had she tried to kill an innocent monster—or at least, a monster who hadn't torn someone she loved into chunks?

"I think I'm going to throw up." For a moment she was in

college again, jammed into a car with six laughing girls, barely sober and immortal because they were all young and nobody's brother had been discovered as a pulped mass on manure-laden dirt.

The monster gave a slight nod, his mouth turning down briefly at both corners. "Understandable."

"No car." She finally blurted it out. "There was no car, how did you get out to his place if you didn't drive?"

"If not for you, I would not be driving now." As if explaining to a toddler, *the sky's blue because of refracted light* or *the wind is trees sneezing.* "I can move over most terrain at reasonable speed, but it's a chilly night. You are still mortal."

Well, thank God for that. "I'll end up a vampire unless you're killed before I drink human blood, right? Is that how it works?"

"No," the monster said, softly but with utter conviction. "That is not how it works at all, Beatrice. You will learn soon enough."

Which seemed to close off further conversational avenues, or maybe Bea's brain-mouth filters decided to re-engage since she wasn't staring down the barrel of her own demise in the next sixty seconds. She tried not to luxuriate in the warmth, the smooth ride, the feeling of gliding further into grateful insanity.

If I'm convinced I'm mad, does it make me sane? All the kicking around of philosophical or ontological footballs with Don couldn't help her now. Was he still alive, or had the monster done something to him?

Could she ask without risking Don and Callie's safety, if the monster didn't already know about them? Her battered brain was not up to any decisions at the moment, no matter how minor—except maybe watching for another chance to escape.

The monster was silent as he drove. He didn't even turn on the fancy satellite radio.

North Bluffs loomed at the end of the Causeway, a dark bulk traced with scattered streetlights along steep winding roads. It was expensive real estate, private gated communities and bougie organic shopping centers plus a few tracts of 'public' wilderness mostly used by jogging housewives. There were a couple semi-rural slices resisting the winds of gentrification, but by and large it was *the* suburb to settle in if you couldn't afford old-money Rhodeshill and Laurel Row neighborhoods or wanted more space than squeezed-together Victorians with postage-stamp yards.

Once they were off the Causeway and free of traffic he let the BMW open up, taking two-lane curves far too fast, barely touching the brakes. Were they being followed, or did he simply enjoy driving bank-robber style?

A twisting, overgrown road swallowed the car, tangled underbrush leaning over the ditches to either side. Bea flinched, but the monster was only reaching into a pocket, fishing out a sleek silver phone in a heavy waterproof casing. "Wrong one," he muttered, dropping it into the empty cupholder—did he ever put a latte there? The car was pristine as if freshly detailed, though it lacked the soupy chemical smell of a brand-new vehicle.

He found what he wanted in his jacket's breast pocket and made a small satisfied sound, very much like a human male.

"How many of those do you carry?" Bea's mouth was back for Round Two. If she somehow got out of this, she was going to have so much good firsthand monster knowledge—but nobody normal would believe her. And she might come down with some kind of weird monster STD, since he hadn't used any protection.

Do NOT think about that. But it was too late. Her brain started wobbling again, wondering about monster babies.

"Tremendously useful little things. Addictive, too, though not nearly so much as..." A glance in her direction, his face ghostly in dashboard light. "As a leman."

What, you like lemon with your blood? Blood lemonade? Is that what you usually put in the cupholder? Her imagination just worked too goddamn well—which was great for planning out a murder during a Roaring Twenties costume party, but sucked ass when you were trapped in small spaces with a fast, strong, apparently unkillable bloodsucker.

Not unkillable. You just didn't get the stake going fast enough. Don was right, should have rigged up a crossbow.

But how could she carry that in? The stake was difficult enough, tucked down the back of her dress and held tight with athletic tape. She'd hoped her quarry would take her somewhere private, guessing she could get to fire stairs on the correct side of the building by a couple different routes; she'd expected to attack on one of the lower floors. Nobody would expect her to go *up* and change clothes before coming back down, taking advantage of a few dead spots in the security cameras before vanishing into the night.

She was Monday-morning quarterbacking her own monster murder. Getting defensive over the failure, as well.

And apparently even bloodsuckers texted while driving. Bea couldn't close her eyes, just watched in silent horror as the car took a few hairpin curves far too quickly while he stared at the phone, now occasionally feathering the brakes, tires clinging with only a faint chirp at the crux of the sharpest bend.

Could he survive a fiery wreck? Was he going to ditch her and the car in one flaming mass, walking away without looking at the explosion, action-movie style?

"There." He tucked both phones away, finally returning his right hand to the wheel—which was comforting, she supposed, if only for the moment. "We'll arrive soon. I should warn you of a few necessities."

Like what? Bea's fingers bit her arms; she was hugging herself tight enough to bruise. It would add to all of her other contusions; she'd be a painted horse before long.

The monster waited, as if he expected a reply. Her lips stayed buttoned, and finally he decided to go on.

"If you attempt escape or self-harm, I will have you; I repeat myself only to be very clear. Also, attempts to recruit any of my staff are doomed to failure, and will result in their elimination. If necessary, I will terminate them in your presence, and I will be cruel. Do you understand?"

So, what, you're holding me hostage? Nobody's gonna pay anything, even Don. She was thinking through sludge. At least pain would keep her awake; this funny floating feeling was probably close to the fatal, gentle drowsiness of hypothermia. "Why not just kill me?" *Come on, man. I stabbed you right in the chest.*

"I would rather pluck out my own eyes and seek true-death than harm a single hair on your lovely little head, kitten." He finally hit the brakes for real; a single light shone on the left side of the road ahead, winking through tree branches. "But if any of my staff are so foolish as to intrude upon our games, I will not brook the interference."

Games? You want to play Scrabble or something? Her head took up a fuzzy ache, the bite-marks on her throat throbbing insistently. If she focused on that, she didn't have to think about any other physical sensation. "So there'll be real human people, where you're taking me?"

"In the morning, at least." The light on the left hopped closer; the car slowed further. "Tonight we have pleasantly to ourselves."

Color me under-enthused. How much more before she started to scream and never stopped? "If someone helps me escape, you'll fire them?" Did that mean he was going to keep her around? Like a pet, or a walking buffet?

How much blood would her body make after each bite? She didn't feel woozy from loss of plasma, but then, it was hard to tell through the exhaustion, the numbness, the reminder of recent activity between her legs.

Do not *think about anything but the next few minutes, dammit. You need all your brains for getting through this.* Whatever this was.

"If any are so disloyal or stupid, I will flay them, drain them in agony, and crush their bones to powder." The monster said it like reciting a grocery list, and Bea found she believed every word.

"Are you going to bite me again?" *Please, just tell me you won't.*

"Absolutely. But not tonight; you require rest."

Golly gee, isn't that nice of you. Bea watched as the mouth of a driveway swelled to the side, pavement overlaid with scattered gravel, the car taking the turn and bouncing slightly as it left the road. The light shone on a huge wrought-iron gate, gleaming as it swung wide. The driveway itself was a curtain of ink until headlights slashed across, revealing a smooth concrete ribbon between thick underbrush, skeletal branches rattling. Probably really pretty in spring, but right now creepy as all hell.

"I don't think you comprehend quite yet, but no matter." Patiently, quietly, as he steered the silver shark of the car uphill. "We have all the time in the world, Beatrice."

That does not sound good. She stared as twinkling lights came into view, a house at the hill-crown peering through sodden, shivering forest. A big old fieldstone mansion, in fact, banks of windows burning in the night. The rain had become heavy sleet, slashing down hard.

The BMW slowed to idle. One of six garage doors was opening—real conspicuous consumption, here. Dripping, the car slipped easily into a brightly lit, concrete-floored maw.

CHAPTER 12

Like any lair held in readiness, the house smelled faintly of polish and disuse. But the thermostat had taken its remote instructions smoothly, the lights were welcoming, and the structure was solid as well as fully stocked. The layered scents of human staff lingered along maintenance tracks; they might be glad of a change in routine—or bemoan it. Either way, those held in readiness for his new cover would serve her well enough. Isolated, well-cushioned, adjacent to more thickly settled areas for hunting, this particular lair was a relatively ideal location for a newly bonded leman's introduction to the rest of eternity.

His prize tensed when he cut the engine and might have bolted from the vehicle had he not laid a hand on her knee, his palm cupped, enjoying a hint of her warmth through the coat's double layers. A single shake of his head, and she waited for him to open her door like a gentleman. She did not demur at being carried, though there was no more sweet resting of her cheek against him. Stiff and pale, Beatrice simply submitted.

His ears told him the house was empty, breathing alone on a winter night. The layout was fairly clear inside his head; it was old habit to install saferooms no matter the cost, though a daywalker did not need such exigencies unless deeply wounded.

The Everly guestroom had not been ideal, this lair's saferoom was properly windowless. She only had a short while longer to enjoy mortal daylight; fledglings were delicate, though with repeated infusions of his own claret she would reach daywalking status relatively soon. Half a millennia, perhaps?

Another pleasant prospect to contemplate. Especially the necessary feedings.

He did not take her to the saferoom just yet. The water-pipes were clear, his maintenance staff no doubt expecting a bonus this year; he set the matter aside as the master suite's sunken tub filled. Steam rose; she looked up at the skylight's dark eye.

This lair's windows were one-way and UV-coated to discourage both prying gazes and sun damage. Such things were marvels, and their presence in bedroom or bath counted a sign of luxury. Were it daytime she could gaze at the sweep of valley, the concrete artery of the Causeway, at a faint persistent haze of smog above the city proper. As it was, only the stain of porch- and streetlights showed indistinct in a dark sea. Her reflection lingered, pallid and beautiful, staring huge-eyed at the pale stone floor, the expanse of countertop, the paired sinks with heavy brass taps, stacks of thick, thirsty forest-green towels.

Then she studied his own moving image on the glass surface, her eyebrows drawing together.

He tested the water—too hot for a still-mortal? Another wonderful problem to solve. "Come, see if it's warm enough. I don't know what you like."

"Why do you…" She freed a hand from hugging herself, pointed at the window. "Is it only silver-backed mirrors you don't reflect in? I mean, there aren't a lot of those around anymore."

"I am solid enough." *Save in lighter mistform, but that might unnerve you.* "Light behaves as it should in my vicinity, unless I force it otherwise. There are natural laws even for our kind."

"Your kind." She swayed, catching herself almost before he had a chance to twitch. "Vampire, right? I hate that word."

Our kind. Enough time for that later. "The proper term is sanguinant, at least nowadays for the European-adjacent."

"Sounds French."

"Much of your language is, kitten." He was doing very well, Lukas thought. A quiet, rational discussion represented progress; he rose from crouching at the tub's side, carefully controlled all through the movement.

Not slowly enough, perhaps. She retreated, blundering away toward the sinks. The mirrors held faint traces of condensation now; in a short while this lair would be alive with her scent and the hum of a well-regulated household.

Approaching a quivering, exhausted leman was particularly enticing. He had not stalked so carefully in many a mortal year. She refused to look directly, gaze downcast, heavy lashes darker than her eyebrows hiding those lovely gold-threaded eyes. When he reached for the front of the buttoned shirt she flinched, nearly cowering onto the counter.

"I can do it myself." A tiny, defiant mutter. "Are you going to drown me? That's not a bathtub, it's a swimming pool."

Ah. Her behavior suddenly arranged itself in a coherent pattern; the shock of realization was exquisite. He would never grow used to the jolts of sensation, stinging-raw, unfiltered by creeping numbness. "You are attempting to provoke me." His fingertips touched the button just over the lump of the necklace, worked it free.

"I've had enough of the psychological torture, thanks." The words shook, her tremors intensifying.

Lukas restrained the mounting urge to rip every scrap of cloth free, set her on the marble, and bury himself in that volcanic velvet heat again. His knuckles brushed white cotton, the T-shirt stretched over her breasts, and the flare of desire was so sharp it tasted of sweet, iron-heavy mortal claret. His fangs throbbed, longing to sink into her once more; he paid very close attention to the buttons.

"You can have the necklace." Desperate now, she was rigid

despite the trembling. "I'll walk back to town, I'll keep going, you'll never hear from me again. I promise. I *swear*."

Too late for that. "The time to flee was before I caught your scent." He slid the button-up from her shoulders; she cooperated woodenly. "Lift your arms. Or I can simply tear your clothes off."

"How many women do you do this to?" More provocation, but she slowly obeyed.

"None." He had to concentrate, lifting the T-shirt's hem. Every inch revealed was a fresh paradise, but he *must* exercise restraint. She was safe, she was claimed, she was *his*. Now he had to keep what he had taken, ease her through the stages of grieving for a mortal life, and deal with the *greiben*.

The last part was easiest. The entire infestation had to go— messy work, but unavoidable. The only quandary was whether or not to allow her accompaniment; the level of violence might be cathartic or traumatizing, depending on her state of mind. "None at all," he continued. "In my entire time upon this earth, you are the only leman I have ever seen."

One heard gossip, of course, but any sanguinant—ancient or otherwise—with the good fortune to find such a prize would not easily allow another to lay eye or hand upon it.

A great shuddering breath. Her face crumpled, and she began to weep in soft, heartbreaking gasps.

Bathing a shaking, crying leman was another new experience; his own nakedness was inconsequential, his personal cleansing accomplished in perfunctory fashion. The last of the *greiben* stench was sluiced from them both as he explored, soaping and rinsing with infinite care, and her sobbing as she cooperated with dreamlike slowness tore at his own chest.

The storm passed as he pressed a fresh towel against her hair, examining wet strands. Soon they would slough the dye; such things did not take to sanguinant well, if at all. Her lashes, wet and matted, stayed down. She was either semiconscious or pretending slumber by the time he carried her thought silent halls to the saferoom, and he laid the invisible seals with care.

This bed was not quite so vast as the Everly's, but the linens were fresh. Certainly the staff were accumulating no little merit; his new cover could afford to be correspondingly profligate with reward.

He settled her gently, pulled white blankets and snowy counterpane high, glanced at the wrought-iron bedposts. Had he chosen this particular stead, or simply had a shopper handle the detail? He could not remember, and it irked him.

His prize curled upon her side; Lukas eased under the covers next to her. Slowly, he gathered her close, damp near-mortal softness sliding against the different texture of sanguinant skin. His knees behind the hollows of hers, a stiff yearning pressed into the firm roundness of her bottom, his arm securely locked about her waist, his nose buried in her hair, breathing in the tang of herbal shampoo and the deeper, far richer aroma of his very own leman.

The twilight came swiftly, unstringing preternatural muscles, slowing his old, powerful heartbeat. He could rest without calcification triggering the wasting lassitude; not only could a hidebound ancient commit an error of camouflage or simple carelessness, but both feeding and necessary rest could end in true-death.

It made a certain amount of evolutionary sense, he supposed. Sanguinant could lay waste to humanity without such winnowing; leman were a scarce, irreplaceable resource. How many of his kind had died of wanting what he now possessed?

"Sleep well," he mouthed, far too softly for mortal ears to hear.

She did not stir.

CHAPTER 13

Bᴇᴀ ᴡᴏᴜʟᴅ ʜᴀᴠᴇ ᴄᴀʟʟᴇᴅ ɪᴛ ɪᴍᴘᴏssɪʙʟᴇ ᴛᴏ sɴᴀᴛᴄʜ ᴀ ʀᴇsᴛʟᴇss ɴᴀᴘ while cuddled with a monster, much less an entire night—or longer, there was no way of telling. She might have slept for a decade, for all she knew.

Sleep was a horrible thing. It crept up on you, even after prolonged spells of terror-induced insomnia, and when it receded you were faced with the problem of yet another goddamn day to get through.

Dead, she wouldn't have to deal with this strange stage set of a mansion, its windows constantly slapped by a real howler of a winter rainstorm likely to fill with ice if the wind kept up, or a persistent dry throat and a monster who kept *watching* her. Every time she snuck a glance in his direction, he was looking.

From the moment she opened her eyes in the bare, airless 'saferoom'—a copy of her first prison but without windows or nightstand, holding only a huge four-poster in wrought iron plus an antiseptically clean bathroom with an untouched round of green, faintly balsam-smelling soap next to the sink—the monster hovered.

He'd had time to get dressed, of course. Maybe he'd even done it with superspeed; the thought of him fast-forward ironing a crease into his own trousers could have been funny if she'd felt even a little bit like laughing.

He wrapped her in a big fluffy white bathrobe and led her up to the mansion's main level, where the rooms were all color-coordinated, designer-arranged, and soulless as magazine spreads. It smelled a little disused though there was no hint of mildew, and her nose tickled with the dusty aura of a house nobody had really lived in for a while.

Still, the place was clean. At least there was that—and it meant people had done the cleaning. Which was great, if she could somehow...what? Get a message out?

To who?

The green-and-gold master bedroom's vast walk-in closet was stuffed with suits and a few other assorted oddments down one side—which was thought-provoking enough, since each piece was clearly tailored and their gradations of color went from charcoal to grey to navy, not a single bright color to be found even in the 'leisure' wear he clearly didn't use very often.

Bea really couldn't imagine this guy in a polo and khakis, let alone jeans and a rock band T-shirt. Even a different haircut wouldn't help. He was just too alien.

The other side of the closet was truly frightening in its impli-cations—a rainbow of women's clothing, heels and sandals and two pairs of sneakers neatly arranged in fabric-covered shoe-boxes underneath. Dresses, sundresses, skirts and blouses hung neatly, twinsets and other tops folded on color-coded shelves, panties and brassieres arranged in deep cedar-scented drawers, a total of two whole pantsuits, no jeans, and certainly no sweats.

Every piece of clothing fit, and there was no mark of previous ownership on even the most delicate fabrics. The shoes were new, their soles pristine; the underthings were laundered but unworn, and none of it was anything she would willingly wear.

She knew some of the labels, and of course everything was quality, including a pair of alligator pumps she would have cheerfully elbowed other shoppers out of the way for during college thrifting.

The monster waited while she wandered through the closet, trying to figure out what on earth she was supposed to do or if there was a secret passage leading to the outside she could somehow trip over by mistake. Her throat kept rasping; she finally found the least objectionable option by running across two drawers' worth of sleepwear.

Blue fleece pajama bottoms decorated with snowflakes and a matching waffle-weave shirt were hardly body armor *or* outside wear, but she figured with them and a pair of stolen boots she could maybe reach the end of the driveway.

She'd freeze to death a few blocks away, but that was a problem to be dealt with later. So much glass, the heating and cooling bills for this place were probably astronomical. She couldn't figure out if the whole heap felt so coldly foreign because a monster had taken up residence *or* because rich people were always a different species.

"These are simply guesses," the monster said from the closet's entrance, and Bea nearly leapt out of her skin. "They do not please you?"

"Um." The persistent swimming sense of unreality intensified. The marks on her neck had faded amazingly, and though she felt tender and thin-skinned all over there weren't any fresh bruises, just yellowgreen ghosts as if the contusions had been healing for weeks. Even her wounded knee looked a lot better. "It's really pretty, but I'm more of a Levi's type of girl." Was she really standing here discussing fashion with a bloodsucking freak who had…

Had he murdered her brother? Doubt had invaded her deep, glowing-coal certainty, and she hated the contamination.

"Ah." He leaned against the side of the doorway, suit jacket unbuttoned and his hands thrust deep in trouser pockets, a peculiarly male-human stance. "Do you enjoy shopping?"

I had a fun time looking at stakes and switchblades online, does that count? Bea decided to change the subject. "Everything fits. Why?"

"Easy enough to tell your sizes. Your preferences are a different matter."

Why do you care? Buying an entire wardrobe kind of argued against her imminent demise, but that could change at any moment.

Maybe he did this all the time and donated the leftovers.

One thing was for goddamn sure: she could not trust a single word the monster said. Bea miraculously found another pair of plain black socks, thankful he didn't try to dress her again, and braced herself for whatever was coming down the pike.

The big guy with the mustache and penchant for bowler hats was named Wren—*like the bird, mum,* he said in a startlingly pleasant tenor brogue, very quiet-spoken for one so huge. The housekeeper, a round middle-aged partridge in wine-red polyester slacks and huge, shivering shell earrings, was Mrs. Martinez. Both referred to her as *ma'am, mum,* or *Mrs. Andranov,* and the last made Bea want to glance nervously over her shoulder.

You are Valentina Andranov to them, the monster had cautioned before they left the green-and-gold sitting room at the edge of the master suite. *Try to remember that; I will deal with the rest.*

Nice of him, or maybe not. Beatrice was at a complete loss how to handle this goddamn situation; what would she be doing now if she hadn't stepped out of a motel bathroom to find him waiting?

Still driving? Already settled two states away, finding a low-level job and compulsively washing her hands?

Others bustled through the house, all human—so far as she could tell—and all appearing blissfully oblivious of the monster. Suddenly he was almost the man from the costume party again, save for the subtle changes to his accent. Now he sounded a little stilted, a faint Eastern European rhythm rubbing through textbook English, and nobody seemed to notice a goddamn thing. More than that, though, he *moved* differently, in some indefinable way.

Chris Everly had walked like a prep-school douchebag. This guy Andranov's body language shouted *thug*.

He complimented Mrs. Martinez on the mansion's 'readiness' and the middle-aged woman outright blushed, smiling broadly. A lanky guy in his twenties, ginger scruff clinging to his cheeks, was Hardison 'the driver'—Christ knew the monster was a menace on the road—and a few others were introduced, their names passing right through Bea's head, refusing to lodge. The staff did not shake hands, instead bowing and smiling like she was some kind of foreign dignitary.

Should've worn something other than pajamas. Bea was past embarrassment—or so she thought, she flinched internally when the monster, as an aside, smoothly mentioned she was jet-lagged.

"A long flight," he intoned, and that smiling mask must have fooled everyone but her, because Wren grinned back and Mrs. Martinez chirped in agreement before hurrying for the kitchen to take care of something or another.

It was so *bright*, too. All the glass meant grey winter stormlight poured into rooms blazing with electric fixtures; Bea's eyes smarted. She should have been ravenous, after...after everything, but even the spread laid out in the huge breakfast nook—pancakes, bacon, assorted fruit cut into decorative shapes, toast, sausages, fresh coffee in a thermal carafe, on and on, Mrs. Martinez and two silent younger women clearly serving as maids hustling between table and kitchen—turned her stomach.

The monster pulled out a high-backed wooden chair with a cheerful green gingham seat cushion, very politely, and Bea sank into it despite goosebumps spreading down her arms at something so dangerous standing right behind her. A second chair without a cushion was obviously arranged just for him, since a stack of fresh newspapers stood to one side of the nested plates and Wren hurried to pour coffee.

"Mum?" The big guy looked almost eager, offering the carafe; her heart gave a strangling, terrified leap. Months spent doing surveillance and attempting to avoid this very fellow's notice was a hard habit to break.

"No, thanks," she managed. Should she pretend a Russian accent? She'd sound like an idiot. "I'm, uh, more of a tea person." Caffeine withdrawals were nasty on stakeouts, and staying mostly away from java meant occasionally slamming some espresso before a meatpacking shift made a positive difference.

Maybe I'd've swung the stake faster if I'd been on a quad latte. The thought was a slap of cold water, and Bea exhaled shakily.

The monster clearly read *The New York Times,* which totally tracked. Underneath it on the pile was the *Causeway Daily,* though, and she caught sight of a moderately large headline.

—*VERLY BUILDING GAS LEAK.*

Could she risk reaching for a paper? Should she say something about catching up on her reading, dare the monster to snatch the *Daily* out of her hands? Bea peered at the letters, wishing the type was bigger, willing her eyes to stop stinging.

"Tea?" Mrs. Martinez was on the case. "English Breakfast, Earl Grey? Or herbal—chamomile, perhaps? We have chai as well. Just say what you like."

The monster's dark gaze rose over the edge of the *Times.* If it was a warning, it was a great one, because Bea suddenly had zero desire to rock the boat. "Whatever you have is fine, ma'am."

"So easy!" The woman beamed pacifically, bustling back for the kitchen—was she on something? Did he drug the help?

I am beginning to think four years of research wasn't nearly enough. They had included a lot of guesswork, a boatload of praying to a god she couldn't believe in after Jared's death, a whole *lotta* assuming. But Jesus, what else were you supposed to do when a monster killed your brother?

And he sat there reading the paper like it was any old day of the week. What would he do if she started screaming? Could she get to an outside door in time? Would the 'staff' help him, or…

Wren loaded his plate and began chowing down Continental-style, knife in one hand, fork in the other. The 'driver' Hardison drifted in, doing the same but with American manners, left hand in his lap unless using a heavy silver butterknife to slice pancakes. The younger man was clearly on best behavior, glancing at the monster once or twice as if for approval. Mrs. Martinez had a spot at the table as well, but the other two maids didn't show up after a certain point and the cheerful woman was up out of her chair so often—fetching, arranging, bustling, refilling—that just watching her was exhausting.

Finally, Bea managed to get a good look at the *Daily*, and she went cold all over for the fiftieth time since waking up.

EVERLY BUILDING GAS LEAK, OWNER MISSING.

That was the big morning news in-city. Chris Everly was presumed dead.

CHAPTER 14

SHE LASTED LONGER THAN HE THOUGHT POSSIBLE OR ADVISABLE, sitting pale and composed in the place of honor, politely refusing so much as a sip or morsel. Persephone at her first feast, watching narrowly as her host set aside a broadsheet in order to peel a tangerine.

Such luxury these days, so much ripe fruit at every table. Mounds of apples, citron varieties, pears, fraises, other berries, bananas in supermarkets, other treasures spilling from the stands; he still sometimes could not fathom how calmly mortals accepted the miracle. Every age was one of wonder, even those plagued by dissolution.

Citrus had a great deal of vibrancy, though it could not match her scent. He did wish briefly for a pomegranate and a silver spoon to free the seeds. Would she recognize the gift?

"Here." He offered the small fruit, wrenched from its protective carapace. "Try it."

A tight, unamused smile. Her gaze fluttered like a wounded bird, evading his; she took the tangerine with delicate care, avoiding even his fingertips, and settled it on her salad plate. A polite noise, her lips moving in what could have been *thank you.*

Yet she visibly trembled. Fangmarks on her slim throat had paled, white and worn-looking as old scars; the healing agents were perhaps overwhelmed by just how much stress her lovely near-mortal body was under. Sleep had done some good but her eyes were still shadowed, the silken fall of her hair haphazardly combed but so irresistible.

A measure of tousling suited her very well—slightly more preferable than the sleekness she'd sported at the party, though that was also decidedly attractive.

Wrenfeldt clearly decided to help the housekeeper bear the conversational burden, complimenting the house and querying politely of Hardison how moving the vehicles had gone, if the garage was up to snuff. Lukas, freshly observant, noted slight changes in social mores, flickers and cross-currents of subtle mortal communication. His new cover felt far more natural than Everly had, both his perceptions and reactions polished to shining.

Such an immense gift, and at its heart this pale, fearful stranger, scorching away uncounted centuries of dust.

"Excuse me." She unfolded, laying a gilt-threaded linen napkin beside her untouched setting. "Not feeling well. Jet lag, sorry."

And she fled—no doubt almost blindly, for her pretty eyes were now red-rimmed. She had blooded him slightly, after all, and was so exquisitely sensitive. Initial effects of the Gift were wearing through, which meant she needed another bite, and feeding as well.

Conversation died, though Wrenfeldt was largely unruffled. The housekeeper looked worried, clearly hoping she had not offended; Hardison hunched over his plate, forgetting laboriously acquired manners for a moment.

"Well done," Lukas allowed, as he rose. "We are under maximum security; you all know what that means."

No more was required. He ambled after her, hands in pockets though it destroyed the lines of the suit.

Did she know how alluring a chase could be?

It was easy to herd a stumbling, fearful leman, even if mistform was denied him during daylight. Lukas rarely needed to use the whispering speed either, since all it took was appearing in her line of sight for his Beatrice to turn and ramble the other direction. The largest problem was keeping her from maintenance or other staff; if she attempted soliciting mortal aid he would have to eliminate the hapless bystander at speed instead of in lingering fashion. The thrall was upon him again, painfully iron-hard, and though modern fabrics were far more comfortable than those of many other eras, he could hardly stand the irritation against his skin.

Step by step, he guided her through the house. Hopefully she was appreciating its bulk and the dim intimation of its purpose —to hold a leman in comfort. If it did not please her, he would find another. Somewhere in the vast world was a place she would enjoy; he would try every permutation until success was achieved.

He did not miss her pause in the cathedral-like den with a rustic stone fireplace; an old housekeeper's trick, burning wood dispelling the cold reek of disuse. A hint of smoke reminding him of other places, other times, but the most important detail was the poker missing from a set of tools upon a decorative hearth-rack.

The shovel might have been a better choice, kitten. Still, this promised to be entertaining, and he turned her wandering course toward the master's suite. She may even have realized his intent, for she lingered in the doorway to the antechamber, staring as if she had not seen the room before, casting a single piercing glance over her shoulder.

Those lovely eyes of hers. Lukas stepped out of shadow, appearing at the opposite end of the hallway.

She gasped, retreating into the trap, and furthermore into the bedroom itself, finally brought to bay. Yes, there was the poker, clutched white-knuckle and held in fencing position; she blinked furiously, a trace of saltwater clinging to one soft flawless cheek, and backed away as he strolled in. He hooked the door with his heel, a quick flicker of motion swinging it to, and leaned back, resting his shoulders until the latch caught. The invisible seal barely took a moment to apply, and he was alone with his leman in an overstuffed green-and-gold suite, rain rattling at roof and wide, crystalline bay windows barred from breakage or spying by a protective shimmer.

Paradise. And a Beatrice to guide me.

"I'm not trying to escape," she informed him, taking a post near the entrance to the giant closet. Had she gauged his speed and considered the bathroom door too far away? There was no lock on either—not that any mortal deadbolt or bar would deter him. "Really. Honestly, I *swear.* I was just…looking for…"

"Of course," he agreed. "You're in some distress."

"Really? Can't imagine why." Quick sarcasm, though her pulse fluttered in her throat. Provoking him again, attempting to exert some small control over the situation.

Were all leman so enticing, or had she been made simply and solely for him? Impossible to tell, so he might as well call it the latter. Once that was decided, all else followed.

"The light's too bright." Lukas attempted a soothing tone, an operation of moderate difficulty since his true teeth were struggling to burst free, painfully sensitive. *Soon,* he promised silently; *we must play the game, but the outcome is not even remotely in doubt.* "And neither water nor wine will touch the thirst. You're only beginning to feel it."

Beatrice froze, those extraordinary green eyes widening. The room almost matched, though nothing could approach the effect of her gaze; being the object of her attention was far more pleasant than he could have imagined.

"Oh dear God," she breathed. "You're going to make me kill them, aren't you. The *staff*. And once I do, I'll be like you."

She must have a head stuffed with folk stories and superstitions, but that was hardly surprising. "That's somewhat of a misapprehension, my dear leman. You are granted the Gift, of course, but I'll do the hunting for both of us, thank you." He attempted to match her accent; very imprecise, he decided. He preferred the crispness of slightly older diction.

"Again with the lemons," she muttered, lifting the poker. The slim iron bar trembled, its tip wavering. "I kill monsters, not people, Mr. Everly. Or is it Andranov? You have a lot of names."

"It's no matter." He lifted one shoulder slightly, dropped it, a subtle shrug. "Call me what you like." The gathering thunder in his bones demanded motion. He stepped away from the door. The sound of the rain underlaid her quick light breathing; her finely arched ribs heaved.

"Don't." The poker stilled. "Look, I'll give you the necklace and go on my merry way, all right? If you didn't murder my brother, fine, I'm sorry about the whole stabbing thing. You have to admit I—"

He could stand it no longer. Lukas moved, snatching the poker; a low terrible sound of stressed metal before he tossed the ruined implement behind him. It clanged against the bedroom door, a muffled *thump* since invisible seals swallowed physical noise. Her shoulders pressed against the wallpaper next to the closet entrance and her slim softness trapped against him, his fangs gloriously free and her small hands flat against his chest, an ineffectual shove.

His head was bent, his nose a bare inch from hers. A heady deluge of performed breath bearing a candysweet edge—indeed, the Gift was scouring through her mortality. Exceptional that it had only taken a moiety of his claret, but a most welcome development.

"Please." That lush, eminently kissable mouth, begging to be plundered. Wet matted eyelashes, her adorable nose pinkened, the feathering of gold at her temples. "Don't make me...whatever you are. Please don't."

It was laughable. "I could not even if I tried. You do not have the temperament for such things." *And if you sink your fangs into another creature, kitten, I will have to tear it to pieces.* Stark possessiveness warred with a certain tender ache, for she was no doubt very lost and frightened at the moment. "My plans are far different."

"What are you going to do?" Her perennial question; eventually she would learn the simplicity of his intent.

What do you expect? The lessons would be illuminating, not to mention deeply fulfilling. "First, I think I shall tear those clothes off you."

Her chin rose slightly. Once more she took refuge in provocation. "The only things I like in that fucking closet, of course you'd destroy them." Her scent was maddening, musk filling his head, a faint sweet note of fresh apples, a salt-tinge of mortality.

And she had finally stated a preference, a wonderful development.

Of course it was too late. His claws were already free, razor edges ripping through his own cloth before turning to her admittedly far thinner garb, careful to merely graze tender warm skin-curves without scratching. She had no time to protest, for the bed was a short distance away even as mortals counted such things.

Glorious to sample her mouth again, to drown in the taste of her. He knew precisely how to breach the gate now, despite her first panicked resistance; at some point he might learn the joy of slow entry but at this moment the thrall demanded otherwise. A single thrust and he was halfway in; simple to brace one arm behind her knee, granting him much better access, and surge deeper.

Rediscovering just how marvelous it felt to be buried inside her—how could he have forgotten in such a short while? Yet every encounter with a leman was fresh, volcanic, tearing away the sharp numbness of age, teaching the wonder of the world and sanguinant senses anew.

Lukas found himself loath to halt the kiss, but the tang of his own claret was unmistakable—he'd sliced his lip on a fangtip, a minor miscalculation. He broke free, gasping, and nuzzled at her throat.

<h1 style="text-align:center">CHAPTER 15</h1>

A silly move, trying to hold him off with a poker; he'd twisted the metal bar into a pretzel and tossed it casually away. Then another of those curious time-skips and he was *on* her, the bed giving with a heavy sigh and his arm suddenly under her left knee. She had never been pinned like this, opened and ruthlessly invaded—her college fumblings, though expected and sort-of-heady in the beginning stages, had been sweaty, alcohol-laced, and ended up deeply unsatisfactory.

Her back arched, her right sock-heel finding the slightly surface of the jacquarded duvet and digging in hard enough to burn, a fuzzy thumping filling her ears—*heartbeat,* she thought hazily, *that's mine*—as narcotic heat dilated from the fangs buried in her throat.

How in the hell...? Useless to wonder just how she'd ended up naked, he had indeed ripped the clothes right off her. Bea's body didn't care about that, it simply thrashed—so far as it could, he was simply too goddamn strong.

Worst of all, a familiar hazy, anticipatory pressure bloomed between her legs. The monster growled, just like in the elevator, and Bea's fingers were claws, nails skipping along the hard smooth curves of his shoulders, muscle flickering against her palms. He thrust again, impossibly deep, tender tissues stretching, a subterranean thrill through her entire shaking, riven body.

Something else rubbed between them, an unerring pressure like a wicked, knowing fingertip against her clitoris. Lightning soared. A moan died at the back of her mouth, her lips slack and open; again and again he rocked, stabbing for her core.

OhGod ohGod ohGod...Was she saying it aloud? Black flowers bloomed behind her eyelids, sealed tight. She was being fucked by a monster, and the hell of it was that he was very good. Slick-wet, bent nearly in half, every nerve exploding, colors strobe-flickering between the black flowers, she had never, *never* understood it could be like this, even with her own hand during the usual teenage exploration of just how to jill herself correctly.

Even worse, it didn't take long at all before a quasi-familiar stillness swallowed her whole. It was inevitable, just a matter of friction in the right spot, orgasm teasing its own inevitability.

The monster's growl deepened, tempo slowing into hard deep thrusts, each accompanied by that insistent probing at her clit. She struggled to avoid release, aware of futility, helpless to stop resistance *or* the explosion.

Long and low, the pulses tore through her. Clenching and releasing around a hot, plundering stranger, her head flung back, sweat sliding between her skin and the strange matte texture of his, a half-strangled cry she recognized as her own stuttering to a stop.

Alive. She was still alive, heartbeat pounding in her wrists, her ankles, her chest, even in her hair. The cessation of agonizing fear was its own reward, even as she shuddered with aftershock. The cock buried in her throbbed, jerking spasmodically, and she couldn't even worry about unprotected monster sex again.

It felt too goddamn good to simply be unafraid for a few moments.

He stilled, and for the first time she was aware of his breathing in deep ragged gulps as well. Had she imagined the fangs? Kisses printed on her throat, working up past her jaw, and his mouth found hers. Tongue, lips, teeth all human again, and he took his time, exploring her response, kissing like a starving man.

Guess he's had time to practice. The crashing realization of what he'd just done hovered somewhere outside a glass bubble, a snowglobe of shock. There was an odd sweet taste to him, slightly metallic, which somehow managed to soothe the dry thirst-pain.

Blood. Probably mine. Jesus.

Though he had obviously gotten what he wanted, the monster remained buried in her, cock twitch-throbbing. At least his weight wasn't crushing—very considerate of him to let her breathe. Hard to think with his mouth doing that—pursuing, demanding attention, *taking.*

Finally, the kiss turned shallower. He pecked at the corner of her lips, pressed more light caresses to her damp, feverish cheek, and finally exhaled close to her ear, hot breath stirring sweat-soaked hair. The sigh turned into words.

"Beatrice." Playing with her name, tasting each syllable. He made it sound absolutely indecent, and Bea had to now deal with the fact that she was spread and nailed under a monster.

And that she had enjoyed it enough to come.

"Say something," he whispered, the sibilants a torrid purr as his cock moved inside her again. "Tell me what you like."

Oh, my God, what the fuck are you doing? More squares on some insane internal bingo card she'd never even dreamed of checking off—fucked by a monster in an elevator, and now this. "Get off of me," she managed, in a breathy, high-pitched little voice.

"Not yet." A faint rasp of stubble as his cheek moved against hers—did monsters shave? "Won't let me. See?"

Another movement, a dragging as his hips rocked, and Bea gasped at the flood of sensation. Postcoital sensitivity meant the smallest shift was magnified, electricity zapping all through her.

A curious feeling, the swelling, almost as if the shape of his cock had changed.

"Barbed, after release," he continued. "Rendering me vulnerable for a short while until the swelling retreats. I cannot leave you, little leman."

Barbed was concerning. *Vulnerable* was interesting. Her cheeks were scarlet-hot, a drenching flood of embarrassment—maybe even shame, she couldn't tell yet. And to top off the entire impossible situation, her brain-mouth filters were failing again. "What is it with you and lemons?" She didn't add *do you have a fruit fixation* only by an effort of will.

"Leman," he corrected. How could a monster sound pedantic after fucking the life out of her? "It means *beloved one.* There are other terms—*imprima, deva, sangdolce. Aima-glyza.*"

Uh. "Please get off of me." She tried to move, to slither away, achieved exactly nothing.

"I already said I cannot, for some short while. Try to relax."

You did not *just tell me to relax.* Maybe males were the same the world over, monsters or not. "At least let go of my leg."

She was bargaining with a bloodsucking fiend. At any moment he was probably going to bite her again. Bea's body gave a low twinge at the thought, and he inhaled sharply.

"Slowly," he murmured in her ear. "Very slowly, kitten."

Sure, monster. Anything you say. But Bea found he would cooperate, though she had to wrap her legs around his waist to ease the strain in her back and hips. The angle shifted as they sank into the bed, her ankles locked against each other, and it would have been nice, it would've been flat-out *great* if he were human.

And if he hadn't killed Jared. Or had he? "Why are you doing this?" She had a limited window here, either of getting him to say something useful or doing her own thinking without the interference of terror.

Come on, Bebe. Use that noggin of yours. Thankfully it wasn't her brother's voice; she didn't think she could stand that at the moment.

Her only weapons here were playing along and thinking ahead. What, after all, would happen when the monster got tired of her? Maybe she ought to be nice, pretend interest, flatter him.

"I'm old." He sighed, and though he still wasn't crushing her, the monster wasn't letting her go anytime soon either. "The years add up, pretty Beatrice. Our kind becomes slow, numb. Hidebound."

"Okay." *Keep him talking.* She tried not to wriggle, tried to not even breathe too hard. Sweat cooled on her arms, her knees, though he was very warm. They were stuck together like some kind of nightmare hybrid—she shivered at the thought.

"Hm." Not quite a growl, as he nuzzled below her ear—a bit awkward, since he was so much taller. The bulk above her might be comforting, protective, if he wasn't a monster. "As we survive, we begin to calcify. Mentally, physically, in every way— a slow death, and unpleasant. The only cure is a leman."

"Cure?" The unappetizing prospect of being infected with a monster's STD rose again, refusing to die just like he had. "Wait, did you give me a—"

"An addiction, to break the spell. It is not like your fairytales, your movies." Did he sound irritated, or dismissive? The monster shifted slightly, propping an elbow near her bare shoulder, and his fingers threaded into her hair. "I did not kill your brother, Beatrice—though if I had arrived earlier and scented you, who is to say? Or perhaps another sanguinant would have found you, since you were actively seeking out the demimonde." His fingers paused, wound in her hair, his hand stiffening.

Uh-oh. "Demimonde?" *Mirror him, let him know you're listening. Men like to talk about themselves.* "I've heard that term." Not often, and always in connection to truly scary stories, the genuinely inexplicable ones that ended up with gruesome body counts, rabbitholing anyone who read too many right into tinfoil hats.

"Many things live alongside mortals." The slow, sinuous caressing of her hair continued. "Few will trouble you, including the *greiben*. I will exterminate the clan which killed your Jared soon enough."

She didn't like him mentioning Jare, especially under current conditions. It felt wrong; so did that other word. "Exterminate?"

"Old and young put to the sword, their spawning grounds sterilized, their halls reduced to emptiness—you may view it as revenging your brother. Will that please you?"

Bea kept her eyes closed. The moment she opened them, she was going to have to reckon with...everything. "Helluva way to treat your henchmen, Mr. Everly."

Saying a dead man's fake name after being fucked by a bloodsucker. If she'd known hunting monsters would end up here, she might never have started. The enormity of what she'd stumbled into made the paralyzing fear threaten a return, nipping at the edges of bodily relaxation.

Her hormones had no goddamn judgment.

"I told you, sanguinant do not stoop to such tools." A fractional tensing, though the cock buried in her had not changed shape again, thank goodness. The monster's lips moved a hairsbreadth from her earlobe, sending shivers down her back with every syllable. "They will continue pursuing the *greisoul*. After all, it is one of their own."

The necklace, pressed between them. At least he hadn't broken it, ripping her clothes off, and she now realized he had avoided smashing the thing through her breastbone during the festivities, too. Nice of him—the setting had some sharp curlicues. But what did he mean, *one of their own*? "You're calling my brother a thief."

"Not at all. If he stumbled into their warrens, he must have been both determined and lucky to escape. Taking a souvenir is understandable, especially since *greisoul* gems are rather enchanting." His chin brushed her shrinking skin, for all the world like a cat's playful nudge. "Nothing to match you, of course."

Okay, sure. Bea was naked save for socks, the duvet was full of scratchy threads, and her hips were never going to forgive her. How long was she trapped here?

The problem was that no subject seemed safe, and in any case the monster didn't pause. "It's Lukas, by the way." A slow, careful enunciation, the final sibilant nearly a shush rather than a hiss. His tension had increased; she hoped it wasn't a bad sign. "My name, when I was mortal. Long ago."

There. That's something to talk about. If she kept him occupied...how long could that work? "How old are you really?"

"Ah." For a moment he sounded very human, and slightly embarrassed. "I do not precisely know. I had the Gift when Akkad was three huts in the mud; I am old and strong enough to be daywalker, and that is enough. Perhaps I am even Archon now."

"Argon?" *Wait 'til I tell Don.* Bea flinched inwardly; the urge to share a new piece of gossip or occult lore with her co-investigator was goddamn near automatic as breathing. She had to find out if he was all right. But how? "No, wait. Listen, what if you give them the necklace back? You can do that, right?" *Because I'd rather not try, though I will if I have to.*

"The *greiben* would consider it an even greater insult, and their nagging grow constant. No, my leman. They must be erased." He stretched, cat-supple, and moved his elbows. Cool air slipped between them—not their lower halves, but he was drawing back.

Looking at her.

Bea swallowed hard, kept her eyes tightly shut. The sweetish taste at the back of her throat wouldn't go away; the fresh bite marks pulsed uneasily. She was acquiring quite a collection.

Was the monster lying? Mixing real details with whoppers, since she clearly didn't know what the hell? Or was he gaslighting her, defense-lawyering whatever involvement he had in Jared's murder?

He couldn't be telling the truth.

Could he?

Silence gathered, blanketed the room. Had the rain stopped? All she could hear was her own breathing. Did he think she was asleep? The sense of being watched was eerily, hatefully familiar. She had a lot to think about, with no idea of how much time she had for cogitation.

A trickle of rasping, unsteady anger collected in her chest. She lay frozen, quiet, and waited.

After an eternity, he withdrew inch by inch. As soon as humanly possible Bea rolled away, stifling a groan as her hips informed her that no, they did *not* forgive her, but it had been a helluva ride nonetheless. Her legs were noodles, the rest of her not far behind. Still, she managed to curl up almost pillbug-tight before the monster proved he wasn't about to leave her alone.

He simply picked her up like a recalcitrant toddler, with frightening ease and no sign of effort. His breathing didn't even change; she kept her eyes squeezed shut, not daring to peek.

It didn't matter. The monster carried her into the bathroom, but not to yet another sunken tub. Instead, a glassed-in shower accepted them both—it was certainly supersized enough, and who needed four nozzles? The water pressure was *great*, though. It was absolutely unfair.

Being washed by a monster was an odd experience, mostly because he was so careful. Scrubbing with a cold trickle and harsh washcloth had become Bea's habit during the monster-hunting years, always while thinking about the next research subject, the next intel dig, the next bit of careful surveillance or sleuthing.

And it had all ended up here.

He even toweled gently, for God's sake.

CHAPTER 16

His prize was still mistrustful. Yet Lukas thought it likely some small progress had been made.

Her physical response was sheerly overwhelming, perhaps because fear lay so close to the survival urge in mortals; eventually, the impetus might be replaced as she learned the dimensions of her new existence. Even the mistake of biting his own flesh had a fortunate effect, in that forcing her to drink from the vein was not quite required at the moment. Eventually the thirst would mount to a point beyond palliating with simple traces of his claret, and he almost lost track of his surroundings while contemplating the future pleasure of her soft, avid mouth drawing upon his blood-channels.

He could not tell whether she was inexperienced enough not to notice certain differences between sanguinant and mortal anatomy, or too frightened to ask. Traditionally one hunted down a leman's previous lovers or mortal encumbrances, if any; modern mores had changed somewhat, and Lukas decided he could indeed set aside that particular custom.

Unless it became necessary. The petty criminal with his podcast might prove useful later; in any case, mortals aged so quickly. Very soon it would be a moot point.

She would be fresh and new centuries from now. Another pleasant thing to think upon.

Beatrice, enthroned in a green velvet wingback chair—a quite agreeable amenity of the master suite's antechamber, these two wide deep seats with the small table tucked companionably between, situated so as to enjoy one of the bay windows, unsealed, though winter twilight blinded the glass. The view was otherwise an expanse of manicured lawn before a tangled evergreen hedge, an incongruous white gazebo swimming in the middle distance.

He would have preferred a more civilized garden, which could be remedied come springtime. If, that was, he and his leman were still in residence.

He had turned the bedside lamps on, and the soft golden gleam was comfortable enough for sanguinant eyes. The *greisoul* gem glimmered, full of its own secret fire. Beatrice had chosen more soft, clinging clothing—nightwear, another set of fleece pants and long-sleeved shirt, candy-striped red and white. Large fluffy yellow socks completed the ensemble; he would make arrangements for more of this attire.

Not only did she look very fetching, but the cloth was too flimsy for outside wear. And she consented to pick at a pleasingly arranged fruit-and-cheese platter carried hence upon a heavy silver tray, the housekeeper doing her best to tempt the lady.

Beatrice did not touch the champagne, though. And her gaze kept flickering to the hall door, standing temptingly ajar.

He was not so foolish as to think her tamed, or even resigned. Quite possibly she might never be.

"It all ends in the same place." He had to speak carefully, for her questions deserved not only clear but appropriate answers, and her understanding of the demimonde was rudimentary indeed. "Attempt escape, inevitably fail, and I will have you. Accept necessity, do not attempt anything unwise, and I will have you. Either way, it will be pleasant."

She toyed with a dusky grape—seedless, a marvel of viticulture, and not nearly so succulent as the lips it brushed or fingertips it rested against. "So no matter what I do, you're going to…" Color rising to her cheeks, a charming flush.

"Yes." *As often as possible.* Even the thought caused a sleepy rumble in the thrall, lingering in preternatural marrow. "It is an addiction, as I said. Leman are passing rare; you are the only one I have ever encountered."

"But…" Puzzlement puckering her forehead, she shifted in the chair, wrinkling her nose as well—a wince, tender mortality somewhat unprepared for sanguinant enthusiasm. The Gift, clearly at work, would swiftly ease such discomfort. "What if you're wrong? What if I'm just some stranger with a grey-man—gryvhen?"

"*Greiben.*" In the dark Teuton forests they had been called other things, and their halls rumored to contain much treasure. Many things burrowed in the earth's skin, hiding from mortal scrutiny until pressed, then reacting with carnivorous force.

"*Greiben*, okay." She took care with the word, attempting to be a good student. "What if I'm just a rando with special jewelry? What is this thing, anyway?"

Are you certain you wish to know? He had to think carefully, parsing modern slang; how stilted and foreign had his speech become? Had his underlings—other than Wrenfeldt—noticed? Business associates would paper over a great deal of strangeness so long as profit was assured, but the risk was still unacceptable.

And he had not even suspected. Lukas reached for the champagne bottle, ignoring the corresponding movement pressing her back into the chair. He poured for two; if she changed her mind, the small pleasure would be ready. "The stronger among *greiben* often consume the weaker. If one does so enough, it becomes an elder—bigger, capable of calling a greater amount of hunting-mist, acquiring far more opportunities to feed and breed. When an elder challenges and consumes another elder, sometimes the core of the eaten condenses in the gut, and a *greisoul* is formed. It eventually kills the eater, with blockage or internal bleeding. The *greiben* consider such created stones holy, and the worship rituals…" Lukas trailed off, for she was distractingly thrilling even while displaying unmitigated disgust. Her collarbones were sweet curves, the fresh glaring fangmarks an unmistakable sign of possession, and that lush, soft mouth begged once more to be kissed as it twisted.

"Oh, my God." She replaced the grape carefully among its brethren and immediately lowered her head, hair swaying as hands flew to her nape. "Oh, *ew*. No. Nope, nope, nope."

Lukas at first couldn't identify the urge rising from his midsection. It turned into a disbelieving laugh—rusty, hoarse, but the first time he had evinced real amusement instead of a controlled simulation in at least two centuries. Another exquisite jolt, burning through him just as the honeyed zap of her blood.

He would have enjoyed rendering assistance, but she had the necklace's catch open in a trice. The chain slithershimmered, loosening to brush her shirt before she held the *greisoul* at arm's length, in one fine-boned, trembling hand. "No way." Her lip curled, she looked about near-wildly as if tempted to throw a rarity into the nearest bin.

Many in the demimonde would hunger to acquire such a thing, despite its obvious dangers.

"It bears no curse for you," Lukas found himself saying. "It was given in love; keep it in remembrance. Of Jared." An old name, pronounced differently not so long ago—but a good one. The boy had clearly been worthy of it.

"Don't." A hard shake of her head. Tiny flakes of black dye already loosening, unnoticed as they scattered, yet another sign of the Gift. "Don't say his name, please."

Four years could be a long mortal while; she had spent it working toward vengeance—and Lukas's presumed demise. Were he tempted to superstition of his own, he could consider her pursuit of him the result of a divine intervention.

To have missed her so narrowly, then been given another

chance just before calcification took him...if mere coincidence, he had won the equivalent of several hundred consecutive mortal lotteries. "Where were you, that night? How did I miss you?"

"Outside. A window." She stared at the *greisoul*'s viridian gleam, the chain dripping from her palm. "I was paying bills, I asked him to take Snowball out. Lost track of time. Then I went looking for...the light in the stable was on." She swallowed convulsively, the shiver of a fragile butterfly.

Lukas's mouth turned down slightly; he sought to dredge the exact memory of that particular night. "Ah. On the west side. If I hadn't exited through the roof, I would have passed and scented you."

Now Beatrice regarded him narrowly. "Why would you go out the roof?"

"Following the *greiben*—there was a hole in the hayloft, pointing quite neatly in the direction of their closest warren-entrance. Mile and a half from the house, I should say, almost due east." If not for the need to halt the annoyance of their pursuit, Lukas might cleanse the warrens simply because they had robbed him of discovering her that night, though it was childish to blame half-sentient excrescences for his own inattention. "Were you wearing the necklace, then?"

"Christ, no." Surprised, as if the very thought were outlandish. "I think it was in my dresser? I'd just moved back from..."

His leman stopped, still holding the *greisoul* stiffly away. Her gaze leapt from the gem to him, and Lukas could not even begin to guess what she was thinking.

He suspected even another few millennia would not help him unravel the barest fraction of that magnificent mystery. Whether the fascination hinged upon an innate quality of leman or was simply the bonding pressing inexorably upon lingering mating instincts—for all sanguinant had been mortal once—did not matter.

He was alive again, and more than old enough to appreciate the fact properly.

Beatrice gingerly set the *greisoul* next to the silver tray. She bit her lower lip as she rubbed her hands together, scrubbing away imaginary foulness, and her eyes shone with gathering tears.

Yet she refused to weep again, simply set her chin and glared at Lukas. Sorrow turned aside with anger, a response both mortal and sanguinant. How many times had he seen the shift in others, across shoals and gulfs of empty time?

"I can't believe a word you say," she said, quietly. "I *won't* believe it."

She would not be so imperious had not doubt entered her pretty, rumpled head. Lukas thought she could hold out against blunt cruelty for some while, but her only real defense against *him* was sarcastic goading and stubborn refusal to admit she might have mistaken the cause of her brother's death.

He had been strictly, scrupulously truthful with his leman since the moment he caught that heady fragrance at the party, strings of red beads alive with movement, her soft bare arms glowing.

He could have missed her twice, Wrenfeldt's mention of an assumed journalist surveilling 'Chris Everly' a not-quite-uncommon occurrence. The thought turned him cold, briefly, a freshly honed emotion-knife, welcome even as it sliced.

Not a single grain of mistruth would she receive from him; yet though her reaction was quite natural, it stung. Even that pain was a sweet hedge against calcification.

Eventually she would learn better. Or not, and he would forever pursue a reluctant nymph.

Champagne was an acquired taste, complex sourness and a short bubbling frisson. Alcohol simply burned away from sanguinant, though some claimed to feel intoxication. It was nothing compared to mortal claret, of course, and even less to a single droplet of his prize. He sipped slowly, considering the next few moves.

"How long do I have?" Another challenge, soft but utterly defiant. "Before you bite me again, I mean. Do I get to know?"

"I could bite you now." *And more.* Indeed he was tempted, especially since she froze, staring deerlike at the nearest wolf. "But you need rest, and I must hunt. When you have finished your meal I will take you to the saferoom; you will rest there. Alone, sadly."

"You mean that big empty creepy place?" Her hands tangled together, knuckles turning pale. "Come on, don't lock me up in there. There's not even a toothbrush."

Ah. He had forgotten a crucial detail of her mortal wants. Fortunately, it was easily remedied, and he could make arrangements for other attire—more pleasing for her, though he found he liked the flimsy sleepwear almost as much as the red dress. "Eat. Or do not, hunger will accelerate the Gift."

"I don't even want to know what that means," she muttered, staring at the glass bowl of melon flesh, ripe colors cut into artistic shapes.

Little liar. "It means I look forward to feeding you. Take your time."

CHAPTER 17

A FEW HOURS LATER HER HEAD HURT LIKE A BITCH, POSSIBLY FROM low blood sugar since she couldn't eat, too busy worrying about this fucked-up situation. If Bea considered *everything* he said a goddamn lie, she wouldn't have to worry about changing into a monster, just about getting killed as soon as she put a foot wrong.

Right?

Attempting to think about something productive took concerted, heavy effort. Trying to piss him off didn't work, and God alone knew what he'd do to her next.

Either way, it will be pleasant. The way he just *said* stuff like that, with utter certainty.

If he was really telling the truth about everything...but no. Attempting to consider that notion caused a deep unsteady feeling somewhere in the middle of her bones, as if the world was about to shred itself to pieces, starting with her own body.

There was nothing about 'lemans' in any occult research she'd done or seen. Sure, witches were accused of fucking the Devil but it wasn't the same thing—was it? And the Brides of Dracula stuff was a relatively modern pop culture invention.

Of course, plenty of legends about goblins and alien abductions seemed to overlap awfully well with the little green hench-men, and word was any type of bloodsucker could get all sorts of critters to do their bidding. Someone out there probably believed bloodsuckers overlapped with extraterrestrials, too.

Imagine being able to answer that definitively, right from the source. She could open up whole new vistas in folklore studies, she could go on *all* the underground podcasts. Don would be avid to hear any details of the Chicago stuff she could dig out of the monster.

If she survived. If she escaped. If Don was okay; the monster hadn't mentioned him. Hope was a torment all its own.

Then there was the brand new toothbrush, set opposite the soap-divot on the 'saferoom's' pedestal sink. A high-end natural tooth-scrubber, still in recyclable packaging. How the hell had he done that? Texting someone when she fled to the master bath-room and hyperventilated, running the sink faucet to cover the sound? She wouldn't put it past him, and it was a far better explanation than FM—*Fucking Magic*, as Don and Jared chris-tened some of the weird stuff they so avidly researched. Bea had been the skeptical voice of reason all through childhood, her teenage years, and pretty much until the night she peered through a filthy stable window.

Now she knew better. Still, it was probably best to attribute whatever she could to regular, normal causes.

She was already crazy enough.

The monster's employees—or human henchpeople, maybe that was a better term—probably hated her causing them more work and trouble. How big a hold did he have on them? They didn't seem like soulless zombies completely dedicated to helping with evil hijinks. Mrs. Martinez was really nice, in fact.

I will return before dawn. I can make you rest until then, or…

He hadn't bothered to threaten. No, he just gave her the options, with a smile saying he didn't mind either way—an almost human expression, tilting his head and studying her intently. Like a reasonably confident guy in a bar, shooting his shot; at the costume party, she would have assumed he was flirting.

Can we talk about getting fucked by a monster? Are we allowed to even think about that? Because if we are…

"Jesus." Her voice broke the hush; Bea flinched, and couldn't even feel ridiculous. "I'm using the royal we."

She wandered to the saferoom's door. She couldn't even tell if it was locked, for God's sake. The way he *moved…*

If she turned into a bloodsucker would she be that scary-fast, that casually strong? Maybe able to tear down human interior construction? Or did he have his houses built vampire-proof?

The strangest thing was a semitransparent sheet of resistance extending inward about six inches from said door. The curtain became almost-visible as she approached, like a force-field special effect in an old sci-fi movie, and rippled into solidity when she gave it a good old-fashioned donkey kick, suddenly solid as a brick wall. Other than that, it yielded with increasing reluctance to slower pressure, causing a prickling up and down her arms like sunshine on already-burned skin.

That was fucking weird, and no natural explanation for it either.

At least she wasn't trapped wearing only a slip. Terror was a lot easier to take in pajamas. Of course, what she wouldn't give for jeans, boots, a sweater and parka, why not some gloves as well? Plus the cherry on top, a way out of this house.

But then what?

He'd let slip that his security had noticed her before the party, so maybe they'd been watching Don too—depending on how paranoid 'Chris Everly' was. Clearly the stake hadn't put him down for long.

Imagine, if he'd woken up while you were on the roof. She couldn't; her brain, usually so wildly hyper, completely refused to run that particular scenario.

"Okay, review." She tried to treat it like a weird story she was picking apart with Don. "Original name Lukas if he's not lying.

Alive for a *lot* longer than we thought, if he's not lying." *Akkad*, the monster had said, and digging that name out of half-forgotten history reading had taken her a few seconds. "Maybe listening to this if the room's wired for sound, fine, oh well. Had security following me before the party, maybe, *if* he's not lying. But found out my name...not so strange, since I mentioned Jared." Hopefully, if room was bugged or camera'd, they would think she was crazy, muttering to herself. Who wouldn't, under these circumstances? "Says he didn't kill Jared." *Again*, if *he's not lying*.

There had just so happened to be a hole in the hayloft roof, as a matter of fact. Pointing eastward, so far as she could remember. Getting it patched was a Jared Project put on indefinite hold when the freaky shit started—the misshapen tracks in the mud, the rocks thrown from the woods, Snowball's barking and growling when the ear-whine started at irregular intervals, the greasy yellow mist at the edge of the yard where undergrowth began. Squishing and rattling at the windows late at night. The time she'd walked up to the mailbox after dark and could have sworn she was followed back to the house by wet, splorching footsteps.

None of that really seemed ol' Chris Everly's style. Or Lukas, or whoever the hell he was. He'd probably honestly believed throwing money at Jared would make her brother fold, and if not, showing up in all his monster glory and applying invisible pressure might do it. Christ knew she might have told Jare to sell after meeting the guy—*if* he'd been wearing the affable, smiling face from the party.

Bea had spent a lot of time wondering about the conversation between her enemy and her brother before the murder; now she could almost believe none had happened. Unless the monster was playing a part with her too, like switching between Everly and Andranov.

He was a third person when alone with her, an unpredictable fucking hurricane—literally. A chameleon with fangs. Each version of him looked slightly different, moved differently, spoke just a little differently as well.

Which sounded exhausting. When he didn't have anyone to perform for, did he just sit and stare?

He's out 'hunting'. You caught that, didn't you?

Christ, she wished she hadn't. Did he treat all his victims like this? If he was busy sucking her blood, why was he out topping up with more? Was he looking to replace her as soon as she bored him? That bullshit about lemons and rarity and not hurting her…

Bea discovered she had drifted back into the bathroom, staring at the neatly packaged toothbrush. Her fingers wrapped over the sink's cold porcelain rim, squeezing hard.

Did she imagine the faint creaking? Was it her bones, or the ceramic? And she realized two things, catching a stray motion in the mirror flush to the wall, probably safety glass. She could find a way to test that later.

First, she was rocking back and forth, her mouth moving slightly as her thoughts raced. And, second, the lights weren't on. It was pitch-black down here. Yet she could see—dim suggestions of shapes, sure, but way more than she should be able to. She'd seen the shimmer-curtain in front of the door, too.

Were there divots in the sink's rim? She ran her fingertips along the edge, and when she remembered there was a light switch she almost laughed. Thin, crazy giggles, boiling in her dry throat.

The lights flicked on when she flipped the switch, decorative frosted bulbs bursting into life. Her eyes stung, watering hard; she couldn't be sure, but she thought maybe there were small cracks at the sink's edge.

Okay. What now? There was no shelf for the white towels, piled on the sunken bathtub's margins. But maybe she could tear up some of the plumbing, give herself a weapon?

He shook off the stake and turned a poker into a pretzel. You're gonna need a tank, Bea. And maybe a grenade launcher as well.

A metallic rattle brought her out of the bathroom, her heart deciding to leap up and block her windpipe once more. The sound, weirdly muffled but definite, came from the door to the stairs—and the rest of the house.

He'd said *before dawn*, had she wasted all night swaying in front of a mirror talking to herself? Or had he lied? Gone out 'hunting', maybe he'd gotten what he needed?

Oh, my God.

The faint sound continued, and with the bathroom lights burning the larger, just as empty room was full of soft shadows. The huge iron bed sat smugly in the center, a tiny green wink near its foot—the necklace, tossed there because if the monster wasn't lying about how it was made...

Rattlerattle. Scrape. Rattlerattle. Tiny sounds, and now that she thought about it, distorted by the invisible force-field.

Someone trying the door? The monster, attempting to drive her even more bugshit? No, he'd probably just walk in and...have her. Bea clutched at the doorframe, her knees pressing together against a hard shiver.

Trap. If I touch the door, does it count as an 'escape attempt'? Or—and here was an awful, sickmaking thought—was it the little green henchmen, coming after the necklace like he said?

Either way, if she was going to escape, she had to wait and plan for a more-than-good opportunity. If he wasn't lying about this leman thing, she might have some way of exerting a little control over the situation—but if she tried and it wasn't part of his script, he might get annoyed and just tear her head off. Or juicebox her to death.

She couldn't decide what to believe, so Bea just stood stock-still, hoping inaction was the right choice. Finally the door quit making those tiny scratching rattles.

In the end she grabbed the white comforter and settled in a corner. She braced her back against the wall—wood paneling over concrete, it felt like—and wrapped the blanket securely. The necklace lay on the floor nearby, glinting at odd moments; had she simply not noticed its habit of random scintillation before? Her own perceptions were untrustworthy as fuck, the world turned into carnival funhouse distortions.

If the little green fucks burst in, she would throw the jewelry at them and run. Bea hugged her knees, put her feverish forehead down, was dimly glad her hair blocked out the surroundings, and eventually drifted into thin troubled semiconsciousness.

A draft of warm air, the sudden sense of breathing presence. Bea lifted her aching, pounding head, peering through clinging strands of hair.

The monster had appeared without bothering to make a real sound, just that soft rush. The door was still shut tight, the shimmer-curtain undulating like seaweed. He crouched before her, balanced easily, elbows braced on knees. White dress shirt with sleeves rolled casually up, silver watch on his left wrist, dark tailored vest, trousers, those wingtips with the tactical soles, his hair ruffled and spotted with a few drops of ice. The aroma of night and fresh air hung on him.

He'd been outside. Lucky him, getting to stroll around.

He gazed at her steadily, unmoving. Which way was this situation going to go? Would he say anything about the trap?

"Ah," he breathed, a soft syllable as if she'd behaved as expected. "The Gift is wearing through quickly."

Beatrice's shoulderblades pressed hard against the wall. Of course, he could lock her down here to starve; she wished she'd had breakfast or more of the cheese platter, even if the thought made her stomach threaten to cramp.

"You must be a bit uncomfortable," he persisted, in a soft, cajoling tone. How could a monster sound so *comforting*? "Lack of mortal food accelerates the process, and leman are so very sensitive."

Go away. But he wouldn't, she could just tell. So she coughed, clearing her dry, dry throat. Even hobbling to the bathroom to get a drink of water seemed like too much effort at the moment. "I thought you weren't coming back."

Good idea, Bebe. Play a few mind games in his direction, see what he does. It could even be a way to winnow out what was truth in this warped new reality.

"That will never be the case." Did he have to sound actually *contrite*? It was goddamn unnerving. "I am sorry to have left you alone. I can help with the discomfort; will you let me?"

You're asking, huh? That's a big change. Had to be another trap. Bea stared at him, mutinously silent.

"So stubborn." A slow smile, transforming his face; the humanity of the expression was enough to steal her breath, knowing what lay behind it. "Have pity on your poor suitor, Beatrice." Drawing her name out, tasting each syllable.

Pity? My God. She longed to kick him, to find a weapon, to hit the door and run, run, *run* away from this place. Run until her heart exploded, until she dropped and they shoveled her, unidentified, into a quiet hole.

He rubbed his hands together, one-two, a brisk dry sound. The monster unbuckled his watch—it looked expensive, she tried not to notice—and laid it aside. He turned his left palm up, still balanced perfectly in a feline crouch, gracefully immobile.

"Watch." He lifted his right index finger. The nail lengthened soundlessly, thinning and tapering to a wickedly curved point, also catlike.

The fear was back, an old friend, a truly renewable resource. Maybe her heart *would* explode, from sheer terror. Her lungs seemed to have forgotten their function, or there was no air left in this prison.

He set the point against his left wrist. "Your head hurts, doesn't it. And you are a thirsty kitten, but neither for milk nor for ale. There is one thing you want, one thing you must have.

The craving will mount unto agony and may be used to break a fledgling, though you will never know that unpleasantness."

Bea had a dim idea what was likely to happen next, yet she still flinched when he made a swift, decisive motion, dragging the claw hard. The sound was like slicing into a very crisp apple, akin to driving the stake into his chest; nausea filled her to the brim, her eyes watering afresh and her throat giving a terrible rasping throb.

The edges of the cut separated, thick dark crimson welling. It didn't drip or spray, simply swelled with its own surface tension. He didn't even *bleed* right; the monster gazed at the wound distantly, his mouth a straight line and tiny red pinpricks lighting in his pupils.

Bea barely noticed. The smell hit her, strange mineral sweetness shifting confusingly through several different iterations—dark chocolate sprinkled with sea salt, a melting-well-done roast doused with her father's homemade barbecue sauce, a brand of fizzy lemonade she hadn't tasted since she was twelve, all mixed with a strange iron undertone. Good things, wonderful things, food-scents meaning *safety, comfort, come and eat.*

They reached right into her head, tugging at the human sense tied most deeply to memory, and the back of her throat felt funny because of the small begging sound vibrating there as she stared at the welling fluid.

"Smells wonderful, doesn't it." The monster extended his wrist, and the blood still didn't trickle or ooze. It simply trembled at a standstill, as if he had control over that too. "Far better than mortal claret, though that is good enough for survival. I hunted well to feed you, my leman."

Did he...had he killed people, sucked their blood, and now wanted her to...

Bea longed to retch, gag, scramble away; she longed to scream, to throw herself at the door until it gave or her skull broke. She *wanted* to—but her body wasn't listening. It stared at the glistening cut, the smell shifting from one delicious, comforting memory to another. Fresh bread, her childhood favorite cherry Pixie Stix, a bottle of very good Cabernet once won at a work raffle, her college roommate's homemade brownies with a thick central ribbon of caramel, all with that distressing salt-copper undertone that should have sickened her but made the rest all the more magnetizing.

He lifted his arm, a subtle offering movement. Patiently, like luring a frightened cat with tuna—it was only a matter of time, really. Hungry enough, any creature would eventually take a chance.

The moan mounted in her throat. Sweet liquid glistened, beckoning, just within reach.

No. I won't. You can't make me.

Except he definitely could, and almost as definitely would. Would she get as strong, as fast? In that case, it might be worth a shot.

I don't want to be a monster. Though she'd stabbed a guy in the chest with a big ol' wooden stake, hadn't she? All the worrying over whether or not she'd been wrong, murdered a human instead of a—

Her eyes overflowed, hot tears tracing a gentle trail on either cheek. Bea blinked, and the tiny movement was her biggest mistake.

The monster, balanced in his crouch, was not bowled over by her sudden scramble. The discarded comforter slid underneath her knee, her fingers—strangely cold, or his skin was oven-hot— seized his wrist, and he made a soft low sound as her mouth fastened on the cut.

A thick burst of heat against her tongue, the pain in her throat blotting out the world as the first thread of filthy monster blood stroked its immensity. Bea was vaguely aware of movement, of the monster staggering as he never did, her back braced against his chest instead of the wall. His other arm settled around her waist, glueing her in place, but she didn't care because the cut was against her lips, his fingers absently stroking behind her ear as she drank.

Her eyes rolled back. The monster staggered again, a more-or-less controlled fall onto the bed taking her along just as it had in the elevator.

The fear vanished. Every pain in the world, from her parents' absence to Jared's murder, was gone. Her cheeks hollowed as she sucked, tongue working greedily, and the monster crooned softly into her hair, cradling her on a cloud. Blessed warmth started at her toes and fingertips, rapidly rushing inward, a skinwarm sea swallowing her whole.

It was *so good*. His wrist moved and Bea's hands locked hard, attempting to keep the flow. The cut sealed itself, implacably; she licked for any possible remainder, uncaring of the source. Lovely, forgiving wellbeing filled her, exponentially bigger than the few tokes she'd sneaked as a teenager or more serious hit-the-bong games in college. And far, far deeper than the biggest drunk she'd ever had, that one tequila-soaked Truth or Dare party in the dorms her sophomore year.

Beer relaxed you, but tequila made you brave. Nothing in the world had been wrong that night, she'd been bulletproof.

Until the hangover hit, that was.

No. Please, God, no.

As usual, praying changed nothing.

CHAPTER 18

The thirst always won. Easier to give it no chance to gain influence, even if too-frequent gorging risked bloodsickness and the craze. Taking without death was a skill requiring a few centuries' practice, beyond the reach of many even ancient sanguinant, but those elders would likely never reach daywalker status.

He closed the cut, whispering in her unheeding ear. Two lines of a poem in the ancestor of the Argive tongue, a phrase popular in London before a great conflagration, a fragment of song from a riverside raider's camp just before the Rus began to know themselves, a line from a black-and-white film popular during the second half of what mortals called a 'world war'. Even, at last, a misty remnant of his mortal tongue, the language of those who followed the Great Antlered God in order to hunt and feast upon him.

When a woman chose among the warriors for a mate the man could refuse, though that cost more than one fur robe since proposals were generally negotiated well beforehand. The acceptance was a single word, meaning *follow-you-home*.

Her hands clasped his arm, the inside of his wrist pressed to her mouth. It was the first time she had willingly touched him, other than to attempt driving a stake through his heart. Her fangs would not arrive until full transition, but even if she were tempted by his radial pulse afterward, his hide was tough enough to withstand a fledgling nip or two.

That game sounded incredibly enticing as well.

Her scent was yet more deeply dyed with his now, and the mix was powerfully seductive. Thrall dozed pleasantly molten in his bones; he was ready as ever, crushed against her taut little bottom. Yet she was so still, so relaxed.

The first taste was a marvelous occasion. Best to mark it with a traditional gift.

"I was a hunter," he said, searching for the modern tongue, a way to express a universe she would never comprehend, the world before his mortal death. "Still am, of course. But this was long ago, before a certain goddess came from the East." Ah, his leman would not understand the saying, but never mind.

"Something preyed upon our tribe," he continued. "Old and young it took, some few who strayed from the campfires. Every few winters a warrior was chosen to attempt a hunt, and those never returned. Thus we paid our toll to the Night Spirit. One year I drew the white stone—it was a fossil, I think—and it was my turn. The funeral songs were sung, my family wailed, and I went."

Her hands loosened, her mouth leaving his pulse. Yet she only moved a fraction, her breath touching his skin instead. The small caress made memory sharper; he could almost smell the fat dripping in the fire, resins burned for the ceremony, the fragrance of those long-ago rolling hills.

"The sanguinant must have been reasonably old, though no daywalker. I thought him difficult to kill, but now I suspect him mostly calcified, for there is no other reason I should have been able to do what I did. I lured him to a pit, though he dragged me down with him, and my spear was capable of entering his throat.

Perhaps in some way he did not wish to live, and allowed his own demise as the Antlered God did to feed our people. I do not know, I knew only the taste of his blood. I lay soaked and broken as the sun rose, and that dusk I died."

Her stillness was neither terror nor tension. The burn of her first true feeding would induce deep languor, masking any discomfort from the first deep physiological changes, altering bodily chemistry, and providing endless intoxication. Any fledgling knew the powerful narcotic effect of their maker's claret, though most were only graced with the honor until the Gift's full bloom made the true teeth break loose.

Drinking only once was a painful way to become sanguinant. Those most inclined to make progeny selected carefully, and repeated feedings ensured survival of the investment.

Still, accidents happened.

The remainder of the tale was unnecessary; he had become a scourge upon his people, erasing them with a lone fledgling's unrestrained appetite before setting out in search of more. Those first gluts had not killed him; afterward, as he gravitated toward more populous mortal settlements, animal ichor sufficed when better could not be had—though only barely, making him weak and stupid. Still, he survived.

He *endured*.

Now she knew a secret even the long-forgotten dead could not whisper. And soon he would feed her again.

A few hours later she moved restlessly, already displaying fledgling sensitivity to dawn. With the Gift's maturation the usual torpor until dusk would set in, and full sunlight deeply injure if not kill outright, first inducing anaphylactic shock before igniting tissues wholesale.

Repeated infusions of a daywalker's strength would help,

but she would still be so very fragile. All the better, though he must be wary of travel, always accounting for her needs.

One small, graceful hand twitched, rose softly. Her fingers moved, and a soft amused sound made his entire body tighten—her first laugh since the costume fête, though lacking the bright edge of that forced gaiety.

He could not remember a single thing he'd said, only the determination to keep her attention a few moments longer. Spout any nonsense, perform any capering dance to interest the leman who had walked into the gathering with head held high, meeting his gaze with a silent challenge, lifting her just-acquired wineglass.

Assessing how best to whisk her away from the party and into the elevator had been sheer, wonderful torture, the fact of a leman shattering successive layers of numbness with every breath, every small comment, every measuring, mysterious glance.

"Trippy," she murmured. "Spiked the punch bowl."

"How do you feel?" *Is it pleasant? Do you like what I harvested?* He had fed nearly to gorging, spreading his attentions among several different mortals unlucky enough to be wandering at that hour; they were left alive, though in some cases so dazed any attempt to reach home or other destinations a matter of chance.

"High as a kite." The last word nearly disappeared in a yawn.

He had to quell an urge to mimic. The reflex was occasionally irritating, but apparently etched too deep into mortals for sanguinant to escape. "Your senses are becoming far more acute. This eases the transition."

"Are you sure it's not...digesting me? Like a spider?" She sounded so wistful, instead of pleased.

"Very sure."

"All right." She lapsed into a long, softly breathing silence, occasionally moving her hand through the darkness and staring raptly at whatever vision the Gift granted one so beautifully made. "You know I hate you, right?"

I know. "It is," Lukas said, "better than nothing. I am not ready to die yet."

"I'm tired."

"Rest, Beatrice. It will be dawn soon."

CHAPTER 19

Golden, rainbowy tracers faded bit by bit as Bea drifted through lassitude. There was a lot of thinking to do, and for once she had what appeared to be plenty of time. Everything was moving so very slowly.

You just drank monster blood. Helluva kick—and was that his plan? To get her addicted, then she'd be a henchman? Hench*person*? Had he done this to Mrs. Martinez, to that Wren guy?

Maybe not since they both seemed so...untouched. Human.

Mortal, the monster kept saying. A term with real *implications,* Jare would interject, both eyebrows lifted as he nodded meaningfully. Her brain kept bouncing between past and present; the sense of an underlying pattern forming into coherence was one she'd had only a few times in her life. Like after Mom's passing, when she realized her parents would never again compare Beatrice to her brilliant, talented big brother, and the recognition of their final, unalterable judgment was almost as painful as the fact that she had never had a chance of measuring up to begin with.

But the biggest pattern-moment had occurred in Don

Bertram's warehouse, the night she pounded on his door in a warm spring rain, probably scaring the bejesus out of him.

Bea, come on, you're not thinking of actually killing someone, are you? Don's worried frown, before she made him spread the papers delineating 'Chris Everly's' businesses—gathered by both Don and her brother when the first weirdness started—on the table, opened a scrounged pawnshop laptop and showed him a copy of the footage from that one camera on the post near the stable, put up to possibly catch the creatures besieging the house in action.

Scrambling out of the house that night with the crammed expanding file folder of Jare's 'evidence', some clothes grabbed at random, a few thumbdrives, and the rosewood box containing the necklace, fleeing whatever had killed her brother—she hadn't even called 911, partly out of panic and partly because alerting complicit authorities was a no-no in Jared's new conspiracy-laden world—and ending up at Don's place three days later, banging on the door like a lunatic, gabbling about little green men...

Don watched the footage, sure, but he hadn't really been on board until the coroner filed it as an 'accidental' death. At the time they were both sure 'Everly' had paid off the authorities and other Noll Mountain property owners, as monsters were said to do, and Bea spent at least a year sick with fear at the inevitable deductions drawn from their discussions.

The horrible drilling whine came back at intervals, warning of the billowing yellow mist and near-naked green henchmen— their laughable size and shape made the grotesqueness even more terrifying. Moving every few months, slipping down the chain of cheap apartments into motel rooms, saving what she could of Jared's occult research, pestering Don for more information, relentlessly scrolling creepy dark-web forums and sites dedicated to the weird—it wasn't paranoia if monsters really existed, right?

I am going to kill him, Donny-Boy, she'd said, grimly. *No matter what he is.*

And by golly, she'd failed, as per usual. All the preparation and work ended up here in the dark, high on monster blood, out of her goddamn mind.

*If at first you don't succeed...*Dad's favorite saying, uttered fondly while walking Jared through a skill or achievement, grimly delivered when Bea brought home B's instead of A's, never quite reaching her brother's academic or creative heights.

Maybe the monster liked telling stories about hunting and tribes and night spirits. Maybe it was the thing to do around campfires in his day. She was pretty sure he was muttering in other languages, too—of course, being an immortal bloodsucker would give you time to practice all sorts of things. Imagining him taking a high-school French test was morbidly hilarious; Bea had to laugh, nearly forgetting she was stuck in a bed with said monster, his hand inches from her face.

The forlorn chuckle shook her entire weary, tripped-out body. The monster's grip on her waist shifted; he had a hard-on shoved right up against her. The guy seemed *definitely* oversexed.

Your senses are becoming far more acute. It eases the transition.

So was she supposed to be a vampire sex toy now? For how long? Was she going to get fangs? Her teeth still felt the same, but she hadn't immediately noticed her eyesight becoming oodles better in complete darkness.

She had to get on the ball, or something even worse might happen.

Come on, Bebe. Think it through. Christ, it was horrible to hear Jare's voice in her head. He wouldn't leave her the fuck alone, ever.

You know how strong this guy is. If you're also a monster, well, all you have to do is get the stake going fast enough.

The worst thing was, her dead brother definitely had a point.

It would be fucking ironic to end up as the very thing she'd set out to eradicate—but she'd do it, if she had to.

Even if he didn't kill Jared? What if…

She had nothing to hold onto except revenge, and maybe escape. But if she got out of here, would she eventually crave human blood? She could work night shifts at another meat-packing plant, probably, and…

Another attention-grabbing burst of visual tracers and deep, hazy relaxation. If she pretended to be okay with the program, would the monster lose interest? Some guys only wanted the chase; the only problem would be if his discard phase included getting rid of any evidence. But if she was stronger, *monster-*strong, she had a chance.

All right. The pattern unfolded, sharp and bright against the soupy semiconsciousness of being zoned. He could probably make a mint with that stuff as a designer drug; was she basically hooked on vampire heroin now? *Here's what you do, Bea.*

She moved, as if needing a sleepy stretch. Arms first, then settling her head more comfortably. A sine-wave going down her body, and she very deliberately spent the most time settling her hips, rubbing in a way guaranteed to give a human guy some ideas—unless he batted for the home team, that was.

Absolute stillness. The monster might not even be breathing, which could be a bad sign.

Bea let the stretch take her legs as well. Another hip-wriggle, more definite this time. *Some* part of him was interested, at least. Unless he'd fallen asleep that way, which didn't seem likely.

If she ever caught him sleeping…but there was that shimmer over the door, probably meant to keep her in the butterfly-jar.

Then he spoke, low but clear. "Enjoy it, kitten. There is much more to come."

Oh, you don't know the half of it, monster. She had a few more ideas, but he was still talking.

"Do you feel that? Dawn. You may noti—"

Nothing. Not even darkness.

Her plan got off to a terrible start; she hadn't passed out in one location and awakened in another, quick as flicking a switch, since college. In other words, she opened her eyes to find herself in the master bedroom, with the monster's nose was less than six inches from hers. Bea choked on a scream, scrambling against sheets and the green-gold coverlet.

"All's well, Beatrice." The monster rose, a single fluid movement—he'd been crouching next to the bed, for God's sake, watching her sleep. "It can be disorienting, the first few times."

The green sheets were nice, but they had her in a stranglehold. At least she still had her pajamas. An emerald glitter on one of the paired nightstands was the necklace, and Bea was shaken with the sudden certainty that the monster wasn't lying about how it was made.

The next surprise was that even though her heart was jackhammering, she felt...actually, pretty good? Nearly every physical ache and pain was gone, a flood of ridiculously intense wellbeing vibrating from her middle outward. The only problem was the *noise*.

Whispers poured into her ears, a confusion of padded drumbeats and sliding movement, creaks and rattles. It was goddamn distracting; she flinched, her hands flying to block the sonic assault.

"Be still, kitten." He was suddenly *there*, the bed giving a sharp groan as the monster balanced, warm hard fingers closing around her wrists. "Let yourself adjust."

Bea froze. The inhuman strength of the monster's grasp was even more apparent, carefully avoiding squeezing hard enough to hurt. More tiny sounds, cold and wetly distinct—*raindrops*, she realized, and the shushing noises were people moving around. Murmurs of conversation, mostly indistinct under the pounding drums. The entire goddamn house was going to shake itself to pieces under that vibration.

Much closer, a sudden startling thump—*ba-thud*. A long pause, then again, *ba-thud*.

She stared at the monster, realizing the bedroom windows were dark. Had she slept an entire day?

Ba-thud.

His hands gentled, one thumb caressing the underside of her wrist—a soft, absent motion, as if trying to soothe. "It will recede," he continued, in a soft inexorable tone cutting through the babble and pounding. "Any moment, now."

And the cacophony did retreat, first becoming a bubbling hiss like water on a pebbled beach before the pressure eased and Bea found she could distinguish individual sounds if she focused. Which she did *not* want to do, it was too confusing.

Better to wait for that other thumping, calm and unhurried, ticking off time. Her hands loosened; she peeled them away from her ears and peered at him. "It's..." Her throat was scratchy, but not terribly dry and aching as it had been. *Oh, thank God. Maybe I'm okay.*

How she could be *okay* with a monster crouching on the bed right in front of her, Bea couldn't entirely say. It was relative, like everything else in life. Impossible things became very doable once a person had compelling reasons, like her brother's body torn to pieces in a filthy rundown stable.

"Mortals. Their hearts will tell you things, in time. The house sings; there is rain with ice, and wind. The trees. Cars, somewhat further away." He paused between each item on the list, and she found she could untangle the different sounds. "The city in the distance, like thunder."

I don't hear that. At least he seemed ready to teach her a few things, though she'd have to test each and every piece of information to be sure.

He could still lie.

Ba-thud.

"What's that?" she whispered.

"Ah." He tugged at her left wrist, gently. Flattened her hand against his chest—he was, for once, just in a very crisp white dress shirt with the sleeves rolled up, and charcoal wool trousers. It was a lot better than the usual costume. Maybe he'd been interrupted while getting into another hilariously, expensively tailored suit. "Listen. Right here."

Hard muscle, feverish warmth burning through undershirt and starched cotton. Another *ba-thud* leapt under her touch; Bea almost flinched. Focusing on the rhythm made it louder. *Oh, hey. That's...*

She couldn't think it was pretty cool, because he was a monster. Bea snatched her hand away; he let her, releasing her other wrist at the same time. He should have looked ridiculous, his knees sinking into a messy bed, his brownish-gold hair as close to a ruffled mess as she'd ever seen it, but the uncanny, barely blinking stillness turned him into a cat watching its chosen mouse move within easy paw-range.

Bea took refuge in confusion. "Did you carry me up here?"

"I thought you would be more comfortable, waking thus." Was that a faint tinge of uncertainty in his tone? "You're right, the saferoom is a bit...bare. And there are new clothes, so you may select what you like. How do you feel?"

Like I've finally had enough sleep for once. Bea shrugged, glancing at the bedroom door—firmly closed, though no invisible shimmer. His heartbeat continued, and she found it was possible to quasi-ignore the noise, like very loud bass from a passing car. "What day is it? Am I allowed to know?"

"Of course." But he paused, his eyes half-lidding. "All Hallows is tomorrow, I think. No, Halloween. The names change, though the festivals do not."

She might've been curious about that—he had to have seen some history, even if he was only as old as she and Don had originally thought. But there were much bigger fish to bouillabaisse, as her college roommate Sami would say.

Bea almost flinched again; for a little while during the monster blood trip she'd thought Sami and Felicia were talking to her, explaining the finer points of what the new plan would entail.

If he was being honest, she'd lost almost a week. Being monster-fucked and high on blood would probably do that to a person, though. Strangely, her mouth didn't taste like morning, just a faint spicy-numb tinge sliding past the almost-gone ache in her throat, very nearly soothing. Her hair was a mess, and she probably looked terrible.

How am I going to do this, then? "Am I allowed to get up?"

"Of course. Shall I ring for breakfast?"

"Can I still eat?" *Let's see how many questions he'll answer.* One of them might even give her an opening.

"Mortal food is pleasant enough, though it does not satisfy. It may slow the Gift a fraction." He regarded her steadily; thank God there were no red lights in his eyes at the moment.

"So...I'm like you, now?" *Am I going to go on a liquid diet? Those guys on the monster-hunting forums would talk about the right way to kill me then, I bet.*

"Hardly, kitten." But a faint smile, as if he found her amusing. Was that a good sign? "When the fangs break through you will be a fledgling."

Fledgling. Okay. She restrained the urge to run her tongue over her teeth; they didn't feel any different. "When does that happen?"

It was his turn to shrug, a supple movement, perfectly balanced. "A few more feedings. It takes so long as it takes, though the end is not in doubt."

Maybe you just want me to think that. I'm doubting a whole lot over here. "So when do I start...when do I start biting people? You know, drinking...drinking blood. Hunting."

"No need." The monster tensed, and Bea got the idea it was a bad question. But he still used the same soft, conciliatory tone; all things considered he was being pretty patient. Maybe this was part of his script. "I will hunt for us both."

She decided to press just a little further. "But shouldn't I start practicing? Like, isn't that the point—you make me into a blood-sucker, and I…" *And I what? What's his endgame? This seems way more revenge than necessary after getting a stake to the chest.*

Although she had no frame of reference for that.

"You will feed from me. Always." He leaned forward, the motion perfectly controlled, and red pinpricks flashed in his pupils before winking out. "You are *my* leman."

I should really be frightened right now. The lack of fear was oddly more disorienting that being scared enough to cry or throw up. "What if I bit someone, though? Would they turn into—"

"If I find your fangs in another, kitten, I will tear the inter-loper to pieces."

Maybe being unafraid was an aftereffect from getting high. Did monster blood produce hangovers? "And kill me too?"

"What?" The intensity didn't fade, but he now looked puzzled as well. "Of course not. No sanguinant will harm a leman, let alone their own. Take you, claim you, certainly. But *harm*? No."

What do you call the elevator, then? And the very bed they were both on? *Taking* and *claiming* seemed like euphemisms. Was all this stuff about lemans a lie? It seemed a pretty complex con to run on a dumb 'mortal' who hadn't even managed to get a stake all the way through, but what did she know?

Maybe it was time to shift to something else, since he was getting a little amped up. And maybe he had a different defini-tion of 'harm' than she did.

That was, in fact, pretty goddamn likely.

Bea braced herself. *Okay. Here goes nothing.* She met his gaze, squarely, hoping those crimson dots wouldn't come back. Did ordinary people ever see them?

It was hard work to lift her arm, shifting among twisted bedcovers; she'd thrashed herself into a knot trying to get away. Still, she managed to free her knees, and he didn't move as her palm met his chest again. Her own heart was skipping along fast and hard, and her cheeks felt hot.

Oh, Christ, am I blushing? I hope he doesn't notice.

The monster stared at her, remote and impassive. Bea patted his shirt; even through cloth the muscle definition was a bit startling. Like carved stone, but giving off stove-heat. "Did I sleep all day?"

"The sun rises, fledglings sleep." His voice rumbled under her fingers. "It is inevitable. You may be able to tolerate sunlight in small doses until the fangs break through. After that, no."

Oh. So that will keep me trapped during the day, if it's true. "But it doesn't bother you."

"I am daywalker, certain things do not trouble me." He blinked, almost deliberately. Cats did that to show affection, but she wondered if he had to remind himself to act human. "Eventually you will share that."

Good news, or just propaganda? She tried to imagine he was human, that her fingers were resting against an attractive man's shirt. "Eventually?"

"A few centuries." The monster finally moved. His hand settled over hers, pressing her palm more firmly to his chest. "It's difficult to say, but eventually, yes. Quite possible."

Shit. Her heart sank—a few *centuries?* When he said it so casually, the whole thing seemed absolutely, horribly plausible. Bea clearly needed to get her ass in gear.

So she let herself hold the monster's gaze, hoping she wasn't about to be hypnotized like a chicken. "That's a long time." *Pretend you're interested. You did it all during the party, you can do it now.* "What if you get bored?"

His hand tightened; his lips parted slightly. No sign of fangs, though, that was good. "Impossible. A leman is an eternal mystery, and you more than any other, I think."

Yeah, well, let's hope you can't tell what I'm really thinking. Self-confidence was probably too much to ask for in this situation, and so was courage. How was she supposed to do what she needed to without either?

A subtle change in pressure. Her fingers moved, trapped but not immobile, stroking his chest. The barest butterfly-brush, answered by a thump—his heart, a strike felt all through her own limbs.

Every outside sound faded, even the rush and splatter of cold winter rain. *Kids must be praying for it to stop before trick-or-treating*, she thought, and hoped her own tricks were up to par this year. The prize wasn't full-size candy bars but her own miserable life. "How do you still have a heartbeat?"

"Mortal death is a process, not a terminus." His fingers shifted, caressing the back of her hand. "It is true-death all sanguinant fear, even Archons. But those are..." Now the fangs were out, dimpling his lower lip. "Beatrice." Lingering over her name.

This might be easier than I thought. "Lukas." She tried to pronounce it the way he had, then rocked up onto her knees, finding the movement easier than she suspected and hoping she didn't lose her balance. Falling over right now would be fucking *embarrassing*, and Christ knew when she'd get another chance at this. The mattress shifted; Bea found herself again nose-to-nose with the monster. "Am I saying it wrong?"

Please. She was doing everything but fluttering her damn eyelashes. If he was just after the chase, this would end pretty messily. *Please, I know I wasn't born to be lucky, but can you throw me a bone here, God?*

She leaned in, and closed her eyes.

CHAPTER 20

her pulse galloped along, sweet thunder. Lukas had barely
enough presence of mind to set the seals, remaining immobile as
her lips touched his. That slight contact burned as well, thick
sugary fire spilling through every blood-channel as her scent
wrapped him in a drugging cloud. So incandescently beautiful,
and *willingly* touching him—she pressed a little harder, and he
could do nothing but respond.

Gently, though. Hardly able to move for fear of frightening
shy, recalcitrant prey.

The thrall woke, arousal a clawed steel bar at the very root of
his being. At the bottom of consciousness, the animal who priori-
tized survival was unbreathing, unblinking, still as a frozen rock.
It gloried in the paired sensations—the small slim hand against
his heartbeat, the mouth teasing at his own. The faint tang of his
blood upon her tongue was even more enticing, if that were
possible.

She explored rather tentatively, perhaps afraid of his true
teeth slipping control. Lukas could barely believe this sudden
turn; he had expected more wild veering between fear and defi-

ance, perhaps another attempt at self-harm or panic-struck escape.

Not this. *Never* this.

The center, the very omphalos of the universe drew closer, her free hand meeting his shoulder, skimming upward, curving at his nape. Delicate fingers, pressing so gently—he needed only the slightest of pressure to obey, leaning into her.

But she retreated, and he froze again. Agonizing, the bare inch between her lips and his own, even if he could drink the nectar of her breath.

"Lukas?" A tantalizing whisper, his mortal name wonderfully altered with her charming, so-modern accent. "Do you want me to stop?"

"No." He could barely remember which language to plead in. *Never. Don't.* If he moved, if he so much as exhaled wrongly, she might take flight. He would pursue, he would have her again...but he very much wanted to see what she intended. The longing was a spear in his chest, a blade so keen it did not hurt at first strike, and he drowned in sensation his numbed, calcified former self had never dreamed possible.

"Okay." A light, brushing kiss, not nearly enough. "But I want something different this time. Can I have it?"

So she grasped, in some way, how helpless he was against her. "Yes." And those incredible, dizzying words—*this time.*

She rewarded him with another kiss, now much less uncertain, and her lovely live weight settled in his lap. Her knees to either side of his hips, her hand on his chest suddenly free because the fabric between them was intensely irritating, so his claws sprang loose to shear the obstructions away. The Gift was in her, strengthening and changing; stronger than a mortal now, yet still so delicate.

She would never reach even an elder's strength or speed; leman did not need such things.

A sweet torment, to wait for what she wanted. She gasped as her shirt was stripped; he crushed her against him, his mouth working hungrily, and almost broke when she wriggled as if to escape.

"Mh. Here." She freed her mouth long enough to whisper again, and her frail fingers pushed at his hands, settling them on the sweet curves of her hips. Still so thin, she needed much more care and feeding—the thrall leapt at the thought, magma filling his bones, and the struggle to keep his fangs contained was far more severe than refraining from the glut.

More mothwing-soft brushes, directing him. He spilled onto his back, every moment of the fall syrup-slow to keep her mouth on his, her slight softness draped across him now, more cloth tearing as he freed them both of any encumbrance.

The kiss grew bolder, though she still retreated restlessly unless his hands stayed where she wanted them—he could caress, though, kneading as she settled, having finally placed her suitor precisely where she wished. Above him she lingered, the silken mass of her hair tumbling loose, the soft velvet furnace of her core lingering just at the tip of his aching, begging shaft.

Her mouth drew away; he longed to keep her. But her lovely seashell hips beckoned, filling his grasp, and she slid with exquisite slowness—down, and down, inch by inch-fraction, closing him in searing, honeyed fire. Her head tipping back, a slight toss of her mane as her teeth caught her lower lip, his leman's face closed and serene.

He was begging, Lukas realized, in every language he had ever known. The words vanished into the thrall's purr, a warning and anticipation all at once.

Beatrice straightened, her thighs flexing beautifully...then settled all at once, impaling herself upon her sanguinant.

The thrall took him, his body a tight-strung bow touched with a single divine fingertip. She *moved*, answering his desire almost before it arose, guided by the subtle shift of his fingers as he held to her satin firmness. Faster, her breath quickening, choosing the angle which most suited her as she pleased herself as well, using him as a tool, an instrument of her own desire.

Watching from under half-closed lids—for she had pushed herself upright, too short to kiss him if she wished to retain this particular rhythm and direction—as his own shape shifted, the secondary prong searching for the most sensitive nubbin high at the crest of Paradise as she suddenly twisted, engulfing him afresh, the movement bowing him once more as he thrust upward, desperate to reach still deeper.

More teasing, or she was still uncertain...but no. A sweet, husky, stuttering moan as she stilled, and he could watch the rosy flush of raw sensuality flood her skin, lush mouth slack as her head tipped back, shudders wringing him dry. His own release burst free, shaking her as well, until she sighed and folded down, coming to rest against him lightly as a leaf, her forehead tucked under his chin.

Miracle. A miracle.

Even if he knew she was still unresigned, even if he suspected she thought to seduce in order to discover a means of escape, he would take it. He would, Lukas discovered, take anything she offered, and more.

CHAPTER 21

AN OLD FANTASY, ONE SHE'D OFTEN JILLED HERSELF ON. BEING ON
top for a change was a nice feeling. And for a monster, he took
direction well. Just disconnecting and letting her body do what it
wanted was hard; shame nipped at her, the old misogynist
double-bind.

But if it helped her survive—or better, if it helped convince
him she was playing along—she'd do it. She would use every
trick her college roommates had giggled about or discussed over
drinks, plus any she could come up with on her own. *Apply
whatever's handy* was a self-defense maxim, equally useful here.

Or so she hoped.

Bea draped herself across a hard, warm chest, and for the first
time in a very long while she was...almost at peace. It felt
goddamn great to have a little control, actually, even if
transitory.

His fingertips wandered up her back, slipping through thin
cooling sweat, tracing an intricate pattern. That also felt good,
until she remembered just who was touching her. But shrieking
and leaping off him wasn't part of the plan.

Besides, her legs probably wouldn't cooperate, and internal
feedback told her she wasn't going be moving for a while. The

shape of his cock had changed, buried deep; every breath caused aftershocks as he twitched, pulsing in response to every slight shift.

Bet that's fun in other circumstances. At least it was proof positive she'd achieved something. If he was just after the chase, maybe he'd leave her alone now.

She'd figure out what to do about fangs and sunshine allergies later. Bea drifted, listening to the steady slow thump of his heart under her ear, and realized the air was hushed, dead still. The house's noise was no longer present. No human heartbeats, no slap of freezing sleet, no burst of laughter from somewhere as an indistinct joke reached its punchline.

God, I'd love to laugh with someone again. Mostly Jare; how her brother would wheeze during Monty Python marathons, or when Bea cracked a few salty jokes in her trademark sweet-innocent tone.

That could never happen again. She might not ever gross Don out with a sudden observation about the implications of weird things again either, or hear a burst of merriment from coworkers—even the meatpacking guys had occasionally loosened up enough to jab in her direction. Often Bea gave it right back, sometimes in gutter Spanish definitely not learned at school.

She'd even like to laugh on her own. When was the last time she'd watched a comedy, for Chrissake? Or even seen a funny commercial?

Don't think I'd want to watch any horror movies, though.

"Beatrice?" Of course the monster wouldn't act like a human guy and pass out so she could have a few moments to herself.

Still, she didn't precisely mind the interruption. Her own thoughts were too fucking grim. "Hm?"

"Thank you. It is…not easy, for a leman. I regret that."

Does this mean the plan's working? If so, she could afford to feel a little cheerful. But it was so hard to tell.

"Yeah," she said, a slow, sleepy murmur. "Me too."

Oh, that's good, Bebe. But are you lying?

At least it wasn't Jare's voice. The deep, vivid tinge of self-loathing was all her own.

Standing naked in a closet was not high on her list of favorite activities, even if the space could have been rented out as a studio. It was also far too soon to know if any of her efforts were bearing fruit.

Rome wasn't built in a day—and she wondered if he'd been around for that. There wasn't a way to ask, and Bea had other problems. He wouldn't let her get in the shower alone, and that was embarrassing enough. But this really took the cake.

"I don't get it." She crossed her arms defensively, wishing she'd thought to grab a towel or something, or a robe if she could have found one. "You had someone reorganize the whole thing?" *While I was locked up in that big empty room with a new toothbrush, or while I was zonked out after monster-blood high?*

"You said you prefer Levi's." He was attending to his own clothes, which was fine—watching a man put on a suit was always an experience. But it didn't make her job any easier, and the graceful precision of his every move was a reminder of essential difference. Somehow he looked a lot less stiffly alien; he was sounding far more natural as well. "And…I destroyed the only other cloth you liked."

I did say that, and I meant it. But what Bea hadn't said was *buy a whole bunch of jeans and rearrange the whole closet, as well as restocking the pajama drawers.* There had to be at least twenty pairs of Levi's in various shades and styles; who in the hell *did* things like this?

Everything pre-washed, too, smelling of fabric softener. She wasn't too enchanted with the idea of other people touching her laundry, either, assuming anything in here could properly be counted hers.

She literally owned nothing now. Even the necklace was possibly stolen *and* a little-green-man magnet besides. "Yeah, you have a habit of shredding clothes. Must be expensive."

"Have no worries, Beatrice." He shrugged into the suit jacket —navy today, very restrained almost-matching tie—and settled the sleeves with quick habitual tugs. Painfully formal or just as painfully hipster, even if he had become incrementally less weird he just wasn't *right* in three-piecers. She was surprised he didn't have a pocket watch, though the heavy gold cufflinks looked antique. The matching wristwatch, though—how many of those did he have? "There is enough and to spare for my leman's comfort."

Blood money? Swallowing the crack took real effort. She was doing really great at keeping a conversation going, but the attempt was close to agonizing. Pretending to be relatively unbothered by a monster was a very new skill; she was getting a lot of practice, yay for her. "Where does it all come from?"

He paused, examining her, which probably meant that was a wrong question. Bea grabbed for a pair of stonewashed jeans— bootcut mid-rise, not bad, but it was creepy to have her sizes just *show up* like this—and a fistful of neatly folded black sweater. "Never mind." She backed for the closet entrance, shaking her head when he took a single step in the same direction. "Can I at least get dressed alone? And please don't rip these off me."

"There are always more. Especially since mortals…" The monster trailed off as she felt for one of the smaller built-in drawers holding underclothes and snatched a handful, still watching him. "I shall restrain myself, so far as I am able."

Is that all I have to do—pretend you're human, and you'll let me get dressed behind a closed door? Bea backed out of the closet, whirled, and marched for the bathroom.

He had *no fucking right* to sound so forlorn. Not with what he'd forced her into.

Strictly speaking, this last episode was all you.

No. Bea *refused* to feel bad over what she did to survive,

goddammit. Using any teensy bit of power she had in this situation had a giant, hundred-and-ten percent ethical pass. She would cling to that, she decided, even as she swept the door shut and discovered the panties were pink, lacy, thong-style, and utterly unwearable.

"Oh, Jesus." Bea tipped her head back, her jaw working, and stared at the night-blind skylight.

What would it be like, waiting centuries to see the sun again? Always assuming, of course, that she wouldn't end up dead well before the event.

She couldn't figure out what to do with the panties. Commando was better than wearing that nonsense; flossing her ass was *so* not on the menu. In the end she stuffed them in the cabinet under the sink, since returning to the bedroom carrying pink lace was more than her nerves could take.

Her hair was drying rapidly, probably because it was so warm in here. Traces of condensation still clung to the mirror over the granite-trapped sinks—who needed this kind of space? *Seriously.*

Bea stopped. Her reflection wouldn't quite meet her eyes, but that wasn't the problem. Neither was the sheen on her skin, as if her pores had shrunk, all of her burnished to smoothness; she didn't want to think about monster-blood beauty care. The toiletries in this suite were expensive organic stuff she could treat like a hotel, sure.

The problem was, the stuff was doing something to her hair. Bea rubbed a strand between her fingers, swallowing hard when tiny black flakes sprang free. Underneath, her stupid natural color—she *hated* blonde jokes with a passion—was darkened by moisture, but still apparent.

Had she cougar'd a guy with flakes falling out of her curls? Uncool. The embarrassment might be enough to kill her, if she wasn't already dealing with so much else.

I am not okay. Her hands trembled. Every edge and color was too bright, too sharp; the noise in the house, while easily muffled, was still far too overwhelming. She watched the woman in the mirror bare her teeth—still familiar, from the slight crowding on her lower jaw and the retainer-straight chompers on the upper, years of tortuous parental-mandated dentistry paying off. But so white, and she hadn't brushed since Don's warehouse.

Were her canines sharper?

Until the fangs break through. What if he wasn't lying?

Now she was even gaslighting herself. *Stay strong, Bebe.*

But oh, it was so hard.

CHAPTER 22

AT LEAST SHE SEEMED TO FIND THE OFFICE MILDLY ACCEPTABLE— more spacious than that of the Everly penthouse, though the shelves were lined with decoratively arranged books chosen solely for gradations of color on their spines, interspersed with unfamiliar curios bearing no significance, sentimental or otherwise. A lingering, longing gaze at the sleek black computer, its blank dark screen at an angle to the leather blotter on a vast oak desk, an examination of the broad, night-curtained windows looking out over what little garden this lair possessed, and his leman finished her circuit of the room by trailing her lovely hand over the back of a leather couch, one of a duo holding conference near a mock fireplace.

The office's secondary purpose was to provide the Andranov cover, more than half a gangster, with an informal meeting space —which accounted for the matching oak sideboard stocked with expensive, unopened bottles plus a clutch of empty glasses and decanters. All Everly businesses had been drained by now, assets transferred, and though Lukas had moved house the control of territory both physical and financial was still assured.

Most underlings would not even notice the change in regime, so long as their paychecks were honored.

"Sir." Wrenfeldt almost tugged his forelock; he had been doing that more frequently of late. "Bit of news." The dogsbody did not add any cheeky observation, though he clearly wished to, and he indicated the stack of files set on the massive desk. The grey in his pomaded hair had advanced a bit; Lukas noted that, welcoming the brief stab of a small regret among his ribs.

The feeling was another luxury, possible only because of *her*. Even pangs of mourning were preferable to creeping stultification.

Black cashmere jumper and those denim trousers—jeans, yes, that was the word, labourer's wear. But she seemed far more comfortable, and the way the heavy cloth skimmed her legs was appealing. She had even selected a pair of dark-blue trainers with something like a pleased smile; his Beatrice touched a silk flower drooping from a decorative basket, fingertips granting the poor thing an unaccustomed luster before she turned away.

The Gift was working in her, gathering speed. Lukas was very much looking forward to the next feeding. "By your tone I assume it troubling, instead of pleasant. Go on." In other words, she could hear anything the dogsbody would say.

A flicker of something unfamiliar crossed Wrenfeldt's wide, comfortable face. Before swearing fealty his nose had been broken more than once; a dogsbody's durability was considerably more than mortal, and such things troubled him no longer. He would be vital until he dropped; that day would be a sad one, though Hardison would step into the duties left vacant.

Hopefully the redheaded youth would prove a little less willing to dip into certain…troubling behaviors, but so long as requirements were met a good lord would overlook much.

"Incursion, sir." Wrenfeldt settled into a posture of relaxed attention, hands crossed before his belt. "From the south, I think. We're at five now, drained and dropped."

An annoyance indeed. Five mortal bodies—it could be traveling fledglings, though any entering his territory should know to keep such things decently hidden, the nest unfouled. "The authorities?"

"Skittish, though burying the incidents as usual." Wrenfeldt did not dare glance at the mistress of the house again; she had turned from her perusal of the sideboard's crystalline wonders. "It's only a matter of time before someone gets curious, sir. Or...vengeful."

A warning, couched in terms a dogsbody could feel comfortable deploying. Perhaps some sanguinant slew the bearers of bad news among their underlings, but Lukas found it much more efficient to encourage a certain fearlessness in expressing opinion. And after all, his Beatrice had been intent upon vengeance. Wrenfeldt was correct in being cautious.

"True." He opened the first file, glancing over the garish crime scene photos, flipping to the autopsy report. *Ah. How very interesting.* They certainly appeared to be fledgling kills, though not bloodcraze-messy. The second was the same, and the third. The fourth and fifth were a double scene, this one entirely consonant with glut.

Very odd. Who expects me to be fooled by this? He returned to the first. It had been some while since he felt this sharply awake while looking over an incident report; a drench of wonderful musky warmth was his leman sidling closer, clearly curious.

Her hair was shaking off the dye nicely. Lukas could still feel her mouth against his, timid before gathering confidence. A terrible bravery, offering herself to the beast; she chattered gamely, displaying brittle bravado, but could not mask the fear in her scent. He did not think it likely a single feeding had accomplished more than temporary détente; no, she would absolutely test his vigilance again.

That will be enjoyable. The thrall gave a sleepy twinge, deep in his bones.

Beatrice was very close. He could pretend to be unaware, but did not; she halted beside the desk when his gaze rose from the autopsy's dry detailing of trauma and decay. Her beautiful eyes widened, either pretending guilelessness or frankly fearful, and he closed the manila folder somewhat decisively.

She almost flinched. Her throat moved—a quick swallow, she was indeed still anxious.

"This is a demimonde affair." Lukas sought a tone of gentle explanation; no need to trouble her with more complex considerations. "I do not think you wish to see."

"I've probably seen worse." Her arms folded, chin raising slightly; a flung challenge. No doubt she was thinking of her brother.

Lukas remembered what the *greiben* had done to the boy's body. Had she approached the broken wreck, after peering through the stable window? Smelled the charnel reek, gazed at the viscera pulled free and flung about?

The thought caused a sharp pang, yet more beautiful, painful heartache.

Very soon, I will cleanse those warrens. He took a single step aside, indicating the slim stack of paper, but did not retreat further. If she wished to view such things, he would at least stand near enough to offer paltry comfort.

She did not betray much—a swift grimace, empathy briefly breaking through. He leaned close, basking in her nearness, and pointed.

"See the damage over the jugular? Opposite, there, is where the lesser fangs on the bottom clamped, for leverage. And there." He indicated the next crime scene photo, wishing she were not staring at such garish, pitiless detail. "The layers of flesh curling in that particular manner denotes a clawstrike. That stipple is where a tip punctured, but the hand was turned before it dragged, you see? This is sanguinant violence; had I attacked your brother, the results might be similar." *Or not, since I learned well to cover any traces long before I could drain without killing.* "The autopsy report states a great loss of blood, yet it's clear from the scene and livor mortis that the bodies were not dumped, they stayed where they fell. A police detective or two is now asking, *where did the claret go?*"

The file folder quivered slightly before closing, shutting away the sight. She settled it precisely upon the pile, then rubbed her fingers against denim, a swift unconscious movement. "I suppose the others are the same."

"Yes." *Mostly.* His suspicions could wait for a more appropriate time and venue. "Would you like to examine them further?"

"I'm good." An extraordinary, almost venomous glance from under her long lashes. "There's whiskey over there. Can I have some, or is it just for show?"

"Of course. It will not halt the thirst, but the taste is pleasant enough." He gathered the folders, acutely conscious of her retreat. "I will handle this personally, Wren. Alert security to watch for the usual signs and run a full check of countermeasures before midnight." It would at least keep them busy; he hoped against hope this was merely what it seemed and not...an event necessitating thorough housecleaning, so to speak.

"So you don't think it's just wee ones, then?" The dogsbody took care to sound only mildly interested in the prospect; his duties were to keep his master's daylight holdings secure, not interfere in demimonde business. A challenge for territory would naturally seek to eradicate such conveniences.

A sanguinant who could protect neither clients nor vassals also could not hold a nest or territory. Nor could a lord unaware of certain troubling signs within ranks of underlings.

"It's best to be sure." Lukas watched his prize stand before the sideboard; she appeared to be reading the bottle labels. "Tell the housekeeper we regret missing dinner and double-check the bonuses for the maintenance staff, then you may be at what ease our security permits. That will be all."

"Yes, sir." Wrenfeldt retreated at his usual pace, closed the door in his accustomed way.

It was irritating—Lukas had planned a leisurely dinner, a

night spent in his leman's company. But this was perhaps for the best.

❦

"Please don't." She did not quite resist when he took her arm, merely stiffened as she realized their destination. Her pleading, however, was very nearly desperate. "Don't lock me up in there again."

"I must deal with this, Beatrice. It cannot wait." Especially since it had been brought to his attention at such a juncture.

"Look, at least put a TV in there or give me some magazines. Anything. Or, here's a thought, I'll stay in the master bedroom, you can put that Wren guy in the hall. I promise I won't try anything. I *swear*."

He could curse his own heedlessness; naturally she viewed him as a jailer, yet it had not occurred to him that she might see the saferoom as an explicit punishment. "I will have a few comforts added, as soon as possible. It is my oversight. I apologize."

"He *apologizes*." A bitter little laugh, and even the edge of contempt was sweet to hear. "I suppose I should be glad you don't just jam me in a coffin. Look, give me today's newspapers, or last week's, dig them out of the recycle. Something."

I would not put it past you to find some means of lighting them on fire. She was an exercise in resourcefulness, indeed. "For tonight, please bear with the inconvenience." The last few stairs receded, and he ushered his leman into the saferoom's soothing quiet. "I have taken refuge in crypts more than once; understand that this is far better."

"Please. I will promise, I will swear on a stack of Bibles not to try anything." Her eyes were shining, her pretty fingers tangled together. She was stiff, just on the edge of outright struggle.

"Beatrice." His hands ached to take her shoulders, ease the

fear swirling through her scent. "This is to keep you, certainly, but more importantly to keep you *safe*."

"Yeah, well, it can't keep *you* out."

It stung, but even that venom was far better than numbing ossification. Lukas confined himself to what comfort could be offered. "No sunlight will reach here; no mortal or demimonde attack can succeed once the seals are set. I will return before dawn to feed you."

"Like a cat. Or a dog, because if I was a cat you'd at least put a dish on the floor." The détente was well and truly over; his prize was nearly aflame with a mix of trembling fury and sweet supplication.

"I am at fault." Even seeing her in this mood was a luxuriously honed pleasure, whisper-sharp, biting deep. "I am old, and my preference for saferooms is space and simplicity. I did not anticipate your discomfort."

"What if you get hit by a bus or something, and I'm locked up here? Please...Lukas." Using his mortal name, a thorny pleasure—she should never sound so fearful. "I swear, I won't try anything. I'll be good."

At least she was not simply, numbly submitting. She might even hazily guess at his unwillingness to cause her more than the minimum necessary distress. Lukas raised a hand—mortal-slowly, though it took an effort—to clasp her slim, soft shoulder, and she froze.

He could lie, perhaps. Or misdirect with not-quite-falsehood. Yet he had been truthful until now, and wished to remain so with his leman; later, she might even count it a sign of trustworthiness. "If I am so careless as to suffer true-death, the seals will release. In that case you might flee and escape notice for some short while, but no sanguinant will let a leman wander. You would be caught, and claimed, soon enough." His true teeth ached, the animal restless even contemplating such an eventuality. "But have no worries. I am too old to be easily slain; I *survive.*

It is my only true talent." A bitter confession, indeed. Lukas would have liked to offer her more.

Far, far more.

Beatrice's gaze swung past him, fastened upon the saferoom door. She watched as it closed of its own accord with a soft, definite *snick* of latch, a deeper sound of deadbolt engaging. It was no great trick, any sanguinant elder could exercise such control upon physical material already sensitized by previous seals.

To a mortal, or a fledgling in the first bloom of the Gift, it might seem otherwise. His leman withdrew, though the physical movement was merely a slight shift, leaning away from him. Closing herself off, a castle on a crumbling shore, determined to resist the tide.

The ocean had time, and so did he. For the moment, however, he anticipated using a certain amount of savagery in dealing with those who rendered his intervention a necessity, just when he had glimpsed how sweet her eventual acceptance might be.

"Rest." Care in enunciating, since his fangs were very nearly free. "I will return before dawn to feed you." *I might even bring a few heads, to lay them at your door. Would you care for that, my so-modern kitten?*

He burst into mistform, streaming away, and the invisible seals settled into place. It was a truly unsatisfying farewell, yet he had little choice.

If he stayed even a few more moments, he might well accede to her pleas despite any better judgment. The calcification was gone, yes...but his ageless heart ached badly at even the idea of her distress.

CHAPTER 23

SHE DIDN'T STUB HER TOE KICKING THE DOOR, AT LEAST THERE WAS that. But Bea hadn't known he could just *vanish*, right out of a locked basement—a nasty surprise, one that sent her stumbling backward while the force-field thingie shimmered into being.

If she hadn't been so shocked, she might not have noticed how the walls developed a thin layer of the same weird almost-visible field, sinking in and going quiescent as she stared. Or maybe her eyes had gotten better?

He was gone, she was locked up again. And though she hadn't expected him to suddenly listen to reason just because she'd semi-willingly fucked him, it was still a crashing disappointment.

He explained some stuff, and you got a peek at some pictures plus some new terminology. Look at the victories, Bebe. Jare's voice, with that note of forced optimism he'd used a lot right after Mom's passing in hospice. *Though the crime scene stuff was kind of gruesome. Maybe he really didn't…*

"Shut up," she hissed. Talking to herself again, in record time.

At least she wasn't in pajamas. The sneakers were an absolute bonus. She'd been afraid he would notice she wasn't practically barefoot, afraid he would know she was lying—getting through a window while that Wren guy sat outside a door had crossed her mind more than once while she promised to be good —and terrified he would rip her clothes off again.

All in all, she could count this as a qualified win. Plus she could dig the goddamn necklace from a back pocket—she hadn't wanted it attached to her throat, but it was even more uncomfortable pressing into her right ass-cheek. And really, she only had Lukas's word about it being made from a dead green hench-thing.

Were they still henchmen if they didn't work for him? The photos in the file folder weren't really the worst she'd ever seen —Don was fully tapped into the thriving trade of weird pictures claiming to be Sasquatch encounters, strange murders, and celebrity deaths with a tinge of occultism, plus she had obsessively studied Jared's autopsy and the sight of his body in the stable never really left her.

She could have gone through the other folders. Lukas hadn't seemed inclined to stop her, but maybe it was a show. How hard would he work to gaslight her? If the pictures were fake, it was a lot of effort getting the Wren guy to put together a propaganda package.

Why would such a powerful monster bother?

Bea studied the shimmer over the door, drawing the necklace out. Warm from her pocket, it settled over the sweater; she still didn't want it next to her skin.

Don't worry about what to believe right now. You have some time alone, use it.

The air was still, close, utterly dead. Now she couldn't hear the other humans in the house again, which might be the invisible field *or* just regular old soundproofing. Her vision and hearing were indeed more acute, her sense of smell not far behind, but plenty of the bigger questions remained. Bea studied the force-field, running fingertips ever so lightly over its near-invisible border.

It gave like warm prickling taffy, unless she pushed hard. Then it hardened right back, nearly throwing her hand away, and the prickles became intense. Which was...interesting.

Finally, she headed for the iron four-poster, and grabbed one of the pillars. Someone had been down to remake the bed; she caught a faint warm scent which translated into a mental picture of Mrs. Martinez, wavering under a far stronger drench of fabric softener.

Wonder what she thinks of her boss ripping up clothes all the time. Bea set her heels and pulled, not expecting much.

Metal made a low, unhappy sound of strain. Bea snatched her hands away. Deep divots were left behind, and the iron post now slanted drunkenly.

"Holy *shit*," she breathed. So this was what monster blood did. She tested her teeth again, running her tongue delicately over familiar edges—they didn't seem any sharper.

If she could get away before the fangs, would she be okay? Folklore said killing the head bloodsucker before an infected person got a taste of human blood was the cure, and it would certainly be a lot easier if she was strong enough to bend metal.

Still, he was bound to be stronger yet, and knew how to use what he had. Bea needed practice, a way to test her new abilities, and there was only so much she could do while locked up. Though the room was pretty big, enough to dance in if she felt the need. And then there was that whole thing about him being the only one allowed to 'feed' her, which sort of argued against the dividing event between monster and whatever she was now—

Rattlerattle. The sound was faraway, deeply muffled but almost familiar. Bea whirled, suddenly afraid she'd lost track of time and had just stood staring for hours, or that the monster had been testing her compliance and would now set about another part of his plan, which might or might not include tearing her clothes off.

Or getting her high on his blood again. A sleepy tickle touched the back of her throat; she could almost taste the thick sweetness, the ever-changing impression of favorite or craved foods.

Rattle. Rattlescrape.

It was the locks on the door, she realized. Should she try to unbend the bedpost, cover up any evidence? Bea watched, her heart lodged firmly in her throat; at least the fear made that terrible little tickle retreat.

Scrape. Rattlerattle. Scrape. The sounds were so faint she almost doubted her ears—but the doorknob twitched fractionally, a tiny mouse-movement.

Bea waited. *Trap. It's gotta be a trap, that's what it was last time. Right?*

But if it wasn't, if she was stronger and faster now…it might be worth the attempt. If he was waiting on the stairs to catch her, what was the worst that could happen?

Well, he'll either kill you or fuck you, or make you drink more blood. Are those consequences you can live with?

Bea sidled toward the door, hardly noticing her sneakers made no noise at all. The necklace warmed, a change apparent even through her sweater—did this mean the little green bastards were outside looking for her? If they were, what had happened to all the people, the 'staff'?

Please don't let them all be dead.

The door rattled a final time, somewhat definitively. The knob kept twitching, and the scraping sound was someone pushing.

It's unlocked. But the invisible stuff is holding it closed. She tried to focus on every clue he'd given about the force-field, backing up nervously in case the little green men came boiling through. The hinges were on this side since the door opened inward, maybe she could work on those?

Finally, after a long nerve-stretching quiet, she edged closer, laid her palms against the invisible wall once more. Once more the prickling threatened when she pushed too hard.

But if she was slow, and patient, maybe something was possible.

Sure, superstrength and speed were handy to have. But tiny, incremental efforts were more often than not surprisingly effective. If he was waiting outside, at a certain point he might make it easier just to draw her out, and then he'd have a reason to do what he wanted.

Just like a man.

Bea pushed, very gently. The prickles intensified, quickly mounting to the threshold of actual pain.

But they didn't get worse. The sensation seemed to top out, and the shimmer wobbled unhappily. Her hand closed over the doorknob; a burst of wild, terrible hope inside her chest made a small whining noise slip between clenched teeth. A slow, slow turn, fighting invisible recalcitrance. The prickles still didn't get worse; the necklace was a hot coal glued to her chest.

The knob wouldn't move any further. Setting her sneakered heels again, Bea leaned back, easing the slab of wood free of its socket. Hinges rasped, metal grinding; half-inch by grueling, painful half-inch the door swung inward.

Holy shit.

Her hand left the invisible field's border six inches inside, and the relief was so intense she almost lost her grip on the still-resisting door. The wooden rectangle fought her, trembling as its inner edge hit the border of the invisible field; she had to not only ease it through resistance at that slow, steady pace but also force it to obey, the pressure calibrated *just* right.

Beyond lay a short landing and the stairs going up, sunk in near-absolute darkness despite the empty archway at the top holding a faint tinge of electric light.

When she pushed a sneakered foot into the field, the prickles intensified. Bea strangled a gasp, listening intently as she worked her leg into the shimmer. Sure, it felt awful, but it didn't seem to do any actual damage.

Which might change if he came back and found her like this, trapped like a fly in sticky paper.

Fuck it. Bea leaned into the invisible field, turning in slow motion, and began easing herself into the tense, resisting gap.

The worst moment wasn't holding her breath until soft black splotch-patterns bloomed at the edge of her vision, nor was it the sudden cessation of resistance after a terrible, squeezing crunch at what had to be the midpoint of the 'seals'. It wasn't popping free and spilling onto the stairs, her body twitching and suddenly halfway up the long flight, nearly overbalancing, her shoulder clipping the wall hard enough to send a hot jolt down her entire right side. Nor was the worst a sudden flood of sound assailing her ears, the volume turned down with a reflex she hadn't known she possessed, or the necklace suddenly cooling as it lay against her sweater, sending a venomous green glitter into the dimness.

The worst was hearing heartbeats at the top of the stairs—two of them, both popping along quickly as her own—and fighting the urge to dive back into her prison, hoping nobody had noticed. If he caught her...

But the pulses weren't Lukas's slow, somehow more intense beat. *Mortal death is a process, not a terminus.*

He could put that on a T-shirt, make some pocket money. Bea pushed herself away from the wall, crimson fear pouring down her back, stiffening each hair, every inch of skin still ringing with that terrible prickling pressure.

Instinct took over. She bolted up the stairs, unprepared for how lightly her feet landed, how each push suddenly provided a lot more oomph. In fact, she was at the top in an eyeblink, whirling, and the house throbbed with voices, movement, bright light, smells concentrated and fired past her because she was moving with inhuman speed.

Someone shouted as she burst from the staircase's gloom and bounced off a wall, her sneakers barely touching carpet before she was at the far end of the hallway. The sound was behind her in a trice, falling away like a train whistle dying in the distance. Her body suddenly knew what to do, careening through brightly lit passageways, and maybe she'd been subconsciously planning because before Beatrice was quite ready her arms had come up, shielding her face as she burst with a crackling tinkle through a wide picture-window looking over the grassy expanse before the mansion.

A moment of weightlessness, then the new, undeniable reflexes took over, tucking her into a compact ball just before she landed. The world turned over, a furrow dug in soaked turf and she was running again, streaking for the driveway's wet glistening. Heavy icy drops pelted her face and hands, her hair stripped back by a stiff breeze mostly made of her own motion, and she streaked down the hill faster than the BMW had mounted it upon their arrival.

Holy SHIT. Crazed glee mixed with a bright white diamond glare of fear—what if he was waiting in the bushes? What if this was all part of the trap?

The big wrought-iron gate reared before her. Bea screamed, a harsh rising caw of effort, and her body, fueled by hallucinogenic monster blood, uncoiled in a terrific leap.

She overcalculated, landing in a tangle of vines and cold-dripping underbrush, but that was okay because *she'd cleared the fucking gate,* and the wild pounding drum that was her heart sang.

At least for a little while, she was free.

The road rose up under her—another leap, she'd somehow also freed herself from the bushes' stick-arms, was over before she could quite brace herself. She hit and staggered drunkenly, the sudden certainty of pursuit, of the trap closing on her, giving fresh hysterical strength to every muscle. The necklace jounced against her sweater, tapping with the rhythm of desperate escape.

Bea put her head down, her arms pumping, and streaked into the night.

CHAPTER 24

Even the ichor of other Sanguinant was near-tasteless now, though it did not stop him from gorging.

Simple matter to hunt down a quartet of fledglings, since a glance at the listed crime scene locations revealed a certain pattern. Even the appearance of their Maker—an elder of some power and potential, perhaps pleased that his gambit had brought a response, however tardy—was dismally predictable. Lukas had thought to question said elder, but the shag-haired beast howled in a guttural tongue from the Teutonic forests before Varus lost his legions, tipped into bloodcraze as the last and probably most favored of his get was drained, decapitated, then torn to pieces in a twinkling.

Really, they should have known better than to provoke a daywalker. Lukas rose from the ruins of the elder's corpse, gobbets of swiftly disintegrating flesh shaking from his flickering hands, the deathdust immediately dampened by rain. Freight cars stood stolidly under lashing sleet, uninterested in the drama; a rumbling of live engines echoed nearby was accompanied by bright white trainlights. Still, any mortal out tonight would be entirely preoccupied with spending as little time as possible in the cold.

Fresh, welcome strength surged through his veins; the most potent claret was that of another predator. Distilled by his own body, it would also strengthen his prize, perhaps speeding her transition. Pleasant to anticipate the event, though speculating upon her likely mood once he returned was not quite cheerful.

The railroad yards were either a wonderful place to hide—screened by cold iron, adjacent to districts where prey was easily found, busy yet deserted at once—or an entirely stupid choice, since it was naturally where the one holding this territory would look first. Especially since the pattern of the few attacks delineated in the files carefully avoided that space.

The elder had survived this long, but perhaps ossified beyond the point of flexible planning. Incursions upon prime territory often came in cycles as populations both mortal and demimonde shifted, and of course Lukas's move from Everly to Andranov might denote enough weakening to provide others of his kind with good hunting grounds.

The only concerning bit was his suspicions in another area, but those could be addressed at leisure.

He made certain all evidence of sanguinant presence was erased, weighing the advisability of taking a measure of mortal claret as well in order to be certain of satisfying his leman's demands.

A short hop over the high fence on the northern side yards, a quick plunge through a dripping greenbelt, and he was in a residential area. It was early yet; winter nights fell during rush hour and many mortals were settling into their homes for dinner. Did she long for an approximation of modern mortal life? Easy enough to provide, especially since she would teach him the proper responses by mere, sweet context. Lukas crouched on the roof of a brightly lit home, watching the yards with an unblinking stare.

Just in case.

I want something different this time. The memory sent opulent shivers all through his ageless frame; sleet starred with tiny snow-granules was chilly, yes, but a few feedings after the true teeth appeared and a fledgling was impervious to most weather. How best to proceed? She might discover a few pleasures in her new existence—travel, luxury, patronage, perhaps even art.

How would she welcome him? He listened to the restless sweep-slap of precipitation, the varied symphony of mortal life inside their ingenious houses—tricks of modern construction were fascinating, and now that he was free of calcification he might study more of the advances in that area. Wise denizens of the demimonde were always interested in science and progress, if only to protect their own existence.

Finally, he judged this part of the problem solved enough. Despite his eagerness to return, Lukas took a long looping route through certain parts of the city between the yards and the Causeway, alert to any further sign of trouble. The rot may not have spread too far; if he were still sunk in the slowly congealing resin of age, would he be conscious of the infection right under his nose? Or had her arrival been the precipitating event?

Even this short absence was uncomfortable. The longer spent away from a bonded leman, the more swiftly calcification would return. The habit of checking his own responses and perceptions was old and very nearly comforting, save for the fact that he had not known how close he was to suffocating in his own hoary pile of centuries before the first tinge of her scent brushed him.

Moving alongside the freeway, he absently calculated the rate of traffic, testing the pattern for discrepancies. None audible, visible, or sensed. Perhaps the plans had not moved very far; yet it seemed her arrival had set certain affairs in motion. She could vivify more than his own existence, clearly.

Meditation upon her responses, even if falling far short of the mark, was a pleasant companion. It did not matter if all leman were so intoxicatingly stubborn; he had his prize, and that was enough. *Adorable* was a much better word than *cute*; he would simply have to be old-fashioned.

Finally, Lukas turned for the lair, plans and contingencies

boiling just under conscious thought as icy water falling from the sky's blind vault sluiced the evidence of battle from torn, fluttering cloth. The thicker-soled shoes held up admirably, a wonderful suggestion on Hardison's part, but he must needs make himself presentable before visiting his lady's bower.

Unfortunately, he arrived to find a house in ferment, a high window shattered, and his tender, vulnerable fledgling flown.

CHAPTER 25

AFTER A RUN OF BAD LUCK, ANY SMALL BIT OF HELP SEEMED LIKE A gift from heaven.

Running down a winding North Bluffs road at superspeed was all right, except when Bea stopped her ribs heaved so hard she retched, leaning against a lone streetlamp. Sleet poured down, sticking the sweater to her torso, and her jeans were soaked to the knee. Her sneakers were sodden, too, but that was okay.

Everything was okay, because she was free.

And what to her wondering eyes should appear but a smear of brightly lit parking lot in the distance, behind a screen of near-leafless trees? She hadn't even known there was a transit center on this side of the Causeway.

The problem of getting on a bus while looking like a drowned rat and without a cent to her name was solved by a heavyset, whistling male driver leaving his big silver craft closed but unlocked before ambling for the brick building holding bathrooms both public and employee. Bea prayed before testing the door, slipped through, pushed it closed—far easier than the resisting oak slab she'd had to wrestle before—and huddled on a seat halfway back, not even peering out the window, sliding down as far as possible to attempt some kind of concealment, hoping against hope.

As if the world had decided to balance out the shitty fortune of failing to kill an oversexed, name-changing bloodsucker, she was dealt another break when the driver returned to find several people waiting to board. Better yet, he opened up the bus and didn't even glance at the interior, being too busy getting the fare-card reader switched on. "Free ride, holiday," he chanted as they trooped up the steps. "Free ride, holiday."

The unspoken public transport commitment to everyone minding their own damn business held, and by the time ten or so passengers had arranged themselves, Bea realized a few of them were almost as soaked as she was. Some were even wearing bits of Halloween costume, which gave a nasty shock to her already-battered nerves.

What day is it? She'd forgotten completely, and further forgotten about the free-ride program for occasions prone to drunk driving. She hadn't had to sneak aboard at all.

Apparently everyone was commuting home from day jobs at the Bluff mansions, probably a thankless task even at the best of times. Bea was glad for the cover; she'd been expecting to be caught, pleading with the bus driver to just let her stay on, giving a sob story and risking him radioing in for a transit cop or two. Which she doubted she had the energy to handle, even if running away and attempting to cross the Causeway on foot was her other option.

She could probably thumb a ride, but why bother? Instead, Bea waited until nobody seemed to be looking before uncurling to sit upright, trying to act like she'd just been tying her shoes or picking up a dropped item. Doing her best to look innocent and self-absorbed, she stared out the window, listening intently for any sign the driver was going to single her out.

It was unnerving to see so many other human faces after...everything. The lights hurt her eyes; her nose was awash with a complex fug of sweat, bad breath, the ghost of what everyone had last eaten, wet clothing, a faint burnt-plastic tinge of public transit. Hearing other human heartbeats made the dry patch at the back of her throat wake up a bit, but running so hard seemed to have accustomed her to new super-senses. The bus rumbled to life, the driver gabbled an announcement into the overhead, and after a patience-straining wait the contraption lunged into motion.

She hadn't looked where the bus was going, but the universe threw her yet another bone—it passed right through the free-ride section around Marymont and the community college campus. She didn't even have to pass the driver to get out, since the doors in the middle of the bus wheezed open once they were on the other side of West 135th, and from there it was a short hop to the subway and a long walk to the only place she could possibly go.

The sneakers held up well, and one lone, dripping woman without a coat on Halloween was nearly invisible. Head down, hands swinging loosely, Bea was surprised she wasn't shivering. It was cold, sure, but that didn't seem to matter so much.

Please let him be home. Please, God, let him be home.

The warehouse's side door was locked, but she heard movement inside and hammered until faint creaks said someone was sidling up to peek through the peephole. Which led to a clearly audible flurry of moving deadbolts, making Bea shiver as the splatters of falling ice apparently couldn't.

Don yanked the door open, wiping one hand on his old Army sweatshirt. "Jesus Christ," he whisper-yelled. "Thought it was fuckin' trick-or-treaters. Get in, get in—I thought you weren't coming back."

"Me too." Bea hurried inside, stepping over the salt line—it didn't stop her at all, and the wall of crucifixes proved no deterrent either. Which could have been hilarious if she wasn't so scared. "Shut that and lock it. Quick." *Not that it'll help, if he shows up*. But the relief of seeing Don—clearly alive, in baggy cargo pants and ancient Sex Pistols T-shirt, his heartbeat almost as quick and hard as hers—outweighed nearly every other consideration in the world.

"What the hell?" Don busied himself with the bolts and chains, then whirled, hands going to his hair. He examined Bea, soaked and wild-eyed in the middle of his hallway for the second time in her life, and his own peepers were wide as possible without popping clean out of his head. "Shit, girl. You look…"

Like a drowned rat. "There's no time. You have to get out."

Don blinked several times, like an owl just waking up. "What?"

"Get the hell out. Not tomorrow, not next week, *now*. I know you've got an exit plan, and now's the time. Stop on your way out of town to pick up Callie, and you guys have to go as far as possible then *stay low*. New names, no contact with anything familiar, the whole nine." Bea ran out of air, had to gasp in a breath.

He had a little trouble assimilating the notion, but who wouldn't? "I thought you'd be halfway to Mexico by now."

"I wish I was, man." Her fingers dripped, so did her hair, and now she was the one hopping from foot to foot. "Why aren't you moving? *Now*, Donny. I don't know how much lead time I have."

"Lead time? You gotta give me a noun, Bebe." But he was already moving, shuffling past her with little *hush-wushes* of his leather slippers.

The warehouse's layered scents were both comforting and overpowering—spaghetti sauce from a very recent dinner, motor oil and hot metal from the chop bays in the larger part of the building, dust, the frowstiness of a man living alone, a yeasty tang of beer. She could even smell the salt, a white mineral note, and didn't bother to refresh the line.

"I fucked up." The admission tried to stick in her throat next to the slowly dilating dry patch. "Didn't get the stake all the way through. He's alive, Donny. He caught me over the state line, and I don't know how long I have before he gets back and discovers I got out. Once you're out the door I'll be gone, but I... I had to make sure..."

"You *gotta* be kidding me." But Don's shuffle quickened; he led her through the kitchen and into the den. Looked like he'd been working on audio mixing; the main monitor above his desk was full of layered tracks, spikes frozen in place, ready to be rearranged. Had he not been watching the security cameras? She'd tried to avoid them, not wanting to leave even that much of a trail. "I thought they covered it up with a gas leak. It was in the paper—even Channel Five had a spot."

"He's using the name Andranov now." Even that might be telling Don too much. "You have *got to hurry*, Donny. So help me, I will pack for you and dump you on a bus myself if I have to."

"Andranov? But that's..." Don all but skidded to a stop. He was cheesy pale now, and kind of green. His heart was galloping so hard it made her feel faint as well.

"I'll talk so long as you're getting ready to go." Bea restrained the urge to stamp her feet like an angry child. "*Move, goddammit!*"

Don flinched as if stung, and headed for the bedroom door. "That's...shit, shit, *shit*. Andranov? You gotta be joking, he just flew in from the old country to take over some business from Morelli and Gazzo, you know, that big oily-haired asshole with all the gold chains? It can't be, he—"

Oh, Jesus. Bea's knees threatened to turn into cold water, matching the rain outside. The sweater soak-stuck to her, so did the jeans, but the shivers were from pure fear. "So he already had that set up ahead of time. Figures. Look, you...you have no idea, Don. You really don't. Promise me you'll get out tonight, and take Callie with you. Please."

"Callie dumped me right after you left. That's why I'm here instead of at the Halloween party." Don banged the bedroom door open, plunging into a dimness only lit by five different-colored lava lamps on a shelf above the waterbed. He hurried between piles of dirty laundry, shoved the closet's curtain aside, and began digging. "Whaddaya mean, the stake didn't go all the way through?"

"I'm sorry." Useless little words; Bea swayed near-drunkenly, listening hard. Would the new super-senses give her any warning if Lukas was even now creeping up on the warehouse? "I really am. It's not like we thought, Donny. It's bad, it's so bad, it's so much worse than…" Her breath failed all at once; her voice broke.

"Hey. Oh shit, hey." Don emerged from the closet's depths, dropping a big green Army surplus ditty-bag with a heavy thump. "Bebe? Oh Christ, what the fuck."

"Don't." She flung out a shaking hand, and he stopped dead. "Don't come near me. I'm not…I might not be…safe."

Because his frantic heartbeat sounded pretty good, especially to the dry spot in her throat. And then there was Lukas's voice, calm and even, terrifying even in memory.

The thirst always wins.

Don froze, and the paleness turned to near-transparency. "Ohshit. Bea, did…are you…"

She pushed her dripping hair back, lifting her chin. "I don't know if you can see it. The marks seem to heal pretty quick after…" Her voice failed; she had to force herself to step back because Don was moving toward her again. "No, don't. Just get the hell out of here. Pick up Callie if you can, but if that's over just *go*. And don't do any more podcasts, for Chrissake. I can't tell if he knows about you."

That was the worst part, the uncertainty. It was almost as bad as seeing Jare's body.

Almost.

"Bea, I know you're really upset, but…"

I have been attacked by little green bald men, fucked by a monster, and I can run almost as fast as a car. I can also bend part of a bed; wonder if I should grab something here and give a demonstration?

"Upset doesn't even begin to cover it, Donny. I fucked up and now you're in danger. You can't even imagine the kind of fucking danger you're in, so *pick up that goddamn bag and get the fuck out of here.*"

She didn't mean to scream; Don actually rocked on his slipper-clad heels. Not only that, but he looked at her like she'd grown another head, and Bea's mouth felt funny.

No. Don't you dare. She tipped her head back, staring at the unfinished ceiling. Sleet pounded down, and the roads were going to be miserable. Thin tremors ran through her arms and legs. *What time is it? I gotta figure out when dawn is, in case I pass out. If I sleep in the sun, will that fix me? Or will I barbecue?*

She'd been doing a lot of thinking on the way over, mostly in frantic circles. She still didn't know how Lukas had found her in the motel; he was probably on the way right now.

Her teeth still felt the same. She ran her tongue over them several times to be sure; when her chin came back down and she glared at Don, he took another hasty step back. The indistinct light in here was bright as noon to her new senses; she saw every pore and pit on his familiar face, microscopic flecks of spaghetti sauce on his shirt.

Not only that, but the rumpled waterbed reeked of sweat and sex. He and Callie almost certainly had a farewell fuck, and *that* was something Bea could have done without knowing.

"I'm sorry." Two completely inadequate words, trembling in a voice she barely recognized as her own. "I really thought I'd done it. I really thought you were safe, but you're not and it's my fault."

"Jesus Christ, Bebe. Quit blaming yourself for everything, willya?" Don swallowed hard, his Adam's apple bobbing. "Jared wouldn't want that."

"Jared's dead," she pointed out, grimly. "So grab your go-bag and get the fuck out of here. I'm so sorry, but that doesn't change anything. Oh, and I need a car too."

"Fuck *me*." Now he was aggrieved, classic Don. "I can vanish, sure, but if I take any merchandise with me—"

"I know where the chop bays are, for fucksake. I can toss your place and make it look like you got robbed." *Especially with superspeed.* It might even be a grim sort of fun. "But I need you to get out, Donny. Please."

"What are you gonna do?"

It was Bea's turn to scrub at her hair, fingertips pressing hard on her scalp, melting drops plopping from her sweater and the ends of her curls. She rubbed at her damp face, her tongue exploring her teeth again—had they changed, were they a little sharper? The sound of Don's heart was quickly becoming an irritant. "I'm gonna drive north for a bit," she said finally, muffled by her hands. Whatever expression she was wearing, it couldn't be polite or comfortable. "There's something I have to do. After that, I dunno. I'll figure it out."

When she was brave enough to look again, Don wore a peculiar expression. "Why don't we team up? Our chances are better together, right?"

Oh, hell no. Not now, for God's sake. It was *vintage* Donny Bertram to pull something like this. At least Bea had a really good answer that didn't require picking her way through a minefield of friendzone accusations. "I saw Jare's body," she said, tonelessly. "I don't want to see yours, too."

The thought of what Lukas might do to her brother's friend was, she decided, so terrifying as to be darkly hilarious. All those threats—flaying, grinding bones to powder—acquired horrible depth not just because he'd said them with such flat unconcern, but because she'd had his teeth in her throat.

And other things, buried in other places. Lukas wasn't human, and God alone knew what he'd do if he caught her and Donny together. Even *trying* to imagine the event made her stomach flip uneasily, though she hadn't eaten anything in days.

Come to think of it, she hadn't needed the toilet either. Which was thought-provoking, sure, but she had all she could handle at the moment.

"Is it really that bad?" Don was braver than the average bear, at least. And he'd done her not just one but several solids, signing onto her quest for revenge.

She couldn't drag him down with her. "However bad you think it could get, it's a thousand times worse. A million, even. You gotta go, Donny. Go and stay gone, and for God's sake don't start up another podcast. If Lu—" She swallowed the name. "If Andranov comes after you, I can't stop him. I can't even slow him down. I gotta know you're safe."

It didn't take much more arguing after that. It took even less to get the key to an electric-blue Dodge Charger sitting in a chop bay, its VIN already chipped and new plates applied; Don threw in a slender roll of gas money despite her refusal.

He even hugged her awkwardly, one-armed, before climbing into his own escape vehicle—a primer-spotted Taurus parked under a tarp on the warehouse's sheltered west side, its nose pointed at a nearly hidden alley giving directly out on Charney Street. Which was nice of him, sure.

But the thunder of his heartbeat scraped the rapidly expanding dry spot in her throat, and her mouth tingled. No fangs yet, but Bea didn't want to push it.

She didn't wave goodbye, but she did watch his taillights vanish as he took a left at the end of the alley, probably a little faster than he should have. The tires chirped, the suggestion of a fishtail skid straightened out, and he was gone.

Thank God.

The sleet was trying mightily to turn into snow; the warehouse stood bleak and slumped, as if it knew it had been discarded like an old snakeskin. Now Bea had to toss the living quarters to cover Don's tracks and then get the hell out of here.

If she managed that she could hit the turnpike going north, drive until dawn got close. If she didn't make it in time, could she pull off the road and find a shaded place to sleep? Maybe the sun would rise, she'd pass out behind the wheel, and all of this would become academic.

Was she hoping for that? Bea jumped; the warehouse roof had creaked—a usual noise, but never so loud.

Her ears were getting *more* sensitive, not less. So was the rest of her.

She hurried back inside.

CHAPTER 26

"We didn't hear a thing," Wrenfeldt repeated. Despite his bulk, he looked strangely small on his knees; Lukas rarely required such flagrant measures, but the instant he appeared both dogsbody and understudy had assumed the ancient posture of repentance. "Master, I swear, we did not hear. She simply…she's fast, like a sanguinant. There was nothing we could do."

"Nothing," Hardison piped up. The boy's pulse was hummingbird-quick; both men reeked of fear. "We was at our posts, master. She just came out of nowhere, *bam*!"

One of the bedposts was bent, the mark of slim fingers printed deep, just where she would grasp. He touched the indentations, gently. "How very odd."

The Gift granted much, and a daywalker's blood was power-ful. The seals had been still intact but humming unhappily, the door locked. Her scent dyed the room, powerfully soothing, but the absence of its font taunted the animal at the bottom of consciousness.

Not to mention the rest of him.

I'll be good. Pleading, tense, obviously distressed. *Please don't lock me up in here.*

Would she have lingered, had he agreed? Lukas did not think so. Yet he could not fault her, young and frightened, all that stubborn bravery and defiance contained in such a small frame. Far more important than fault was swift action. Very quickly both the thrall and the addiction would punish him—as if he needed any further spur other than deep aversion to the return of calcification.

Hardison was still gabbling. "—just vanished. We ran out into the driveway, but she was gone. Not a sign, Master. We checked the door, locked tight, and Thomas said—"

"Thank you, Hardison. Now be quiet." For if the boy did not, Lukas might simply break both him and the dogsbody, then every other servant in this empty shell. Robbed of its beating heart, the building was useless; his prize now wandered the night.

When he stilled, turning inward and filling his lungs with a soft slow inhale freighted with her scent, the fury almost, *almost* retreated. But not quite. The dogsbody and understudy had crept down to the saferoom door, had they? Verifying she was gone? But neither could alter or affect the seals, and though she was exhibiting a portion of fledgling strength, the reinforced door and multiple bar-locks should have been more than enough to keep her contained.

The seals would not harm his leman, especially with his own blood fueling the Gift; it was just barely possible she had discovered some way through from the protected side. Even so, the door should have stopped her—unless Lukas was mistaken, which could be so. He could not rule out his own ineffectualness.

What a bare, cheerless room. What had she felt, standing here, iron softening under her slim fingers? He was surprised she had not torn the bed apart in a fit of pique, but such was not her temperament.

No, she was altogether more deliciously complex and resourceful, his beautiful, evanescent Beatrice.

The greisoul. Had she been wearing it? Ah, he remembered. Tucked in a back pocket of those denims she liked so much—but this was not among the item's many uses, not that he was aware of.

Both dogsbody and understudy were still, breathing hoarsely, pulses absolutely uncontrolled. Their fear was not to be soothed, although he supposed he should be grateful her flight had been so swift as to preclude any damage from ill-conceived notions of trapping or delaying their master's prize.

His inward attention fastened on a soft, nearly imperceptible tugging. It was not the bright crimson thread of an open blood-trail, as he had followed to a cheap lodging-house—no, *motel,* that was the proper modern word. Yet it was stronger, for she was his bonded leman; even more importantly, she was his very own fledgling, the only one he had ever made.

And a Maker could always find their own.

Lukas turned, his gaze settling upon the pair of kneeling mortals. "Burn this lair and the Andranov cover." It was far from the first time he had been required to kill a just-acquired identity, and would not be the last. "Every servant here may have the bonuses already accrued, then go upon their way. As for you two…"

Hardison flinched, his gaze fixed on Lukas's shoes. Wrenfeldt had seen the effects of repelling incursions or taking new territory upon his employer's clothing many a time, and so was presumably less fazed. Besides, he had also watched ossification creep upon an ageless being with increasing speed and depth for how long, keeping his own counsel?

Such patience was middling-rare. Lukas reached several decisions at once. "How long have you been in my service, Thomas?"

"Quite some time, Master." A faultless reply. "Almost two hundred years, I should think."

Which was not very long, in the scheme of things—but it no

doubt felt so to a mortal. "Faithfulness deserves a reward." He watched several microscopic flickers of expression cross Wrenfeldt's face; in a state of heightened emotion, even a century or so of practice could crack.

Before she had struck his accumulating chains, he might not have noticed or cared. Now Lukas found confirmation of unpleasant suspicions, but this was a small matter indeed. He could find a dogsbody with even less trouble than a fleeing fledgling.

Best to simply let all other pots boil elsewhere for a moment.

"Master..." Wrenfeldt's shoulders bowed slightly, but even as he dropped his chin and stared at the floor, a flash of avaricious expectation crossed his broad face. Lightning, there and gone in less than a moment.

Enough. Come dawn she would be asleep, and the pull nonexistent until dusk. Lukas must move with some speed now, for if she chose the wrong bolthole to shelter in the effect could be disastrous. "Be about your work with good cheer. Keep yourselves in readiness; I shall make contact soon."

He burst into mistform, streaming for the doorway. Hardison squeaked; Wrenfeldt elbowed him, quite ungently. "*Shhh*," the dogsbody hissed.

It was all so much noise; Lukas knew what he must do. He could take a few moments with the desktop computer upstairs; unlike many other underlings, it did precisely as it was told, no less and certainly no more. Which was comforting in a way, yet could not be the entirety of service.

In any case, a few among his underlings would learn soon enough the folly of oathbreaking.

It had been some while since he used his speed in this fashion, gliding along terrain features as only a sanguinant could, avoiding mortal notice where possible. A flash in the night, a cold breath upon the nape—in earlier days, the folk would know something was abroad in the night. If any were so unfortunate as to be away from shelter, they might well spit a bean into the darkness, mutter a prayer to a favored god, or clutch at an amulet. Nowadays, they simply hurried about their business, doing their best to forget the hint of something ancient and inimical crossing their path.

Northward the call led him, and he could even use the shining metal conveyances of this time, so long as they were proceeding in the correct direction and large enough to crouch upon. To do so conserved some of his strength, though he could —and would—not stop until his prey was run to ground.

Yet it was fortunate she had chosen to flee thus. He had an inkling of where his wayward prize would be wending, since certain matters weighed so heavily upon her mind. Lukas leaned into the howling wind of transit, snow and icy rain ignored as they soaked tattered clothing, velocity combing his hair. The intimation became certainty as the night grew old, and though the thrall mounted deep in his bones and the fact of her absence turned from shock to rising torment, he still had occasion to be grateful.

Dawn found him parallel to the freeway, since little traffic was moving in the direction he wished and the terrain had begun to look familiar indeed. Old hills which had once been mountains glowered; the call shifted slightly before fading all at once as the sun's fiery rim lifted over the horizon, underlighting a heavy eastern pall of storm moving in.

She was asleep for the day, hopefully tucked into some safety —it was unlikely her true teeth had erupted, though the protection of mortality against sun-damage would be swiftly fading. Cloud cover would also help shield her.

The tide had turned, All Hallows was over.

Lukas had another means of finding her, and it lay in the bowels of a nearby peak clothed with bright patches of maple and birch still clinging to a few painted leaves, crowded by hemlock and spruce ready to withstand whatever blast would issue from the northeast.

His paced slowed, though not much. Yes, the terrain was familiar indeed.

He was thirty miles or so, as the crow flies, from the foothills of Noll Mountain.

CHAPTER 27

Winter dawns were late, but she'd spent too much of the night on buses or subways, not to mention impersonating a hurricane in Don's living quarters above the warehouse. His bosses might not even realize the blue Charger was missing, since she'd also done her best to light the place on fire before heading out.

If Donny got cold feet and came back…but that wasn't Bea's problem at the moment. She'd done all she could for him, including committing arson for the very first time, and now she had to save herself.

Of course heading south or west might have been a better idea—a lot more country to lose herself in, if she could hope to do so. The feeling of being watched by invisible eyes waxed and waned, and honestly at this point it was almost an old friend.

Not really.

At least the high drilling whine of the little green men didn't appear. By the time she left the turnpike, filling up at an Irving station thankfully still crouched at the end of a long exit as it had been four years ago, it was well past 5am and a hideous, unwelcome numbness was creeping up her fingers and toes.

It had taken her three tries to find a place open for cash instead of deserted filling stations which assumed anyone passing by would have a credit card. The yawning clerk gave her a cursory glance before taking payment, and she bought a cheap sunshield as well. She was still damp despite the Charger's heater going full-bore and the luxury of heated seats, but working the night shift in a boondocks stop-and-rob probably accustomed the clerks to a whole lot of strangeness, purely human…or otherwise.

Dawn found her close to the ultimate goal, rattling over the washboard ruts of an abandoned logging road she'd once hiked under muttering protest. A few miles up the side of a frowning hill the gravel track widened before petering out, and she pulled the Charger into heavy shade at the end.

It'll have to do. She just hoped nobody would get curious, but people in this part of the world often knew how to mind their own damn business. Now Bea wondered how much of that was closemouthed rural tradition, and how much was these mountains being older than God and crammed with weird shit.

She barely got the sunshield up before passing out—though the hanging boughs of a regrown spruce draped over windshield and roof—at the exact moment the sun crested the horizon.

No dreams, no hallucinations. Even the foggy sense of time passing in the blackness of sleep was muted.

Consciousness burst into full flower, and Bea found herself slumped sideways over the center arm-rest and console, the cupholder digging into her ribs and her cheek pressed against the passenger seat's upholstery. A faint breath of new-car smell —whoever this beast had been stolen from was probably having a bad week, if they weren't rich enough to afford the inconvenience.

Hope they've got insurance. Her mouth was full of a strange almost-spicy taste instead of morning breath, and she ran her tongue over her teeth while pushing herself upright. All in all, for spending the day keeled over in the driver's seat, she didn't feel bad. No stiffness, just the urge to stretch every limb nice and hard.

It was disorienting to both crash and wake up in darkness, though, like pulling long night shifts at the packing plant. Even more odd was the hazy sense of physical well-being, though her throat was awful scratchy.

And though she knew it was night-time, her eyes were working better than ever.

Take it while you can, Bebe. Her brother's voice sounded cheerful. *You're still a couple to the good.*

"Yeah," she muttered, trying not to think about what might happen if Lukas caught her. Her breath halted for a moment; the resultant shiver wasn't entirely unpleasant.

Don't dwell on it. Maybe he only got you the first time because his people were already watching. That would mean he was aware of Don—but hopefully she'd given her brother's best friend enough time to get good and lost. At least she could hope, and the fact that she'd spent an entire day sleeping unmolested in a stolen car was a good sign, right?

The blue Charger roused obediently when she twisted the key. Not having to pee in the woods was a goddamn luxury, really. If the bloodsucker-making process was reversed somehow, she'd have to go back to scanning for bathrooms at every opportunity.

Her vision was now so good she nearly forgot to flick the headlights on. Even the foglights were unutterably bright; getting back down the logging road was a matter of taking it slow, letting the shocks do what they were designed for, and wincing at particularly bad jolts.

She wasn't quite on home ground, but it was close.

The road's tunnel through dense greenery wavered slightly, and she realized her eyes were hot and full. Bea swiped angrily at her cheeks, and kept going.

❧

Small changes accumulated over four and a half years. The mailbox listed heavily, nearly buried in a drift of vines; the driveway's mouth, butting up against ancient seamed two-lane paving, had crumbled at the edges, the concrete drainpipe underneath—meant for runoffs in wet springtime—half-choked with detritus from more than one storm. Undergrowth scraped at the car's sides as she negotiated the familiar rise. There was no porchlight shining through winter's last dusk-gasp, no star of floodlight atop the post at the edge of the turnaround or its twin near the stable's dark, leaning bulk.

And there was the rambling knockoff colonial, her brother's pride and joy. *Four bedrooms, I'll use one as an office. You can do something too—an art room, or meditation?*

"When the fuck am I gonna meditate?" Bea murmured, the old conversation raw and aching in memory. He'd been so goddamn *proud*.

We have acreage too. Goes a fair bit up the mountain, it's a big-ass lot. During hunting season we'll have to wear orange. And the den looks right onto the back meadow, I can put my desk there and have the trees while writing.

The windows were scabbed over with boards, the wraparound porch he'd been so proud of visibly deteriorated. The forest had crept across a good portion of the back meadow, looming closer than ever. Bea shuddered—the weird stuff, like the tracks of tiny misformed feet or horribly savaged bodies of small wild animals, most often happened along that line. Now she remembered each and every incident, including the ones passed off as imagination, hypnagogia, or just plain bullshit.

Can you just not be an asshole, she'd yelled over the phone, right before giving in and leaving college for good. *You're going off the deep end with all this alien abduction shit, can you just* fucking *not? I should have known you wouldn't let me get my degree!*

Her heart hurt, thinking about that fight. Turning off the headlights and cutting the engine meant the foglights also died. Night rushed at the windshield, swallowing the car whole. Even the trickle of cold air through the inch of rolled-down window smelled familiar—fresh air loaded with balsam and the faint iron tinge of running water from the creek at the west edge of the property.

Months of being under siege in this house, afraid to even go into Noll Corner for groceries because when she came back something was sure to have happened, Jare wild-eyed and pale, the noises near the windows in the dead time between midnight and 3am…

The Charger's door swung shut with a heavy, decisive sound. She was halfway to the house before she stopped, one drip-dried sneaker hovering until she realized she'd frozen mid-step and put it down.

She couldn't go in there.

Nope. Not today, Satan. One of Don's favorite little jokes. Had he stopped by Callie's place, had he been able to convince her to flee with him?

"Worry about yourself, Bea." Her voice broke the hush. The trees sighed, ruffling under rising wind. She should have been shivering, with no coat, no gloves, no hat.

But she wasn't. The tremors came from an entirely different source.

She turned, and it took a few steps before she was on track. Yes, this was exactly how Jared had approached the stable that evening. Neither of them liked being out after dark by that point, but it had been a nice spring day, warmer than late April usually got, and Snowball usually did her business in a hurry at that hour.

There was the window Bea had peered through, a cataract eye filthy with dust and pollen outside and cobwebs on the inner surface. Scraps of faded crime-scene tape fluttered near the doorway, and even though it was a cloudy moonless night, rain or worse threatening on a rising nor'east wind—she could tell by the way it sounded climbing over Noll Mountain's shoulder—her new super-senses were pitiless, because she could see every splinter of the stable's leaning walls. The long-ago haze of horse, hay, and manure tickled her nose along with a deeper, darker thread.

He came along here, Snowball was barking but I didn't hear her because I put my earbuds in. Bea took one last lingering look at the window before backing up to walk along the path he'd taken and sidling through the doorway—Jared wouldn't have had to turn sideways, but it was frozen half-open now, probably swung to during a storm.

After the body was taken away.

Oh, God. She didn't have to go inside very far. Rotting wood, mildew, and that nasty hideous brassy note, still terribly present.

Death.

The stain was faded, yet obscenely visible. Bea found the right angle and sank into a crouch, tilting her head just so.

Right here. He was right here, looking at…and Snowball was over there, they threw her after they…

It wasn't that hard to believe a monster, after all. Bea turned, staring at where she knew the window was. Lukas hadn't heard her heartbeat for some reason—the wind rattled and moaned at the stable roof.

Quite possible, since the reek of greiben was strong and they are noisy in withdrawal. She could almost feel his breath in her hair, and hunched her shoulders before unfolding.

If she looked at the stain anymore, she might start to cry again. Instead, she half-spun, and looked up at the hayloft. Maybe she could leap there, with her body's new super-reflexes...but she used the rickety old ladder anyway, holding her breath and hoping it wouldn't crumble under her weight.

Would she get heavier? Lukas certainly was.

With each rung, another damp, nasty scent intensified. It

reminded her of greasy yellow fog, big black insectile eyes, their horrible little mangled paws and naked buttocks.

It was looking more and more like she'd tried to stab the wrong monster. Now Bea had to wonder what else he was telling the truth about.

I really don't want to think about that, either.

The hole in the roof was a lot bigger now. It pointed due east; cold air whistled past, her sweater's hem flapping and her hair lifting in a cloud, almost worse than the roof of the Everly building. She found her fingertips resting against the gem at her breastbone, and its humming tingle could have been imaginary.

Oh, what the hell, she thought, and took a few running steps, gathering speed. The leap flowered underneath her, just as it had at the North Bluff mansion's big overdone gate, and her body knew what to do, twisting in midair to avoid branches, her sneakers hitting forest loam, the rest of her driven into a crouch like a cat jumping off a slightly too-high counter.

"Holy *shit*." Now she was talking to herself in the middle of the woods at night. If this kept up she'd be a crazy old lady living under a bridge, muttering about abductions and monsters and…

What the hell's that?

A faint, terrible rumbling underlaid the wind's rising moan. Bea straightened, very glad her new eyesight had no trouble with tangled underbrush at night, and hoped she wasn't about to get herself lost in the wilderness.

Faint, horrible sawing shrieks could have been the storm coming in, but an odd nervous thrill spilled down the back of her arms, goosebumps rising all over, her nipples hard as chips of rock and her hair tingling at the roots, curls flirting with moving air. Shadows moved as she picked her way deeper into the trees, and when she touched the necklace again she realized the emerald—or petrified henchman, ugh—was faintly but definitely glowing.

"This is so goddamn weird," Bea whispered, and hesitated. It was best to run away, wasn't it?

But she had to know.

Slowly at first, then moving with more confidence as her new super-senses proved more than adequate to this new challenge, she moved towards the noise.

Due east.

CHAPTER 28

THE EXCRESCENCES HAD BEEN DRIVEN DEEP, THE NORTH SIDE OF THE mountain now scarred with at least two mineshafts full of poisonous cold iron. In the close fungal-scarred tunnels they festered; he moved through methodically, reaping a harvest of death.

Their defense was truly desperate before the highly flammable spawning grounds, but not nearly enough. Mistform was peculiarly suited to this manner of extermination—it could not properly be called a battle, so very one-sided, and neither could it be named a hunt for he took nothing from them but their half-vegetable lives.

The peculiar blue flame needed for cleansing was mildly dangerous to fledglings, a nuisance to elders, and almost an afterthought for daywalkers. It was said an Archon could dance across lava at bright noon and take no damage, and some part of Lukas wondered if he would ever try such a thing.

Unlikely. And yet.

Though they spent the majority of their time below, the *greiben* were sensitive to solar cycles—torpid during the day, more active at night. Dusk arrived as he was in the deepest part of the warrens, the last spawning field exploding in noisome liquid spatters as piled, green-glowing eggs popped, flooding the flames with fresh mucus-thick fuel. Nearly formed *greiben*-nymphs writhed, dead before birth.

The only problem was keeping a specimen of proper size alive, since both juveniles and elders were reckless in defense of the eggs. Victory was a foregone conclusion, though a messy one, and he had to make a final circuit of the spawning ground while holding a desperate, nearly roasted *greiben* by its skinny scruff, ignoring its scrawny windmilling limbs and attempts to crack its own spine, twisting to bite the intruder despite mist-form's refusal of such maneuvers.

An occasional shake to settle the hissing, desperate thing sufficed.

Perhaps he was a little more savage than necessary, but better that than the alternative. And the battle might even have frac-tionally blunted the rage burning in his bones, both the thrall and his own temper increasingly uneasy.

The more he mulled, the more irritating the entire situation became.

Finally he swept upward in mistform, every sense scanning for lone survivors. Only two had escaped his dive into the netherworld, one far less charred than what he held, so he killed the hapless extraneous with vicious efficiency, taking his new hostage up with a warning shake. Rising, rising more, smoke and the terrible rumble of a sanguinant's killing rage reverber-ating in every cavern, along every large or oozing-thin passageway.

Now all he had to do was hope she had not rid herself of the *greisoul*, and this little green rag would sniff her out no matter the hour. If Lukas was wrong, he would simply have to hunt her at night...but why would she flee so far northward unless she meant to make a visit in this vicinity?

Let me be right. Let her be safe, and whole.

And nearby.

The excrescence's struggles intensified as the surface approached. Lukas did not throttle his own growl; bouncing, overlapping echoes would warn him of any twitching survivors, just as mistform's sensitivity to living heat would catch those too wounded to flee yet still clinging to some manner of existence.

He had done his work thoroughly, and in good time. He wheeled through a pillared forest of stalactite and stalagmite, cathedral-crafted over geologic ages by dripping water—a process close enough to calcification as to slightly unnerve him. The stiffness was already invading, mentally and physically; with a bonded leman's absence from their sanguinant, the ossification returned swiftly, galloping where before it had crept.

A flutter of acceleration, the *greiben* struggling with the enhanced strength of a creature which knows its own survival deeply in question, and he searched the higher tunnels swiftly, finally coalescing in the throat of a vast worm-hole chewed into the rock. The stink was immense, titanic, and he ignored it just as the struggles of the lone survivor.

Outside the warrens, the wind had mounted. At the end of this tunnel, past a tangle of confusingly braided dead-end passages meant to trap outside creatures and alert the *greiben* to their presence, was a familiar black mouth half-hidden in shrubbery upon the mountain's southern slope.

Lukas listened for a few moments, predatory instinct alive with warning, and finally decided he had fully cleansed the infection. Thin runnels of caustic smoke would solidify into poison char or escape the warrens in shreds through entrances like this one, vanishing into the maw of a winter storm.

He was about to shake the struggling, scrawny child-sized creature into quiescence and give it to understand its task, but a soft, almost-inaudible note intruded upon the sough and groan of moving air.

A sweetly familiar rhythm, indeed.

No. Not possible. Once more he was luckier than any soul upon the tired earth could possibly be—or creeping age had decided to swallow him whole, and he was hallucinating after a last paroxysm of violence.

The whispering speed impelled him to the heart of the trap-passages, and a single breath of clean, fresh outside air swept past, pushed by some vagary of atmosphere or physics.

And upon it rode a trace of lovely warm fragrance, musk and tenderness, silken hair and large, mistrustful gold-threaded eyes. A hint of burning, a splash of cold rainwater, and the wicked warm honey of arousal, whether fear or something else.

He burst from the entrance into a tangle of vines, under-brush, and trees tossing their arms as the night combed a dark, gorge-ridden mountainside. A convulsive movement broke the *greiben* in his hands, for at the edge of a small clearing a familiar shape stood, head upflung like a startled doe, her curls lifting in a bewitching, shining mass and a green gem upon her breast.

Her scent burst upon him again, stripping away creeping numbness. Lukas was suddenly aware of half-frozen water sluicing from the sky, the mountain whistling and rushing as it bathed.

Beatrice's lush, tender mouth moved slightly. The Gift burned in her, the grace and control of sanguinant merely polishing what had existed before. She whirled, plunging into the trees, a dryad surprised in primeval forest.

Lukas dropped the crushed rag of last, hapless *greiben*, and bolted after her.

CHAPTER 29

Being chased through the woods was a common nightmare, sure. Zipping between trees with that strange flickering speed, wrenching herself aside as trunks or giant granite boulders reared before her, leaping like Supergirl—all that was new, and so was the terrible dilating pain in her throat, the dry ache returned with a vengeance.

One moment she'd been staring at the black, rumbling hole in the hillside, alternating waves of hot and cold flashing all through her. The next, that immense growl halted and Lukas resolved out of thin air, his suit torn to ribbons, thick dark splatters dripping from arms and legs, holding one of the nasty little green henchmen casually as a struggling kitten.

There was no sound behind her save the wind and mounting waves of raindrops piercing the forest canopy, but her back crawled with that instinctive sense of invisible eyes following every move. The terror was immense, red-tinged, vying with the pain in her throat.

The thirst.

Hiking eastward on the mountain had taken quite a while, but it seemed like only a few seconds later she burst from a line of trees just past the leaning wreck of the stable, sneakers brushing softly instead of smacking in mud. The rain was silver curtains loaded with ice; sheer unthinking desperation, beating behind her heart like a second pulse, pelted her for the house.

Boarded windows, locked doors, the porch shuddered as she leapt onto it and hesitated, skidding...

...and a warm living weight hit her from behind, driving them both through the front door with its beveled glass insets, still whole despite abandonment.

Or it had been. The entire doorway shattered, splinters and shards flung across the foyer; somehow Lukas's arms were around her; he turned and took the impact on his shoulder, a half-familiar movement. She barely had a heartbeat to realize he must have done the same thing in the elevator before they tumbled, rolling, all the way across the foyer, ending at the foot of the stairs.

Disuse, neglect, mildew—the house reeked of all those things. Under the sad rotting smell an uninhabited structure quickly acquired was familiarity, from the ghost of floor polish to the even fainter trace of Jared, and a tinge Bea almost didn't recognize as her own preferred laundry detergent and the perfume she'd discovered in college.

Memories crowded her, a flood she managed to keep dammed during waking hours. Her own voice, sharp and needling or sarcastically dismissive.

Can you take Snowball out? I'm doing the goddamn bills...do you always have to make everything weird...it's raccoon tracks, or something...I guess I'll come stay for a little while...Jesus Christ, don't listen to everything Don says...

The warm, heavy weight was on top of her, and Lukas inhaled harshly. His cheek had ended up pressed to hers, a rasp of stubble, and more frightening than the strength in his fingers or the deep growl something human-sized shouldn't have been able to produce was the fact that he wasn't crushing her, and his fingers around her right wrist didn't squeeze. He simply held that arm pinned, the rest of him stretched over her, and Bea froze.

Oh, shit.

He was sniffing, she realized. Great deep gulps, and both of them were soaked clean through. In his case it was probably a good thing, because the guck he'd been covered with was unpleasantly acrid; she probably didn't smell too fresh either, after being drenched, drip-dried, then hiking through the goddamn woods in yet more pouring sleet.

The growl petered out, but he stayed atop her. Bea didn't dare move, she hardly dared *breathe.* The curious stillness was expectant instead of peaceful, the last moments before a thunderstorm breaking.

"Beatrice." The same lingering over each syllable of her name. He shuddered, a wave passing through his much larger frame, and at the end of the movement his knee was between hers. "You are...unhurt. That is good."

It's probably gonna change in the next few seconds. Staying frozen was hard work, especially when he moved again, his knee sliding up, and she felt a very familiar insistent probing against her thigh, prodding through his ruined trousers and her wet, clinging jeans. *Oh, hell.*

"The door unlocked," she managed, in a husky little whisper. It sounded less terrified, and more...provocative, since the thirst was torment-teasing again. A terrible dry need hit her sideways, swamping her entire body, filling the deepest pit of her belly with molten heat. "I s-swear it wasn't me, the door unlocked and I..."

She wanted monster blood, she realized. *His* blood. The swimming lassitude, the deep warmth—it was like needing chocolate once a month, or the salt cravings at infrequent intervals.

Do bloodsuckers have periods? Why did her brain rabbit-jump everywhere, why couldn't she think of something useful? And why, oh God why, did she *cry* when she was terrified? Her eyes were full of hot welling water.

"Yes." As if he'd expected it, but did he believe her? "I suspect so. And yet."

That does not sound good. "Please," she managed. "I believe you. I do, I promise. I'm sorry. I shouldn't have staked you, please just let me go."

"We are well past that point, kitten." Rough, as if his throat hurt too. His knee pressed upward, pushing her legs apart a little further. "Had I seen you that night I would have taken you then. Do you doubt it?"

At least she wasn't laying on splinters, but the floor couldn't be clean. Cold hardwood, in fact, and the stairs a rising shadow to her left. "We could just be calm, and talk about this. Couldn't we?"

"We will," he said, grimly. Another deep inhale, another shudder. "I will have you, I will feed you, then we may speak of anything you like."

Oh, boy. Bea erupted into motion—or tried to. A slight lurch, rocking a few inches to her right, was all she could manage.

It was like dropping a lit match into gas fumes. His mouth fastened on hers, and she was lost.

The floor was freezing, he was fever-hot, and the sound of tearing cloth along with cool air brushing bare, damp skin told her he was in a clothes-ripping mood again. It might even have been a relief to have wet denim explode from her legs in shreds, but Bea was far too occupied with scooting away, her blindly questing left hand hitting the bottom step before finding the newel post at the end of the banister, curling around and hauling with hysterical strength.

That same numbing-sweet taste, his tongue pursuing, taunting, *taking*; a single trickle ran across the thirst-spot and lit a fuse, sparking all the way down her spine. She was faster now, stronger, capable of putting her fist through the walls of Don's warehouse or the monitors hanging over his desk, able to run down a winding country road fast as a car.

But he was swifter, heavier, and had leverage as well. One wrist trapped, he had the other in a trice—though there was a splintering sound as she heaved blindly, she forgot it because his hips settled between her legs and a familiar hot, hard tip probed just at the most sensitive, aching part.

At least slow down, she wanted to say, but her mouth was stoppered, and he didn't bother waiting. The growl was back; he moved, muscle rippling in a single hard thrust, and Bea's hips jerked, half in protest and half in pure blind reaction.

Her entire body turned liquid. The new sensory acuity extended to touch as well, and sheer sensation drowned her. More wood splintered, the growl vibrating in his chest sending waves of heat down her back as he thrust again, driving deep. More fire, that wicked little questing caress finding her clit, and it was official, she was being fucked at the foot of the stairs, her fingers clenching and lungs heaving as she tried to scream.

Any sound she made was swallowed, lost in the deep thrumming noise he made or his hot, insistent mouth. Again and again, hammering home, the pressure building, a dagger-sharp splinter poking at her shoulder. She flinched, and he snarled.

Weightlessness, an iron-hard, fever-warm bare arm snaking behind her back. Then they landed, wood cracking, dust billowing, the angle of the invasion changing because they were on the stairs somehow, her hands clawing at his shoulders because he had let go of her wrists. His free hand was somehow under her left knee, pushing upward; she was trapped, her bare hip pressed against the wall, the rest of her shaking as her back arched, cooperating blindly as the pleasure slammed again and again, setting every nerve aflame.

No warning, and no mercy—climax hit like a freight train, body bucking and the scream still trapped in her throat next to the thirst spreading in a rasp-haze. It lasted forever, hit after hammer-hit, and each time she thought it might end he moved again, sending a fresh series of jolts from toes to scalp.

Even when he broke away from the deep voracious kisses, it was only because he had let go of her knee, a swiftly lengthening claw dragging across his naked chest just below the collarbone. Then, somehow, her mouth found that shallow slice—and the blood trembling at its edges with its own surface tension.

An endless, searing gulp hit the back of her throat, spread in a slow summery haze. Again the world vanished, every terror and every uncertainty blotted out. The warmth rushing inward from her fingers and toes met orgasm-aftershocks; she trembled between the two, drinking voraciously.

Feeding.

CHAPTER 30

Every pull against his blood-channels was liquid honeyfire; to feed her while buried so deeply after his own release was another form of concentrated Paradise. He closed the wound, though he would have liked to let her draw forever, and she nuzzled sleepily for the last droplets. Every movement caused a subtle, wonderful reaction in the velvet fire enclosing him. Lukas pressed his lips to the top of her tangled, adorable head, inhaling the fragrance of leman, night air, winter rain.

He reeked of battle, but it could not be helped. The relief of finding her was almost as exquisite as the deep sigh she gave, turning her chin and resting beneath him almost as if resigned.

Or almost as if...content.

No. Focus on what must be done. Clarity of thought was restored to him, the fear of quick instead of creeping ossification vanished. Losing even a sliver of this lucidity was an extremely unpleasant prospect.

Yet she lay quiescent as if satisfied, at least physically, and it was sweet to think at least he knew how to please her in one respect. The rain hissed with ice, falling in waves against an abandoned house, and though mildew and disuse had settled in this place, it had once been well-loved. The ghost of beeswax polish said so, as well as the solidity of construction and a faint, pale, nearly ineffable tang of his leman. Nothing compared to the reality in his arms, of course...but she had lived here for some while, and the walls remembered.

What must it be like, to return? And to find a *greiben* hole on the mountainside—so she had listened to his explanation, resolved to test it? He did not like her so close to such things. A fledgling could hold off the excrescences long enough to gain escape, but she did not even have her fangs yet. A chill walked down his back.

"Oh, my God," she murmured, singsong-soft, clearly lost in the narcotic haze of feeding. "We broke the stairs."

He should apologize, Lukas knew. Yet he did not feel repentant in the slightest, not about this. "Better to break them than injure you."

"I think you just like ripping clothes and smashing things." A soft, experimental twitch—testing her surroundings, or thinking of escape.

Or both.

"Perhaps." His arm tightened under her back. At least with his hovering, the night's chill would not reach her skin—not that she would notice, with the Gift rising to the surface. He still longed to shield her from that minor discomfort. "The thrall is...energetic."

"Thrall?" She even sounded curious, though she shifted again, hips performing a delicious little wriggle threatening to undo him.

"The mating instincts are very strong. Every sanguinant was mortal once, after all."

"Mating, huh." A pause, as she absorbed this. "I'm, uh, not gonna have little vampire babies, am I?" A tone of sleepy near-horror, though her maker's claret would be insulating her from anything save warm relaxation.

Lukas could barely believe his ears, but the query made sense. The gaps in her knowledge of the demimonde were both amusing and mildly horrifying. "No. Sanguinant are bitten, not born. We do not...procreate." *Though the attempt is quite pleasant.*

Another restless shift. "Can we at least move a little? There are splinters."

"Slowly, in a moment." He had to think very carefully about how to shift them both; the lower third of the staircase was very nearly a ruin. "I must find something to wrap you in, and we must travel some distance before dawn. I do not wish to shelter you here."

"Yeah, I haven't been home since..." A wave of trembling passed through her slim softness, tension fighting with post-feeding languor. "What are you doing here?"

"Following you, of course. Lift your arms...there. Hold fast, I will shift us both." Lukas could now see how to untangle them from the forest of splinters. She obeyed slowly, and he could not help but enjoy the event. "Though while I was here, the warrens needed cleansing; I attended to that while you rested. They will not trouble you again; other *greiben* clans will dislike your possession of the gem, but it is not their elder. They will not dare pursue you."

"No way." Light, laughing slang. She clung to him as he moved, one limb at a time, with infinite care. "You've been busy. How did you find me?"

"You are my leman." No more need be said. Lukas settled into sitting, his shoulders braced against the wall; she had cooperated beautifully, her legs wrapped about him, and gasped as they finished settling upon a patch of damp, relatively clean floor.

He could stay in this position forever, his lap full of leman, her heels tucked behind his hips, her head nestled below his chin. He could tangle his fingers in her hair, slide his other hand under sodden cashmere—the jumper had held up remarkably well. The *greisoul* was a hard warm lump pressed between them, though not digging, and best of all, he was still buried in her, as close as possible to the breathing, irresistible heart of all existence.

"But *how*?" Persisting, curious, his kitten even settled herself more firmly upon his shaft, the heat of her core enough to proof him against any chill even were he not sanguinant. "Tell me."

Brave enough to demand, now. It was a cheersome turn of events. "Do you think I could feed you and not find you? Your blood cries out to me, lady mine." *Ask for more. Ask for anything, save escape.* The rattling ice-rain intensified, and the problem of how to bring her to another lair before dawn was a troublesome one.

Though not entirely lacking solution.

"But…" She halted—perhaps in trepidation, though he made neither move nor sound to provoke such caution.

Explanations might soothe, and there was time. "It was more difficult to find you after the fête, but I had a blood-trail then— the wound on your knee. Now you've been claimed, and fed. Much easier." His fingertips slipped through damp, curling silk. The texture of her hair was a continuous marvel, as was her skin, the arches of her ribs. "Rest. You are still very near mortal, and the rain may be less than pleasant until I find a vehicle to carry you in some comfort."

"I've got a car." Amazingly, his leman laughed, a low sensuous chuckle. "I can drive."

"Let me have the honor. I am older, after all." So easy to pretend he had some measure of her trust, instead of another mere temporary, tentative détente.

"Yeah." Sobering now, a quicksilver turn of mood, though she still rested against him. "Sometimes you're almost a funny guy, Lukas."

It meant little—simply the warm lingering relaxation of her maker's blood. Still, he was absurdly touched, and stung at the same moment.

There seemed nothing else to say. For that short while as the storm mounted outside, freezing wind mouthing the shattered doorway, he was at peace. Perhaps she was as well.

Though he did not think it likely.

The car was a heavy electric-blue item gilded with freezing, its interior saturated with her scent and a faint note of a previous owner underneath; clearly she had slept in its embrace. Lukas decided not to ask its provenance, though he did note the plate number for later investigation. The upholstery was a trifle damp; regardless, it performed its duty admirably, and with his leman —wrapped solicitously in a knitted blanket taken from the dwelling, which still held all manner of ephemera from her previous tenure—settled in the passenger seat, he was very nearly content.

Apparently the house had been sealed just after her brother's misfortune, as if during plague times. She had given a longing glance at the now-shattered stairs, but shook her head and turned away when asked if she wished to linger a few moments. *There's an afghan on the couch in the den, I'll just use that.*

Carrying her swiftly under dripping, ice-freighted trees to find the vehicle was very nearly pleasant, though far colder than he liked.

Languid from feeding, she occasionally lifted a hand from the blanket's protective depths, moving her fingers and staring in rapt fascination. Still struggling to snow, the storm had to settle for a mix of small flakes and ice pellets with an increasingly rare fraction of liquid drops, but it would not be long before temperatures plunged and Boreas howled from polar wastes to take his due.

Despite the conditions, there was just enough time to reach the lair he had in mind. Lukas focused on controlling the machinery, alert to the possibility of accident or impasse; really, the labour mortals spent on roads, when they could afford it, was one of the most compelling arguments for their status as a truly cooperative species. A small army of large vehicles for spraying salt, spreading traction-grit, or scraping away snow was held in readiness to meet the challenge, and weather prediction was no longer solely a matter of sailors' wisdom and guesswork—though plenty of the latter remained.

His prize stirred as the valley descent was completed, the car handling with aplomb a long, ice-freighted turn onto a highway heading south. "What happens if we get pulled over?"

Does that truly worry you? Still, mortals might look askance at a well-wrapped leman and her rag-clad protector. Or perhaps not, since oddities of their own kind filled the night. "There is no reason to do so, but I am well equipped for the eventuality. Should a simple piece of identification not suit, a little of the *quietus* will. We will be left to ourselves, never fear."

"Great." She drew the word out, perhaps with a hint of sarcasm. Which was another happy indicator; even outright mockery was better than constant, devouring fear. "Where are we going? We've only got half a tank."

"South. Fuel is easily acquired."

She shifted, gazing out her window at the trees left to shield denuded slopes beyond from the view of bored travelers. He thought the silence companionable, until she sniffed slightly, as if upon the edge of weeping.

Even the bravest of mortals, carefully shepherded through the Gift's first stages, might well mourn for what was lost to them—though most fledglings actively sought the blessing, carefully chosen progeny aware of their own value. For a leman, caught and claimed, it was no doubt often otherwise.

"All will be well, Beatrice." An awkward promise, of little use or comfort to her at the moment. Yet he was helpless not to offer it.

She did not reply.

CHAPTER 31

'SOUTH' APPARENTLY MEANT UPSTATE NEW YORK, AND THE LAST LEG of the trip was spent with him checking yet another phone screen instead of paying attention to the road as mixed precipitation turned to actual snow. The wind veered a little more eastward than north, but was still stiff enough to send gouts of whirling white across the highway. If not for the weird numbness of dawn approaching in her fingers and toes, Bea might not have known the sun was on its way.

She barely cared. Huddled in the old, lumpy afghan from the back of the den's couch—she'd forgotten its scratchiness, the gaps in crochet patched with scrap yarn, the melted cigarette hole off-center in a petal of the one granny square made with Red Heart—Bea was too busy trying to think through the warm, intense high of monster blood, attempting to gain a little perspective.

This time Sami and Felicia weren't talking, and neither was Jare. She was left with her body's glowing, incredibly pleasant sense of well-being, and each wave of painless warmth or burst of golden-rainbowy tracers swamping her was a distraction from the fact that she'd wasted four years of her life setting out to murder a guy who, even if he hadn't killed her brother, was still...whatever he was.

Monster. Vampire. That funny word, sanguinant.

It was amazing he had a phone to look at, though this one was in what looked like a military-grade case. There was no reason a vampire in the rags of what had been an expensive three-piecer should look so effortlessly in control of everything around him, as if other people wearing whole, unstained outfits were the weirdos, not him.

She'd spent enough time to get a double-major degree on researching the paranormal, the occult, the unexplained. But he was something else entirely. And that term, *demimonde*, only used by the contacts who were into the *really* scary shit.

The reflex of disbelief was easy, seductive, and could probably drive her even further around the bend into cuckooland. Sure, he could still be lying—the little green things *could* have been working for him, he could have been pulling the strings from behind a curtain, driving her brother mad and finally murdering Jare that awful, unseasonably warm spring night. It could be a complex, long-running con, and he could be lying about everything else as well.

There was just as much evidence that he wasn't, actually. And why would he bother? If he got his rocks off terrorizing random women, buying them entire wardrobes before strangling them, or if he was even a bloodsucking Don Juan, addicted to the chase...but that didn't wash, either.

It was far more upsetting to think she'd been entirely wrong about Jared's death, pursued vengeance with obsessive focus, and landed in this mess all on her own. Sure, she'd been right about a few facts—'Chris Everly' was really an immortal bloodsucker, he had a reason to be interested in the Noll Mountain property, her brother was truly dead, half-naked pint-size green goblins actually existed—but the associated assumptions had really chewed her ass, as Dad used to say.

That's not where he bit you. Bea kept getting distracted by the tracers and her own increasingly bleak wonderings. All of a sudden they were off the freeway, negotiating slippery surface streets.

Finally Lukas touched a button, his window rolling down. A keypad on a concrete post festooned with carefully trimmed ivy leaned close; the Charger's nose pointed at yet another giant gate, this one more utilitarian than the North Bluffs place.

An honest-to-gosh gated community, in fact. The sign said *Saratoga Oaks*, and the wide sidewalks were already sprinkled with glittering de-icer under streetlights made to look like old-fashioned lampposts, some already fading as the sky bleached to the particular predawn grey of *get ready, winter's about to kick some ass*. Tiny snowflakes whirled; the storm was following them, gathering strength. These houses were much smaller than the North Bluffs mansion though clearly more expensive, heavy on the brick and brownstone, and each was determined to ignore its neighbors.

Jesus. How much real estate does this guy own?

He *still* barely glanced at the road, though she could feel a concerning amount of slip in the Charger's tires. And she was still seeing tracers when the world went away, sunrise sinking her into a black hole.

High-grade ecru carpet. Bare blank white walls with peach undertones. A blocky birch bedstead, avoiding the four-poster designation only because the square pillars were so short and fat; the linens were white with pinkish pinstripes. A violently patterned afghan tossed across the foot, not quite out of place— in fact, it made the room look almost homey, almost lived-in.

Almost. The bathroom was white tile, antiseptically clean grout, black geometric accents repeating on hard surfaces and pinstriping the pile of neatly folded towels, a rosette of plain white soap, lily of the valley scent.

And a sleeping bloodsucker.

Lukas lay supine, one arm flung out, tucked under the pillow bearing a dent from her own head. His other hand rested on his bare chest, strong fingers against sharply defined muscle and burnished, flawless skin lightly fuzzed with dark hair. Head tipped back, eyes closed, mouth relaxed, he was either barely breathing—or not at all.

Funny how unconsciousness could make even a monster look vulnerable. He hadn't moved when Bea eased out of bed, or when she grabbed the still-damp afghan and wrapped it around her shoulders, when she made a circuit of the room to inspect the invisible force-field. Each apprehensive glance returned the same answer; Bea realized she was nervously tapping the necklace, her only real option for nervous fidgeting.

At least it was warm enough to walk around in the buff, or with a crocheted laprobe reeking of mildew and winter rain. She didn't even want to think about the heating bills for all these places. Or the window repair for the mansion.

Bea considered the bedposts. She looked at the built-in shelf the towels rested on, even gave the afghan a long hard stare. *If I ever caught him sleeping,* she'd thought more than once, but now she had and there was no weapon to hand.

If there was, though, what would she do?

Say you had the stake. You're a lot stronger now, and he's laying right there. Didn't he say the seals would release if he…

He hadn't murdered her brother. In fact, he'd been trying to get Jare out of the way, but pigheadedness was absolutely a dyed-in Dunlevy trait, and she should know. The truly, bleakly hilarious part was that if she hadn't thrown herself at this guy with a red dress and a stake, he might not have ever known she existed.

Were her teeth sharper? She couldn't really tell. *A few more feedings, it takes as long as it takes.*

It was so *strange* to see him asleep, to think of him getting tired. Did he ever hurt? Was he ever afraid?

Her fingernail made a slight sound, striking the emerald—or whatever it was. *Happy birthday, Bea. Girls like jewelry, don't they?* She'd found the receipt for the chain while filing a mountain of paperwork he hadn't had time for, finishing the third draft of his second book.

The one that was supposed to really make his name, since the first one had done so well commercially.

A terrible thought tiptoed through her head as she yanked the afghan up her bare shoulder once more. If the monster was telling the truth, why in God's name would Jare give her the stupid thing? Had her brother gone into a hole on the side of Noll Mountain and come out with a brilliant stone set in something that looked like titanium? Had he seen the *greiben*-things in there? If he had, why would he blame the little green men on 'Everly'? A natural mistake, or...

It consumes, unless given with love.

She didn't know what to think. It was pretty bad if your brother was just plain crazy, but in the vast scheme of things, that was livable. Far worse if he was murdered by monsters, and light-years more awful to wonder if he'd *meant* to give her a cursed...

No. Jare loved you, and you loved him, even if he was a grade-A asshole sometimes. What brother isn't?

Her heart gave a terrible, wringing leap.

Lukas's eyes were open. He was looking right at her, and Bea was next to the door, her hand flat on the wall for support. She realized it had to look like she was trying to get through the seals again, and snatched her fingers away as if the flat painted surface burned, nearly dropping the afghan in the process.

"I w-wasn't," she stammered, aware it just made her look guiltier. "I w-was j-j-just..."

He curled up to sitting in one fluid, controlled motion. Tilted his golden-brown head from one side to the other, stretching his neck. It was a very human movement, all things considered.

Then he just *looked* at her, dark eyes level, no sign of anger or amusement.

Oh, crap. "I d-didn't want to wake you up." It sounded like a completely lame lie, mostly because it was. "I was thinking about my brother." That part was unequivocally true, but he probably wouldn't care.

Lukas nodded slightly. "It must have been...difficult. Seeing the house, again."

That's one way to put it. Of all the responses she'd expected, that one wasn't even in the ballpark. "Yeah." Her cheeks felt hot—Christ, if she was blushing, there was no way to hide it while only wearing some granny squares. "I haven't seen you sleep before."

"I spent the day arranging a few matters. The weather is somewhat uncertain, so deliveries were minimal." He paused. "Even a daywalker occasionally requires rest."

I guess so. Bea squared her shoulders, and though she tried to march across the room, she probably looked more like a stray cat creeping under a porch. It was kind of undignified, since she was only wearing a blankie.

He didn't move when she perched on the edge of the bed, though her hip sank into the mattress next to his blanket-covered knee. He simply watched her, probably not sure what crazy thing she'd do next.

The feeling was emphatically mutual. But Bea took a deep breath, fixing him with what she hoped was a no-nonsense look. "I've been thinking."

No response save a further fractional head-tilt, maybe faintly puzzled, maybe saying *go on*. Which meant she had to take the plunge, or feel even more ridiculous. "I believe you," she announced. "About my...about Jared. "

"Ah." Did his shoulders hunch, ever so slightly? "I regret not moving sooner on that matter."

So far, so good. "And I'm sorry for staking you."

"I did not mind so much." A very slight smile, growing as

she watched. His chin dropped slightly, and he shrugged, muscle rippling on his shoulders. "You seemed so determined, how could I refuse?"

Yeah, well. It was awkward to get her right hand untangled from the afghan; still, she managed. "Hi. I'm Bea Dunlevy. Nice to meet you."

The smile remained, though he examined her fingers hanging in midair like he didn't know what to do with them. Bea was beginning to think she'd violated some kind of bloodsucker etiquette by the time he took her hand in both of his.

"Hello." Quiet and grave. "I am Lukas; it is an honor to make your acquaintance, lady mine."

He lifted her hand, turned it over. Bea didn't resist. Lukas pressed his lips gently to the inside of her wrist, and a soft, entirely inappropriate jolt of lightning flooded her entire body.

My hormones are so stupid. "You're not going to let me go, are you."

A small headshake, his mouth turning down for a moment. "No." He studied her for a moment, maybe expecting her to scream, and when she didn't he continued. "For a fledgling, every feeding is a temptation to glut, and every feast risks bloodcraze and true-death. When dawn loses its grip we are elder, but the risk of lethargy increases; we may starve from sheer anomie. The older one gets, the more calcification threatens and spreads; to stay flexible, engaged with the world, is extremely difficult. True-death looms ever closer, and the only cure is a leman. To be renewed with every moment spent in your company—do you think I would willingly give that up?"

Jesus. "If it's so bad being...what you are, why would you ever make another person go through it? Am I going to—"

"Leman are immune to glut and ossification both—and to the killing sleep as well, though you will never achieve the speed and strength of an elder. You are a miracle, and will never know what you save your sanguinant from." The soft earnestness was almost disarming, almost completely *human*. "Do you see? None of my kind would willingly let one of your kind escape."

"Is it this thing?" She couldn't free her hand, had to tuck her chin to indicate the necklace. "Because if it is, I can just—"

"It is not the *greisoul*." Patient as Jared explaining one of his conspiracy theories, accompanied by what very well might be an awful ring of truthfulness. At least he didn't hint she was stupid for not knowing, or for not listening more carefully to any explanations before now. "It is rather some intrinsic quality—we do not know how or why, only that leman are rare, and to be prized. Consider that eventually my blood will grant you daywalking, and another sanguinant may be even less to your taste than myself. I am, at least, the beast you now know."

That's not really a plus. Bea's chin set, the trademark stubborn look her parents always despaired of. Jare thought her mulishness deeply hilarious; nobody ever understood it was her only defense against an entire goddamn world constantly finding her far less than second-best by comparison to him. "So what now? What happens next?" *Let's get it over with, whatever it is.*

"A few small matters must be attended to. Afterward, though...what would you like?" He cradled her hand in both of his, gently enough she could very nearly forget the crushing strength. "What does Beatrice Dunlevy want from life?"

I never thought much past the staking, honestly. Bea found herself staring at his hands. His thumb moved slightly, stroking the underside of her wrist where his lips had pressed. His skin felt normal now, not feverish; it was actually kind of soothing to be touched so gently. "I don't know," she heard herself say, dully, and the familiar bite of shame from having to use those three little words was almost worse than sitting naked in a mildewed blanket or being pinned under and ravaged by a monster.

Next would come the disappointment, the withdrawal, the knowledge of never quite measuring up. And it was sounding like she had a longer-than-average lifespan to endure that curse, probably as payment for being the Dunlevy sibling safe in the house while the better one was dismembered.

"How wonderful," Lukas said, softly. "When you decide, tell me."

Bea's eyes prickled. It wasn't fair for a monster to sound so...she couldn't find the word. "Okay, sure. Right now, though, I could do with a shower. And some clothes—that won't be ripped off me," she added, hastily.

"Of course." Immediate agreement, though he didn't let go of her hand. "I will do my best, kitten. Always."

CHAPTER 32

E HAD NEITHER DREAMT NOR THOUGHT SUCH THINGS POSSIBLE—
first the luxury of twilight rest without fear of true-death, then
arriving at consciousness to find his leman somberly, shyly
willing to grant him singular grace. The quicksilver turn nearly
left him gasping like a landed fish.

He took her in the shower's warm embrace, her back against
warmed tile wall and her damp cheek pressed to his, the thrall
riding him unmercifully as she whispered *slow down, just a
little...oh...there, yes*, and her willingness was far sweeter than the
Gift had ever been. Her pleasure arrived in great gripping
waves, nearly robbing him of the strength to resist his own
release. Following her rhythm, her sweet husky little cries echo-
overlapping, wringing one last honeyed spasm free as his fangs
sank slowly into her throat. A single smoky, delicious mouthful,
merely to confirm she was very close to full transition, and he
regretfully withdrew; rinsing a languid, relaxed leman was a
more diffuse but no less exquisite experience.

Her hair had fully shed the black dye; gold with coppery
tinges edging many a sleek wave, it was pure sanguinant glory.
The tender damp satin of mortal skin was sleek and burnished

now. He had heard leman described as *lamps in the night*; now he knew why.

Once the seals were taken down, however, there was no time for anything but careful attention to their surroundings. This lair was furnished in overstuffed, deliberately almost-shabby style, an imitation of actual comfort. Outside, a soft hiss of falling snow rose and receded in waves, the peculiar sound meaning small flakes not quite convinced of their own inevitability; his senses dilated as he shepherded a towel-wrapped Beatrice to the decoy bedroom.

No hint of other scent in the luxurious little brownstone, no untoward rustling in the nearest neighbors, either. These were largely vacation or second homes, retreats from more frenetic city existence; mortals of a certain status were fond of such things.

"So, do you have these places built or remodeled? They can't all come with saferooms." Beatrice scrubbed at her damp hair with casual roughness; the offerings, paltry as they were, seemed to meet with her approval. At least, she let out a sigh of presumed relief upon seeing a selection of her preferred denims, and chose a wine-red jumper with an intriguingly steep V-neck as well.

She disdained the underthings, for some reason. He had no complaint.

"It depends. Even an unfinished space may serve, so long as the seals can be set." He kept a wary watch upon the windows, though most were blinkered by slatted blinds and heavy drapes. Instinct told him it would not be very long now; still, this was not a tactically sound place for what he suspected. "Your trainers were nearly unsalvageable; the new ones should fit."

"*Trainers.*" A sly, engaging half-chuckle as she laid the towel aside; she dropped onto the cheerful yellow-draped bed, bending to tie shoelaces, and he was hard-pressed not to have her again. Especially when the jumper's neckline showed that lovely freckle, peeking at him from a generous slice of décolletage. "When did you come over the pond, sir?" A mimicking of his speech-pattern; he had not thought he sounded so...stilted.

"In the latter half of Victoria's reign. I thought it would help me shake off a degree of calcification." Two new slim silver cell-phones had to take precedence over more civilized accoutrements; Lukas disliked the absence of watch or cufflinks, but he had been lucky to secure even these supplies. Mortal weather-watchers predicted the storm would only intensify over the next handful of days, laying the foundation for further waves of packed icefeathers. To the north, the sleet had already turned to freezing rain.

"Yeah, you were in Chicago. 1905, right?" A quick, calculating glance, almost fearful, though her pulse did not change much. "The Comptain Murders. You know that's still being argued about? Everyone's got a theory."

"It was nothing extraordinary. A battle for territory, incidental mortal casualties necessitating a change in identities." He checked the phone cases once more, then tucked them away. The thought that she had traced that particular thread gave him a half-chary, half-lovely frisson; it irked him to have left even muddled traces, yet her attention was most welcome. "Most mortals simply do not wish to know of the demimonde; the rest have short lives and even shorter memories. A few alterations, and they will not recognize even one they held as a friend."

"Yeah, you have this thing where you look different every time you..." She straightened, and despite the lightness of her tone, those wide, liquid eyes held more than a touch of fear.

"Simple tricks," he assured, gravely. "Playing to mortal expectations. Often they see only what they wish, and that is a great aid to passing unnoticed. All the same, I am aware I have grown somewhat...stiff. You will teach me better."

"Huh." Not quite convinced, she nevertheless granted him a rather timid smile. "How am I supposed to do that?"

"No need for effort, kitten. Your mere presence is enough." He still heard nothing untoward outside the lair; he was loath to break this small enchanted interlude, for what loomed ahead might unnerve her. Yet the sooner dealt with, the sooner he could soothe her, and begin the business of teaching his prize the more enjoyable aspects of her new existence. "Tell me, do you like trains?"

"Like, the subway?" Puzzled but not suspicious, yet the ghost of trepidation still lingered. A bright, fragile bird, no longer battering herself against the cage bars—but any untoward movement might startle her into frantic flight. "It's fine, I guess."

"No, passenger trains. If you dislike such things, we can drive."

"You'll let me drive?" She leaned back on her hands, giving a few charming trainer-kicks, a little girl asking for sweets. Yet her smile held a knowing edge, testing a boundary, curious what a measure of seduction could grant.

If only you knew, sweet Beatrice. "Not tonight."

She tensed, kicked a few more times. "Then when?"

"After a few loose ends are arranged, perhaps." Lukas was entirely aware a reminder of any escape attempt's inevitable end would certainly distort if not shatter this momentary accord—especially if she lacked plans in that direction at this moment. Best not to mention it, and also best to restrain the urge to answer her challenge with a different game. The thrall was a sleepy murmur, ever and always ready to be roused. "Allow me the honor of making our travel arrangements tonight. Please."

"Fine." Sudden watchfulness. "Can I at least ask where we're going?"

"Into the city." Perhaps it was old-fashioned to refer to it that way, but he found the tradition pleasing. "There is a meeting tonight, one better handled sooner than later. I could obtain only two coats in your size; choose one, and we shall leave."

At least he had not calcified to the point of eschewing modern electronics; the things were so utterly *useful*. Still, he missed the days of private railway cars. Leaving last night's vehicle at the station was a relief; the upholstery was still slightly damp, and the scent of dead *greiben* unpleasant at best.

A calculated risk, to take her among mortals—if she suffered an attack of sudden mistrust or attempted to interest them in what she might view as a predicament, he would be forced to far less comfortable measures. Yet this was a mode of transport his current prey would not suspect, and his leman surprised him once more with cheerful semi-docility.

She walked under his protective arm at the station, and her furtive glances at the mortals hurrying to their own destinations paralleled a rise in the soft thunder of her pulse. No doubt the sudden noise and relatively bright lights were overwhelming to newly fledgling senses; at least his timing was sound and they did not have to wait for boarding. Nowadays first-class was called business and 'first' meant something else, but he had taken the precaution of purchasing several other seats in the same car and thus there were only a few scattered travelers.

She gazed out the window, worrying gently at her lower lip. No sign of true teeth yet, though everything else about her shouted of the Gift. Tiny dots of melted snow jeweled her mane, dusted the shoulders of the red woolen peacoat she had chosen, and she perched with every evidence of enjoyment as the train accelerated.

His prize gave him many a curious, lingering look, holding her peace for quite some while. The night would be in its deepest part when they arrived; half an hour into the journey a buzz from one of his pockets intimated his orders had been received, if not quite honestly answered. The last part of his trap was set.

There was some question as to exactly how deep and far the rot extended; it was possible, though not very likely, that a few among those present tonight would be innocent of wrongdoing.

Nevertheless, this would be a violent lesson. His leman

would not enjoy some aspects, certainly...but perhaps she would be comforted in some measure by its rationale.

Settled in a reasonably comfortable seat, the linchpin of the universe at his side, Lukas let his eyelids drop to half-mast, and contemplated each likely scenario in turn.

CHAPTER 33

Jared had gone to New York a few times for meetings with his agent or a potential publisher, but Bea never had despite the relatively short distance. Now, headed that direction—even if only to New Jersey—she couldn't even feel excited. The urge to fidget crested and receded, rose again.

You could start screaming. Flag down the conductor. You could've done something at the station. She could even, she supposed, claim she had to visit the bathroom—though it was anyone's guess if he'd buy the lie—and try to throw herself off the train.

Into a developing snowstorm, though that was the absolute least of her problems. Even dimmed for night travel the lights were too bright, and the human heartbeats were distracting. It was better when she focused on the absurdly slow, steady sound of Lukas's pulse, and she wasn't sure how to feel about that, *or* about the fact that she was quietly going along with the program.

Whatever the damn program was, at this point.

The sky was an orangish sheet speckled with small multicolored jewels. She peered out the window, wondering if it was a leftover hallucination from a monster-blood high—except he hadn't 'fed' her tonight, just bit her in the shower. The place at the back of her throat where the thirst had settled wasn't aching just yet, though she was very aware of its existence.

And her teeth felt odd. Not quite painful, but certainly sensitive, as if invisible braces had been tightened after a cleaning.

Lukas lounged catlike in the big, comfy aisle seat, dark eyes half-closed and his legs stretched out. What 'identity' was he inhabiting now? Unshaven, tieless, and slightly rumpled, though the black wool coat was high quality and the eternal three-piece suit was charcoal as well—he looked like he'd had a hard weekend, and she wondered what others would assume about her own quasi-dishevelment.

Nobody would guess the truth. Or would they? She'd sat on hundreds of buses, carrying around the loaded secret of Jared's death and her own planned vengeance as well as the terrible, much larger consciousness of weird paranormal shit lurking in the dark cracks of the world's foundations.

Nobody had ever looked twice.

How could she even begin to explain? *Hi there! This guy's an immortal bloodsucker and I'm...*What exactly *was* she? A pet? An emotional support sex kitten? Plenty of the stories and movies made being a vampire look pretty cool—papering over all the onscreen murders, sure, but action movies had a higher body count and everyone loved those, too.

The reality of bloodsucking, at least as described by the guy next to her, sounded more like a curse than anything else. Was she actually *pitying* a monster?

Go figure.

Multicolored sky-lights shimmered, and she finally realized what they were. Bea shifted, damn near pressing her nose to the glass. "Stars," she blurted, helpless to keep quiet. She was seeing right through heavy, snow-pregnant cover. "But it's snowing."

Lukas stirred. "Hm? Oh, yes. You'll enjoy the next full moon, I think. Quite the sight."

Wow. That is something. It was bright as noon outside, between the glare of a huge city, the sky's cloud-dome reflecting, and the snowflakes getting thicker. Up north they were probably having a real howler; it hurt a little bit to think of Jared's abandoned house, a hole where the front door used to be. And the afghan, discarded at the other place as if it didn't matter.

It was probably better to take nothing with her, ever. If she dropped the necklace under her seat, would whoever found it pawn the thing, thinking themselves lucky? Or maybe they'd turn it into the lost and found, and it could be auctioned off in a few years.

Train-rhythm was absurdly soothing, a metal heartbeat partially drowning out the human ones.

Mortals. Even thinking about it caused a squidgy sensation behind her breastbone, though she hadn't eaten anything in what felt like forever. Her biology was all whacked-up now.

"How long is this going to go on?" She kept her voice down, hoping she wasn't about to piss him off.

"A little over four hours. Are you uncomfortable?" Now there was a faint hint of worry, just the slightest shading to his tone. He was sounding a lot less weirdly robotic, that was for sure. "There's a diner car; mortal food might—"

"No, I mean *this*. One empty house after another, with you all over me and having to...to feed." The last word was a hateful, bitter-tasting little syllable, but at least she kept her voice down. Yelling would probably be a bad move. "Is this what your life's like?" *Because it sounds like hell.*

"These are rather exceptional circumstances. There are a few matters to clear up tonight, then we can go wherever you like." He gazed at the front of the train car as if lost in thought, his profile familiar from brooding nightmares, yet the invisible sense of his attention was firmly on her, and almost, kind of, very nearly comforting. "Abroad, if you prefer. Choose a house, and you may fill it with whatever you wish. There are some necessary precautions—new covers every half-century or so—but it is more than possible to pass unnoticed. You have not seen the more pleasant aspects of sanguinant existence; I very much wish to introduce them to you."

Lots of promises. "Anywhere I want?"

"Name the place, kitten."

It wasn't the worst nickname she'd ever had. "I want to go back to school." *Try that one on for size.* She'd been so close to finishing her degree, but she'd probably have to start over again. You couldn't get transcripts for a woman who didn't exist anymore. "Night classes would work, right?"

"Or private tutors, certainly."

See what else he'll tell me. "What's this meeting we're going to?"

"Housekeeping." A ghost of a smile, and for a moment he looked *incredibly* human, not to mention flat-out anticipatory. Which should have been jarring, but instead was somehow both strange and even a bit intriguing.

"If you won't tell me, just say so." Bea couldn't help adding a little bit of bitchiness. "God knows I shouldn't believe anything you say."

"I have vowed never to lie to my leman. Tonight may be unpleasant, but will swiftly be over. I would have you remember..." Now he looked fully awake, dark eyes uncomfortably sharp and direct, though he still stared at the front of the car, the door to the next carriage closed tight and secretive.

Is he going to threaten me? "Remember what?"

Lukas was silent for a long moment full of train-rhythm and scattered human heartbeats, all working together in symphony. His own unhurried pulse blotted both out, each slow beat providing a moment's worth of respite. "That you bear no responsibility for what may occur. What I do tonight began long ago, and is necessary."

That...does not sound very comforting at all. "Okay." There was no good answer, really, so she decided to shut up. A faint itch ran under her skin, the sound of the iron wheels growing by increments, though thankfully the thumping human heartbeats remained drowned out by his.

At least she could look at the stars. So she did, turning as far toward the window as the seat permitted, wondering if she would ever see sunlight again.

Theirs was the last train into the station, and of course Lukas looked like he knew where he was going. He even acted like a solicitous boyfriend, rising first, offering his hand to help her to her feet, stepping down from the carriage and turning to help her debark, settling an arm over her shoulders and drawing her close. It might have been nice to stroll with someone like this, especially someone tall and broad enough in the shoulder to discourage unwanted attention.

But all she could think of was what other passengers, or the hurrying figures on the street in front of the station, would do if they knew something so old and strange stalked among them.

The snow thickened, drifting lazily down, and despite the hour there was a great deal of activity. A low grumbling drowsed in pavement and buildings; she wondered if it was the city itself, masses of heartbeats all stacked together. The streetlights didn't seem to interfere with the stars, and she might have walked right out into traffic trying to look upward, marveling.

The sidewalks glittered with small stacked ice crystals, bits of mica, a crazyquilt of cracks. The flood of detail was overwhelming—she could lose herself in the shape of a stranger's coat-buttons, the crystalline flakes settling on fabric or concrete, the rough pitted surface of bricks, traces of corrosion on lampposts, the tiny reflective particles in sign-paint. Once off the train, it was as if some fog-grimy lens had been whisked from the world. Color, noise, and sensation swamped her afresh.

Tiny cold kisses against her cheeks. Traffic humming by, each car a glowing jewel, diamond-sword headlights cutting thin swirling sheets of individual snowflakes. A musical note of wind sliding between buildings, a dim whisper-lapping accompanied by metallic tang shouting a river was nearby. Even the thick clotting reek of exhaust was borderline pleasant.

She wished her teeth weren't so sensitive, though. Even the pressure of her lips was irritating.

Am I high? But he didn't feed me. Bea stared at a discarded plastic bag skipping along the street, dancing with the snow-laden wind. Her hair felt alive, every individual strand buzzing like the streetlights, the traffic lights, the golden windows behind which people were going about their nightlives.

It was weird, but no weirder than anything else lately. Bea blinked as a concrete monster swallowed them—no, it was just a parking garage, its shell filling with echoes of her footsteps. The soundwaves broke and reformed, and she had the idea if she listened carefully she could tell where everyone was parked.

Is that echolocation? Huh.

The entire concrete wedding-cake felt deserted. Buzzing fluorescents, a stairwell not nearly so nice as the Everly building's, and Lukas's arm around her was warm and constant, a gently guiding rope as they descended. Even the necklace was making a low noise, singing to itself in a thin reedy whisper.

They passed through an open archway into the long-term parking section. Lukas slowed, glancing over the shiny metal beetles crouched obediently between painted lines. Bea shivered, settling back into her body with an entirely internal *thump*. The sensory flood swirled and receded, losing no intensity but becoming far more manageable. It was like crossing the invisible tipping-point during a college all-nighter or a long shift at the meatpacking plant, from *I wish I were in bed* to *might as well stay up*.

Crisp and clear, the world was still in hi-def, and the echoes still packed with information. But she could handle it a lot better now.

"Silly," Lukas murmured. The parked cars became sparser—

of course, everyone wanted to cluster near the stairwells. They seemed to be heading for a black SUV, parked all by its lonesome at the far end of this level—at least, they were until he stopped, which meant she had to as well. He guided her to the side of a support pillar, placing her very gently. "Stay here for a moment, please."

You're not afraid I'll make a break for it? Bea was almost grateful to lean against the post; its thick yellow paint, chipped and cracked, glowed reassuringly. An engine had started on the floor below, someone determined to get out of Dodge by the sound of it. She could *hear* tires gripping, the slight chirp as it took a corner maybe a little too quickly. Sounded like a fairly heavy vehicle. Another followed.

Her mouth wasn't dry, but there was a strange taste—sweet, as if he'd kissed her again. Bea's nape tickled, an insistent warning.

He was almost to the SUV, approaching at a careless amble. The prickling wouldn't go away.

"Lukas?" Her voice sounded very small. "Something's—"

BOOM.

The car exploded, a giant orange chrysanthemum, belching black smoke.

CHAPTER 34

HE HAD EXPECTED THE BLOW AND TURNED AT THE REQUISITE ANGLE to deflect, shrapnel slicing past and a sudden acrid stink of burning petrol—a faint ghost of almost-lemons as well, which meant C4 without an odorizing marker—ballooning outward. His leman was safely behind a concrete shelter, no doubt a little startled; her scent was far more pleasant than this, though fluctuating heavily since the last half of the train ride as the Gift burned toward the surface.

The flame-burst caressed him—a sanguinant's ancient enemy, living fire. It had been some time since his eyes watered or his nose stung like this.

A pop, a zinging; he realized it was a fusillade, bullets humming like bees, chipping bits of the floor and walls, ricochets almost musical in their rhythm and intensity. A simple matter to locate the guns, and that was interesting—they were set on tripods, no doubt remote-controlled.

Of course, he would hear the pulse of a mortal assassin, and sniper fire was easy enough to dodge. The bomb had been triggered remotely as well—he had not tripped anything mechanical, so perhaps a laser beam, or a hidden camera.

Several impacts at once, metal rosettes exploding on impact.

A new type of ammunition, and the fire's caress attempted to burrow inward along paths opened by bullets.

Engines gunned, drew nearer. A screeching of tires, metal grinding as a mechanism unlatched—a door, opening. A short, hopeless cry his entire body wished to answer, but his concentration could not be broken at the moment. A burst of pistons slamming as fuel was dumped into spark-chambers, and the bullets were really quite a nuisance. An elder would be bled out in moments if the explosion had not set him alight; as it was, Lukas's discomfort was slowly mounting.

His suit might be ruined. Again.

Footsteps. Barked orders. More firing. Yes, they had hidden below, probably in soundproofed vehicles—which rather argued for hidden cameras. The meditative state did not waver, though Lukas decided this affair had gone quite far enough.

He burst from burning wreckage with a snarl. Yes, multiple vehicles—two black vans and one blue, plus a set of taillights vanishing at the other end of the floor as someone made good an escape. Several mortals in what they called 'tactical' gear, spilling out of the vans and spreading out, four already firing, all yelling, their scents a heavy wave of sweat, bad food, garlic, gun oil, acrid excitement. More missiles, dry clicks as the remote-operated guns ran out of ammunition, mortal male pulses clipping along high and hard, and a blow to his cheek snapped his head aside.

One of their so-new bullets. It actually caused a brief burst of something like pain, luxuriously sweet without the buffer of ossification.

He was on the first assailant in a moment, the one with a white cross painted on the chest of his black body armor, like a crusader of old. That was enough of a giveaway, though the religious amulets most wore would also have been a clue. So would the feathers tied in one man's coppery hair, the tattoo of an occult symbol just visible upon the cheek of another, the cowls and cravats of old-fashioned chainmail, in blackened metal so as not to give away location with a stray gleam.

Hunters. The chainmail was to protect them from sanguinant feeding, the body armor a new type of flexible honeycomb ceramic; however, mortal bodies still did not take to bludgeoning well. Their cries became fear instead of combat-howls, his own growl swallowing the snaprush of flame and bursts of automatic fire. Thick black smoke swirled—they might even have disabled the structure's fire suppression system.

He found a certain amount of force would overcome the ceramic armor's resistance, and plunged his hand into the chest of an assailant. Viscera exploded. He could have gorged, true, yet he did not wish her to see the animalistic feeding necessary in such conditions, draining in single gulps, tearing, the spray and the bathing in hot life-giving claret. This was business requiring cold precision, so he attended to it with smoking clothes, his coat in tatters but the suit underneath still mostly whole.

Did they think me a mere elder? Or did they expect the explosive plus an additive in the petrol—and this ammunition—to turn the trick?

There was a third possibility, one Lukas considered as he tore the head cleanly from another hunter, ignoring the mortal's attempt to sink a shining kukri into his chest. It was a beautiful piece of craftsmanship, worthy of a better owner; he would have liked to retain it, but did not think his leman would appreciate the memento. Instead, he ripped the mortal's ribcage asunder, snarling.

The animal was free, though not blinded by bloodcraze. He could feel his leman's mouth, shy and sweet under his, hear her quiet, husky murmur.

So what happens next? Her most-favored question. She did not seem to realize her own fascination with the world was exceptional, her sensitivity extraordinary. Her eyes could level mountains, if not with their own incandescence then with a single flicker in his direction, for he would do whatever she required.

He did drain the final hunter, but with his back to her refuge so she would not have to see his jaw distended, hear the gulping covered by the roaring of the fire as it settled into consuming whatever fuel remained. The smoke was merciful, though acrid.

The claret was merely nutrition, no longer a pleasure. Still, he swallowed the mud gladly, only realizing when he dropped the empty shell that he need not have bothered to hide the act.

His leman was gone. Another escape attempt, taking advantage of temporary confusion?

No. The fleeing vehicle, he decided. This trap had another dimension; she was not yet completely taken by the Gift, and showed distinct signs of disorientation. Perhaps she was even confused, thinking them a manner of rescue. Interesting indeed, and now not only had he been betrayed, but the traitors had completed their own ruin by laying hands upon what belonged to a true predator.

Lukas paused only long enough to toss the bodies upon the burning vehicle, bursting into mistform just as smaller explosions of unexpended ammunition began to pop and ricochet once more, a mock-battle echoing in an empty concrete well.

CHAPTER 35

THE BACK SEATS HAD BEEN TAKEN OUT, LEAVING ONLY A CAVERNOUS
cargo space. Bea was nearly thrown against the sidewall as red-
haired Hardison took a corner so fast she was sure the vehicle
was momentarily on only two wheels, but the guy Wren—she
almost didn't recognize him without his bowler hat and three-
piece suit like Lukas's—had his shoulder jammed hard against
the front passenger seat, and the very large rifle pointed at her
looked like a serious piece of business.

"Stay still!" Wren barked.

She was trying to, but keeping her balance inside a slaloming
van was difficult when she was so distracted. Their pulses raced,
twin drums beating a frantic tattoo, and she'd just seen Lukas
blown to pieces.

"Fuck, fuck, fuck," Hardison chanted. "Did they get him? Tell
me they got him."

"Keep your eyes on the goddamn road," Wren barked. "Dunlevy? Dunlevy, you just stay still. Don't make me shoot you."

It was almost a shock to hear her own name. Bea's right hand
was clamped over her mouth; her nose was full of smoke-reek,
and the moment kept replaying inside her head—the ball of

violently orange flame, the wall of heat slamming against the concrete pillar, the sudden raucous burr of bullets.

They'd been *shooting* at him. But she hadn't heard any heartbeats. The air inside the van was curiously still and dead despite their obvious speed; its interior was coated with thick foam cushions, peaks and valleys like the cardboard containers eggs were sold in.

Soundproofing. Huh. Her hand felt feverish, jammed over her lips; her teeth were so sensitive even breathing past them hurt.

They had just killed a super-old sanguinant. Her own efforts with the stake seemed laughable, but then, she hadn't had the pull or resources for a car bomb and what sounded like an entire army's worth of machine guns. This van had screeched to a stop right next to her, its side door opening, and Wren hopped out like the bird he was named for. He was *strong*, too—nothing compared to Lukas, of course, but enough to pick her up and toss her bodily inside.

There was a faint burning edge to his scent and Hardison's, vaguely familiar. It reminded her of monster blood.

What. The fuck. She stared dopily at her new kidnappers—or rescuers? What would they do when they figured out she was halfway to bloodsucker? Of course they probably already knew, and that couldn't be good.

Both Wren and Hardison were in some kind of black body armor, cop cosplay, real weekend-warrior shit. Bea's gaze roved the interior—if the side door was locked maybe she could kick out a window, hopefully before they picked up much more speed?

The last thing she needed was to bail out at freeway velocity, though. Comforting to realize she was still working out contingencies even if drowning in sensory overload, not to mention confused as fuck.

"What about her?" Hardison's voice broke. "How's it looking? She got it? Can you tell?"

"Fuckin' 'ell, Hardy." Wren's brogue was now thicker than

split-pea soup. "Don't get us noticed by the fuckin' gardie *or* in a fuckin' accident."

I'd like you better if you weren't pointing a gun at me. Bea's poor overworked brain was right back at square one, except nobody was holding her against an elevator wall. Still, this did *not* look good.

"If she ain't got it, what are we gonna do?" Hardison persisted.

Were they after the necklace?

You can have it, if you want. Good luck with it, too. Bea let go of her mouth, slowly, and lifted both hands, trying to look harmless. There was a funny twitching as if her teeth had come loose, reminding her of the hated retainer worn for so many years. Her tongue touched the back of her top front incisors and shied away, sensing razor edges.

Crap. That's not good either.

"Oh, that's no problem at all, Jimmy, there's a river here. But we'll not be using it, will we, Miss Dunlevy? I can see she's got what we need, and so could you if you didn't need to *keep your eyes on the sodding road.* Christ Jaysus, lad, it's snowing so will you please just *drive*?"

"All right, all right. But do you think they got him?" Hardison was still pretty excited, though the wild swerving evened out a bit. Headlights splashed against the windshield. An eerily muffled sound—someone honking, probably at his driving, and no doubt accompanied by a good ol' New York Salute.

Or New Jersey, depending. Bea had no fucking idea where they were at the moment, and didn't care. All she wanted was for the big, meaty guy with the handlebar mustache to *not* pull the trigger.

So weird. I would have stabbed myself in the throat a couple days ago, but now I'm staring down a barrel and I kind of want to live. I really would like to go back to school—if I can survive this, I can manage to redo my degree. Easy-peasy, no sweat.

Hell, she might even be able to resurrect her own identity, considering how the world simply didn't care enough to pursue her. Maybe she could even find Don and apologize for fucking up his entire life, now that Lukas was...

Oh, God. Was she actually upset over that?

"They'd better have," Wren said, grimly. "Now shut the fuck up, laddie. Miss Dunlevy, let's not have any sudden moves."

Bea nodded. *Sure thing. You got it.*

"That's the spirit. You nod for yes, shake your head for no. You thirsty right now, Miss Dunlevy?"

Bea shook her head, considered the question, and tried a tentative shrug. *They did kill him. Oh, my God. They actually killed Lukas.*

She couldn't tell how to feel. Her entire body was numb except for her mouth, where her teeth were moving as if conscious. The sensation was right out of a nightmare, and the necklace, tucked under her coat, was far warmer than it ought to be as well.

"Well, your eyes ent glowing and you ent leaping on me, so I think you're all right." Wren peered at her, a flash of teeth showing through his mustache. "You just stay in control of yourself now, you hear? I'd hate to have to shoot you."

"If you shoot her, will it work?" Hardison wanted to know.

Bea's eyes widened, and even though the van's interior was dim for humans Wren could clearly see as much. "Jaysus, Jimmy, that's no way way to talk. Besides, she has to be alive or'n it won't work, so far's I can tell."

She strained to *think.* Maybe they didn't like their boss, so they'd...

Oh. Oh boy. And now they're discussing what to do with me. Why didn't they shoot me too?

"Miss Dunlevy?" At least Wren was being polite. And if he suspected she was a bloodsucker, holding a gun on her was a pretty smart move. "Don't mind young James here, he's just a bit excited. Once we've gotten what we need, we can all go our separate ways. I've no desire to kill ye, lassie, but I *will if I have to*. Understand?"

Bea nodded. Several times, in fact. The motion made her teeth even more sensitive, which was a *really* bad sign.

"Hot damn," Hardison said, and the van swayed as he took another corner at slightly more than advisable speed. "We did it. We really did it!"

He sounded super happy. Bea kept her eyes on Wren, waiting to find out what the hell.

"We did *some* of it," Wren corrected. "Now there's the rest, and we'll live forever. Just so long as Miss Dunlevy here keeps a calm head."

Her mouth had calmed down a bit by the time the van stopped; the sweet taste was near overpowering, numbing the inside of her throat as well. The goddamn thirst had begun to tickle, and she hoped they couldn't tell.

It sounded like they wanted something, but for the life of her she couldn't figure out what. She hoped it was the necklace, but they could just shoot her and take it, right? Killing Lukas was way more difficult than getting rid of one tired, worn-out whatever-she'd-become. Leman, fledgling, sanguinant.

Monster. You're a monster now.

Now that her chompers weren't shifting around, they felt normal when she ran her tongue nervously against them. But behind the dull ache masked by sweet novocaine—apparently she could make her own oral analgesic now, which was both interesting and faintly disgusting—she sensed other shapes packed against her jaw, under her cheekbones. She wondered if she'd have to learn to talk again, or if she'd sound drunk trying to speak with a mouthful of painkilling spit.

Hardison got out; when he opened the van's side door everything outside poured in, sound and scent plus pale fluorescent light. Impressions of space, metal girders, thin walls, lapping water, concrete pilings—this place was near a river, and it sounded big.

Warehouse big.

Wren duck-walked to the door, keeping the gun trained on her the entire time. Bea did her best to look nonthreatening. It wasn't hard, she just wanted to curl up in a corner and hyperventilate for a while.

A long, *long* while.

"Come on out, then. Slowly." Wren backed up. His big black boots squeaked on stained, smooth concrete.

It was indeed a warehouse, jammed with what looked like mounds of trash and rotting corpses of heavy equipment. Tiny squeaks and scurries were probably rats in the walls, and Bea shivered as she eased out of the van. Her legs shook.

A few things were now clear. Both men didn't just dislike but actively hated their boss, though Hardison's fear was almost as strong. Wren was the one in charge now, and he clearly felt Lukas had stiffed him of something.

"This way." Wren indicated with the rifle; Bea moved very slowly. She wasn't sure if she could use superspeed right now; her limbs felt both weak and leaden. She couldn't tell if it was from shock, fear, the thirst, having a night that crowned an entirely insane however-long she'd been dealing with all this bullshit, the approach of dawn, or sheer rage.

Because she was *furious*. Sure, she'd tried staking a semi-innocent bloodsucker, so it could be argued this was just the consequences of her own damn actions.

But for God's sake, it was *ridiculous*. Why couldn't they just go complain to their employer, leaving her the hell-and-breakfast out of it?

Tucked against an outside wall, the warehouse's office was a surprise—clean and cozy, done up like a studio apartment. Two futon couches on unvarnished wooden frames, a trim little kitchen with a two-burner countertop stove plus a mini-fridge, a foldable dinette set with a pair of spindly chairs, and clean, practically new blue carpet. One corner held a small empty desk, its surface covered with a light scrim of dust. The place smelled unused, but that was the only problem.

Wren motioned her to one of the couches; Bea hobbled in that direction as Hardison rummaged in the kitchen. The younger man seemed a bit more relaxed now.

"Sit down." Wren's fixed smile was not at all comforting, and his left cheek twitched at random intervals. "We told our hunter friends that you tried to ram a stake through our master's heart, and for that they'll let you live. But you do anything unwise now, Miss Dunlevy, and you won't just have to worry about my wee popgun here. They're professionals, and have done for many a sanguinant. Nasty way to go, fire."

Bea nodded, sinking by degrees onto the futon. It felt great to sit down, actually. She couldn't tell if the numbness creeping into her fingers and toes was the approach of that black needle-skip of having to sleep during daylight.

What would happen at dawn? If she passed out…

All will be well, Beatrice. God, how she wished that was true. She'd prefer to hear Jare's voice inside her head, or Don's, or even her mother's. Anything but the soft, deep, intimate tone belonging to a dead monster.

It was difficult to believe they'd killed him, just when she was starting to almost, *almost* not dislike the guy.

"Can't believe we did it," Hardison piped up.

"He's been going downhill for a while now." Wren eyed Bea as if he expected her to disagree, but her neutral expression was the same one she kept plastered on for family dinners, retail work, and when the guys at the meatpacking plant got rowdy. "Near two hundred years I've done the barstid's bidding. And what do I have to show for it? Money, aye, but naught else."

Two hundred years? Some of her shock must have shown, for Wren gave a tight, humorless smile under his mustache. "Didn't know about that, did ye? *Dogsbodies* they call us, the daylight hands and eyes. Supposed to be loyal as Fido. Well, I tell ye, lass, every dog has his day."

Oh, man. All of this was super interesting and maybe Don would love knowing the details, but Bea was more interested in figuring out what the hell these guys wanted with her. She tested her teeth again—still human, though the lower half of her face continued to ache, a faint diffuse prickling. Could she talk them out of whatever it was they had planned for her?

"We got everything," Hardison said, bending down to peer through the space between the cupboards and counter. He'd piled various items—white plastic packets, glass bottles, something that looked like a centrifuge—there, and his blue eyes shone avidly.

"We might not need so much. The way Miss Dunlevy's looking, she's starting to develop wee biteys, just like a little cobra. Listen to me as God's writ, young lady, when I tell you we don't want to harm ye. All we want is what he gave ye."

What the hell? About all she'd gotten from this was several sets of clothes ripped off. And some volcanic sex, but she hoped like hell they weren't talking about that. If so, she was going to see just what using whatever superspeed and strength she had would get.

Even if killed her. Even if it made the thirst wake up.

"I'm gonna go to Texas," Hardison weighed in. "Eat me some cowboys."

"Will you please shut the entire fuck up?" Wren snapped. It cost him a visible effort to smooth his face and his tone when he addressed Bea again. "Now here's the deal, Miss Dunlevy. All we want ye t'do is bite us, same as *he* did to you. You do that—and give us a bit of your own red stuff, enough to start the change—and God's my witness you're free as a bird."

What. The hell. Bea stared. It felt like her eyes were close to bugging clean out of her head. "You *what*?" Her mouth was finally working again, thank God, though she sounded hoarse and couldn't quite give her consonants the usual bite.

She sounded tipsy, in fact, but without the giggles.

"I didn't sign up to be a fuckin' chauffeur for a century." Hardison rounded the corner from the kitchen, bouncing slightly on his toes when he came to a stop, giving her the once-over. "Hey, I been wondering, what happened to your hair?"

I've been kidnapped by a psychopath and a dipshit. Her lungs suddenly filled all the way, and she felt a curious sense of both mild relief—and honestly, a bit of letdown. The gun was scary, yeah, but these were just...humans.

Other than the *two hundred years* thing. Sure, she'd known bloodsuckers had servants, but not that their lifespans could be extended. Go figure—though if this was where it ended up, maybe Lukas would've been better off hiring temps.

Wren started up again. "If you decide to be troublesome, we have other ways. Jimmy here knows all about phlebotomy; he's quite the whiz with needles. We can probably get enough red stuff even if I'm forced t' shoot ye. Nice shiny bullets, designed specially for those like *him.* Young ones like you ent nearly so hard to kill."

Jesus Christ. "Uh." Bea raised her hands, very slowly, palm-out. "I'm sorry. I d-don't understand. You actually *want* me to...to bite you?" If she enunciated slowly, it was all right. For the moment, her teeth were behaving. "You m-mean, like, infect you? With vampirism?"

"The Dark Gift." Wren's dark eyes held a faint flat shine, somehow scarier than red pinpricks and extendable fangs. "That's what it's called, and why he chose to give it to a..." The twitch was back in his cheek.

"She's not so bad." Hardison said it like he was doing her a favor. "A little old, but that's okay. Like, you'll live forever now."

"You hired hunters to kill..." She almost said *Lukas,* stopped herself just in time. *Your boss* was probably the wrong way to put it as well. "To kill *him?*"

"A small fee to the Church and miracles are possible. Love the work they do, the mad lads." Wren's grip on the gun changed slightly, with a dry metallic sound. "Now, Miss Dunlevy, what's it to be, then?"

"I, uh…" *Think fast, Bea.* The thirst tingled slightly, a cough refusing to make up its mind and break free. "I d- don't know exactly how. I mean, he didn't exactly do a lot of explaining."

"*He* likes that, aye. It was fifty years before I found out how old *he* really 'us." Wren's mouth pulled hard against itself, a bitter grimace; his accent was getting thicker. Irish, Scottish, or Cockney? She couldn't tell. "But no worries, lassie. Our hunter friends have made quite a study, and they like to talk when they drink. So, you just give us both a wee bite, we'll have a bit of a 'sup from your own red stuff, and then you can go."

"Scout's honor," Hardison said, holding up three fingers.

Bea highly doubted the redhead had ever been a fucking Cub Scout, and furthermore doubted that these two would let her walk if by some miracle she managed to do what they wanted. "I don't think you know what you're asking." *They're not going to be reasonable. Why am I even trying? The psycho will shoot me unless I think of something, quick. And even if he doesn't, that numb feeling is definitely dawn.*

How much time did she have?

"I've had three whole lifetimes to savvy it through." Wren managed to sound both patronizing and avuncular at once. His finger was awful tight on the trigger, Bea saw, and the realization didn't make her shudder only because she was afraid he'd squeeze if she twitched. "And don't think I don't know what time it is. Sooner ye give us a nip and a gulp, sooner ye can be somewhere nice and dark when the sun rises."

CHAPTER 36

THE TUGGING IN HIS BONES, THE YEARNING IN HIS VEINS PULLED HIM onward, slicing swiftly between snowgusts in mistform, bursting through the whispering speed when needing to cut against the wind, across rooftops. A foot brushing a cornice, the glass of an office building showing a subtle glimmer as light refracted from disturbed flakes, the startled bark of a vehicle's horn as he touched down in the middle of a street, pushing off again with a crimson flash—his eyes glowed from lid to lid now, showing the rage of a sanguinant whose leman had been harmed.

Had been *taken*.

He might have expected earthbound prey to use a winding way, many a doubling and turn to throw off pursuit, but they had not. Still, constrained by roads, their route was longer than his; he arrowed for earth, the pull loud and clear instead of attenuated to a mere whisper by distance.

There. A large, ramshackle structure, its flank jutting on pilings over a polluted river, was all too easy to infiltrate. Mistform thickening as he streamed past piles of ephemera and sullen, long-abandoned machinery, swirling once about a grey delivery van, its side-hatch left open and the small interior light gamely carrying on. Every third fixture overhead was live, fluorescents buzzing to themselves and emptiness.

A pair of unsurprising scents; the traitors had spent some time here, making arrangements though hardly improvements. There might be security cameras pointed at likely approaches—he heard heartbeats as well, all three familiar yet only one welcome.

And a thread of glorious, wonderful scent reaching even into the the mistform's haze, drawing him onward. Was this a second iteration of ambush, using his prize as bait?

Voices, now, as he swirled toward the source of the pull. While their interesting new ammunition was merely bothersome to him—necessitating some small attention paid to resealing wounds and keeping the claret where it belonged, two skills any daywalker was more than conversant with—it could quite possibly bleed his fledgling to the point of exhaustion, and she would require much care afterward. There was the risk of more open flame as well; even if he had proved his own immunity, she was still vulnerable.

He could celebrate his new status later. Lukas gathered himself, mistform clotting into the mortal-visible range as dense crimson fog, and followed the clarion call of shared blood toward the other end of the warehouse, downstream and shoreward.

Almost there. All will be well, Beatrice.

A gunshot boomed sharp and jarring between piles of rubbish, echoing against the roof's exposed bones.

CHAPTER 37

"Look, I'll do my best, I just don't know how." Bea stayed very still, the spring inside her coiling tighter and tighter. Could she get going fast enough to burst through whatever they had walling this office? She couldn't tell if it was more than drywall. "You can put the gun down, okay? We can figure this out together."

"Oh, I think I'll be keeping it." Wren was getting more worked up the longer conversation went on, and that was a *very* bad sign. "Jimmy, lad, bring out your needles. I think we'll get the red stuff early, just in case."

"Sure thing." But the ginger guy hesitated. "Guess that means I'm going first, since you're holding the gun. Right?"

From the crackling silence which ensued, Bea got the idea they hadn't quite thought out this part of the plan. Which was kind of stupid—but then again, she'd only shown up a few days ago, unless this Wren guy had already known she was some kind of bloodsucker sex kitten?

No, probably not. They had Lukas's murder planned to a T, this felt like extra credit.

Don't worry about that, worry about getting out of this room without being shot.

Wren visibly made up his mind. "Age before beauty, Jimmy-boy. There's a pistol in the kitchen, get it. Then she can bite me."

I really would rather not. Bea forced herself not to grimace, to keep that steady, neutral expression.

"I dunno." Hardison didn't move. "Maybe we just need her to bite, since we already have some of *his* red stuff, you know? So I should go first, to check."

That's interesting. Lukas had definitely given both of these guys monster blood. Was it a regular thing? Did they get high off it, and that was how bloodsuckers controlled their daylight hires? She just didn't know enough, but that probably wouldn't matter.

"Jimmy, for fuck's sake." Wren's cheek was back to twitching, tiny plucking motions now regular and constant instead of random. "Do what I fuckin' tell you."

"Don't I always? I'm just *asking*, Thomas, you don't have to be so—"

It happened fast. The gun's nozzle swung away from her, an eye-scouring flash and the roar was massive, world-ending. Bea cried out, clapping her hands over her ears, her body instinctively throwing itself aside, but before she landed on blue carpet Jimmy Hardison's entire head was vaporized.

*OhGod, Jesus Christ, oh no...*Blinking furiously, her ears ringing, Bea peered through her hair.

Wren's ribs heaved. A fine, sparkling mist of blood hung in the air as Hardison's body folded, landing with a wet thump, and Bea discovered that even if she hadn't eaten for days and might be entirely on a liquid diet from now on she could still be nauseated enough to retch. A heavy, coppery reek mixed with the acrid smokiness of gunfire, accompanied by a distinct tang of shit; her new vision was acute enough that even half-blinded by muzzleflash she could clearly distinguish white bone-chips and greyish brain spread in a blotch on the cabinet doors, all over the countertop and its medical paraphernalia.

Shouldn't the blood smell better? The thought provoked another flare of nausea.

"Fucking kid," Wren muttered. Faint vapor lifted from the gun's barrel, its single eye very big and dark indeed. "But I guess it works, eh? Look at that."

No, thanks. Bea decided the nearest wall was good enough to try. If there was rebar or something she couldn't break through—

"Get up off the floor," he continued. 'And by God and Mother Mary, ya bint, if you don't stop stalling and do what I—"

A shimmer in the air, a warm breeze ruffling her hair. A small scream of stretching, overstressed metal; the rifle, twisted into an unusable hoop, was flung across the room, landing on the slumped mess which used to be Hardison. A blurred streak resolved into the shreds of a black wool coat, thin curls of smoke rising from the fabric. Underneath, a three-piece suit, torn and peppered with holes; atop the tatterdemalion a sandy-dark head, damp hair bearing a frosting of rapidly melting snow-crystals.

The wall next to the desk shuddered like a drumhead, dust rising from the table-surface. Wren hit hard, leaving a dent in drywall before sliding down.

Another burst of warm air caressed Bea's cheek, stirring tangled curls. She stared at the shadow looming over her, still blinking away afterimages, and the immediate flood of hot, bone-deep relief was so intense she flinched. Her hip banged the futon couch's base, and Lukas's hand halted in midair.

He was soaked almost clear through and oddly gaunt, stubbled cheeks hollow and his jaw working. His eyes were no longer dark but *red*, a wet vivid glow spreading in tiny droplets which winked out on invisible updrafts; he smelled of cold night wind, burning, and a clear colorless scent she recognized.

Pure, unfiltered rage. Her own anger was a single droplet to that ocean.

He crouched easily, regarding her, head slightly tilted. His largest fangs touched his lower lip, pressing gently; the truly scary thing, she realized afresh, was how *controlled* he was.

Lukas grimaced slightly, and the fangs receded. "All is well, Beatrice." His hand didn't move, palm-up, offering.

Oh, God. She reached for him, almost blindly, and let out a sobbing breath when her fingers met his.

He steadied her, clearly unworried about Wren's presence; Bea couldn't decide whether to keep an eye on the gasping heap who had just been holding a gun on her or stare at the monster who brushed at her shoulders, peered at her with those strange crimson eyes, and finally leaned close to inhale deeply.

That seemed to help, because when he withdrew the red glow had shrunk to those almost-familiar pinpricks. He held her shoulders, gave her one more long examination.

Under a heavy layer of smoke and winter night, he smelled so very familiar—the dry almost-musk of a healthy sandy-haired male. The thirst dilated at the back of her throat, she had to swallow hard against it.

"I thought you were dead," she managed.

"Hardly." A ghost of a smile; the crimson pinpricks vanished. His eyes were dark again, and strangely warm. The change was so sudden it almost robbed her of breath. "I have not enjoyed your company nearly enough."

Really? After being blown up and shot at? Her gaze skipped past him—Wren was moving, it looked like he'd gotten his breath back.

Lukas's hands tightened fractionally on her shoulders, a brief, consoling squeeze. "Are you hurt? Tell me."

She managed a headshake. *But it sure looks like he is.*

"Very well. Sit, if you like. This may take a moment." He let go of her, though lingeringly, as if he didn't quite trust she could keep herself upright without the help.

She found she could, and watched Wren try to push himself back against the wall as Lukas bore down on him. Even in rags, her monster strolled as if in complete charge of everything the room contained, and honestly she couldn't say he wasn't.

"M-m-master..." Wren's teeth chattered, chopping the word into quivering pieces. He had gone chalky, with a decided greenish undertone, and the black tactical breastplate creaked as he tried to scoot further. An invisible rippling descended upon him, both like and unlike the seals. He froze, though his ribs still heaved with deep panting breaths. One of his arms hung at a peculiar angle—looked like a humerus fracture.

Bea winced in sympathy.

"Be still," Lukas said, almost kindly. "I did not mind the money you embezzled; you earned more than that with hard work. I did not mind your contact with hunter cells either, for it saved me the trouble of tracking them." He stopped, very close to the other man, and folded gracefully into a crouch once more, balancing easily. "I cannot even blame you for covering up incursions for half a year hoping another sanguinant would topple me, for that is my own incompetence. I had calcified almost to the point of no return."

"Master..." Wren's mouth worked, spittle collecting at the corners, sliding down his chin. He trembled so hard the wall creaked like his body-armor, though the invisible weight forestalled any other movement. "I...I was misled."

"Were you?" Lukas's tone of gentle interest was downright chilling. "I suppose we might call it that. Still, all those things matter little. Even luring me away with months-old reports of an incursion was a good ruse, though a tired one. And yet."

"I won't ever do it again. P-p-please, Master." It was jarring to hear such a big, brawny guy whine, mostly because Bea knew what it was like to plead with such overwhelming power. "I promise, I *swear*."

"It is good to have a tool one knows the measure of," Lukas said, softly. "But you attempted to break into a sealed saferoom where my leman rested."

What? It took Bea a moment to realize what the hell he was talking about—the North Bluffs mansion, and the door unlocking itself.

So he *had* believed her about that. At the moment, she was just very, very glad he was occupied with something else. The rifle, bent nearly double, lay atop Hardison's body; she hurriedly looked away. There was the door...but that was kind of useless, wasn't it.

And really, why would she run? He was a monster, yes. He'd also come to get her, and Bea discovered it was incredibly comforting to be the person someone dropped everything and ran to help.

Had Jared felt this way when she showed up at the house on Noll Mountain? The loosening in the chest, the sudden sense of being able to breathe again, the *oh, thank God, someone else, I don't have to do everything alone*?

Huge greasy drops of sweat stood out on Wren's face, matching the shiny spit coating his chin. "Two hundred years," he spat, suddenly. Looked like he'd gotten past fear and into defiance; Bea could absolutely relate. "*You were never going to change me!*"

Lukas was silent for a moment, leaning back slightly on his heels. "Of course not, Thomas. You do not have the temperament for the Gift."

"It's not bloody fair." Wren's lips skinned back, dark eyes now blazing. "You could have let me try."

"My friend, I gave you all the life I could. Now you will die slowly, in agony, because you dared lay hands upon what is not yours to touch." The scariest thing wasn't what Lukas said, but how—level and emotionless, simply stating facts.

Oh, hell. Bea's hands were fists. She could break for the door, hope to distract him, maybe? That might give Wren enough time to get away. Not that she liked the bastard; for God's sake, he'd been holding a gun on her just a minute ago, and he was enough of a psychopath to want...what he wanted.

But looking at Hardison's body was difficult enough,

reminding her of Jared, of brutally detailed autopsy and crime-scene photos. She absolutely never wanted to see another corpse ever again.

"Lukas?" Her voice cracked, the thirst spreading. Now her entire throat was dry and scratchy, the craving intensifying since the source of what it wanted was right in the same room. "Please, don't."

He didn't move, yet that invisible sense of his attention settling on her was undeniable. "No need for fear, kitten. You may simply look away."

That's not the point. She tested her legs, found out they would hold her, and took a step. Then another.

CHAPTER 38

Contemplating the ruin of a friend was always difficult. Under other circumstances, he might have simply unseamed a traitor from nave to chops; he certainly had before in the course of a long, long life. There could be no such quick mercy for one who had dared interfere with his leman. The difficulty would lay in holding the corpse to quivering agonized life while Lukas meted out a lesson any approximation of a soul would take screaming with it into the afterlife—and be deformed by ever after.

Tentative, near-staggering footsteps behind him, softly musical. He was still contemplating where to begin when the fragrance of his leman closed about him.

Her hand touched his shoulder. Warmth flooded from that slight contact, both the animal and the thrall snarling within him, restrained by the thinnest spidersilk leash.

"Please," she repeated. "It's almost dawn. I don't feel good, I want to go somewhere else. I don't want to see another dead body, Lukas, *please.*"

Wren's gaze flickered between them. A ratlike, chewing little gleam of hope lingered in his pupils; he no longer struggled against the *quietus.*

"This dogsbody not only betrayed me but could have injured my leman," Lukas pointed out. "It may do some good, for you to see the consequences."

"I've seen enough." So frail, her fingers, not even bearing a fledgling's full strength. Still they held him chained, far more effectively than any iron mortals or the demimonde could ever manufacture. "Can't you just let him go?"

Oh, my little leman. "You wish me to simply release him?"

"I want to get out of here. You said we could leave." A soft sobbing breath, her grasp shifting slightly. "Prove I don't have to be afraid of you, okay? Just...let him go."

Lukas weighed the suggestion. Wren's gasping continued; he was perilously close to mortal shock. Not only was his arm broken but at least four of his ribs, plus a possible femur fracture. He reeked of complete terror, and the dry, slightly oily fur-scent of dogsbody.

"I would like very much to flay you," Lukas told him, finally. "Slowly, making certain you are conscious of every moment. Then to reduce every bone save your skull to splinters, and last take your eyes and hearing while I crush your head by slow inches. I can make it last, Thomas; I kept much from you, but you know enough of my abilities to understand this is but the bare minimum consequence for your crime."

"Lukas—" His leman's fingers tensed.

"One moment, my Beatrice." His true teeth extended, and he showed them in the ancient snarl of dominance and battle, knowing the kill-light was again in his eyes.

Wren sought to scream, could only produce a papery whisper. His color was very bad indeed.

Regaining blunt camouflage teeth took an effort. His fingers flicked, releasing the *quietus*; Lukas straightened and turned.

His prize did not retreat. She simply gazed up at him, the visible pulse in her throat quick but not hammering. Wan and exhausted, no doubt feeling dawn's soundless thunder grown very close, she still had the strength to plead, not merely with voice but with those beautiful gold-threaded eyes.

Prove I don't have to be afraid of you.

She meant well, certainly; she could not know a castoff dogsbody faced expiry by inches as its Master's mark slowly leached from tissues and bone. The doom was almost comparable to slow suffocating calcification.

Beatrice did not flinch when he cupped her face in his hands. He was sodden, soot-streaked, and blood-spattered; she was disheveled and slightly trembling. Lukas leaned close, allowed her scent to enfold him as he pressed his lips to her forehead. A bit too cold; she needed feeding and a safe place for daylight rest.

"Very well," he murmured against her flawless skin. "But only because you ask it of me, sweet Beatrice."

"Can we go now?" A pained, little-girl whisper.

Given Wrenfeldt's age, it would not take more than half a year—if that long—for his physical dissolution to become total. It was an agonizing death, and another sanguinant could not save him. Not that another would be inclined to welcome such a discard; why bother, when a much younger and less suspect item could be acquired with so little trouble?

"Of course." He ignored the whimpers behind him; the release of the *quietus* allowed pain to begin piercing the veil of shock. The dogsbody might not even be able to leave this small, dusty room. "Clasp my neck, kitten. We must move quickly, and the snow thickens."

Her arms stole upward, fingers interlacing at his nape. Lukas swept her up, and took her from the small charnel-house.

They were far away when Wrenfeldt began throat-cut howling, but Lukas was certain she did not hear. His leman was so weary, after all, and as he pressed her head to his chest he also covered her other ear with his palm, his fingers tangled in her clinging, windblown hair.

❀

There were certain places well used to hosting the demimonde, though their employees remained largely unconscious of the fact; what money could not accomplish among mortals, a certain amount of invisible pressure inevitably managed to overcome. He had planned to use this hotel anyway, and the iron-haired clerk at the front desk—though eyeing Lukas's ruined garb somewhat askance—was familiar enough with the quality of fabric speaking more loudly than any parlous condition.

Besides, no desk clerk was averse to earning a little extra cash, especially two crisp, folded bills proffered in the politest, most acceptable manner. Such maneuvers had not changed for centuries, and no doubt many travelers were stranded by the gathering storm. Most importantly, the credit card Lukas produced for an identity Wren had never touched was of the requisite type to impress, another subtle signal.

And the rumpled, sleepy angel leaning against Lukas's side was beautiful enough to daze any onlooker lucky enough to catch a glimpse. She bore only a few smudges of soot on clothes of the same understated but extreme quality, and that was enough of a passport to overcome any residual uncertainty.

No luggage, but a yawning bellboy was nevertheless roused to show them to the suite—the clerk was either earning his own bribe or that rarest of creatures, a manager eager to spread good fortune. Nevertheless, Lukas wildly overtipped the young man in his scarlet uniform as well, and made certain both blinds and curtains were drawn.

Beatrice swayed with fatigue near the foot of a very large bed clad in a patterned pale-green duvet and likewise spring-colored pillows. There was a little more taste than usual in the suite's decorating, but it hardly mattered; the walls and door took seals just as any other bolthole would, and he was careful to hang the *do not disturb* tag beforehand.

Too exhausted to be skittish, she let him slide the red coat from her shoulders. The *greisoul* glimmered, full of its own secret fire, and he longed to strip her, run his fingertips over her curves, reassure himself of her wholeness. Yet she was so pale, nearly transparent, and dark smudges rested under heavy-lidded eyes.

He dragged a claw over his wrist, let the flesh part. "Drink."

His leman did not demur, but fastened on. Her true teeth had arrived, and their sliding into his flesh was an exquisite sting. Lukas eased her down upon the bed, letting her draw again and again. The thrall poked and prodded; he pressed his face into her hair and did his best to enfold her in his larger bulk.

He closed the wound in stages; her fangs slipped free as dawn took hold. Beatrice sighed, fading into a fledgling's rest.

Anything Wren or Hardison could possibly have uncovered was suspect. Once more it was necessary to burn a network of influence and assets to the ground, moving elsewhere as the flames faded. Eventually new growth covered ashes.

Along with fire, it was the only certainty. Normally he would feel the urge to mourn, if only to keep ossification at bay with a grief as sharp as the stony, clinging fingers.

Not now. Nor did he move to rise just yet, though there was daylight work to accomplish—travel to arrange, luggage to acquire, hunting just before dusk in order to feed her once more when darkness covered the world. All that could wait a few short, luxurious hours.

Every ending also means a certain freedom. A harsh lesson only time could grant, carrying its own reward. Lukas closed his eyes, and the blackness for once was kind.

He breathed her in, ignored the thrall's discomfort.

I thought you were dead. As if that were possible when he now had so much to enjoy, the world a dangerous garden to experience through her shining eyes. Eventually she might even understand what it meant that her sanguinant was no longer merely daywalker but Archon.

Time enough for anything, now. He cradled Paradise in his arms, and listened to the imperceptible sound of his fledgling's deathly sleep.

EPILOGUE

Full moon hanging over a harbor, bioluminescence tinting warm lapping waves, stars crowding a sky too soft to be truly black, a breeze redolent of garlic, salt, cooking meat, roses, car exhaust, and a liquid golden tang reminiscent of olive oil—Bea braced her elbows on the stone balustrade, enjoying the last left-over sun-warmth leaching from its roughness.

The nights were still getting shorter, but at least this faint echo of sunshine lingered well after dusk. The study's windows were floor-length, more like doors and easy to prop ajar; she liked this terrace a lot. Sneaking out to look at the night despite having a lot of studying to catch up on was a time-honored tradition.

If she unfocused her gaze, the town's lights shimmered star-like as well. Bright interweaving threads of violin, accordion, and guitar drifted up the hill, fading in and out as the breeze shifted. Learning how to use super-senses hadn't taken long, and now she wondered how she'd ever gotten along in the world without the sharp edges, the interplay of colors never before dreamt of, hearing every scratch and whisper of the night as well as the drowsy thunder of human heartbeats, each pulse distinct and unique.

She sensed him before he spoke, of course. Lukas resolved in the shadows, linen shirt and loosely elegant summer trousers glimmering faintly. It was fun to dress him; he no longer looked like a starchy, near-clumsy old man trapped in an awkwardly young-seeming body. He'd grown his hair out too, though shaking it from his eyes every so often might have annoyed him. His habit of ambling along with hands deep in his pockets certainly helped him look a lot more human.

"I know, I know." Bea heaved an only partly theatrical sigh, taking a last long look at the moon's cratered, beautiful grin. The vast luminous disc was yellowish, prickling her eyes slightly—reflected sunlight, after all, even if robbed of hurtful power. "I should be working. I'm so behind on the stupid math requirements I might never catch up."

The study's lamps burned softly, casting golden squares and triangles on the terrace; he stayed in deeper shadow, as usual. A whisper of cloth moving was his shrug. "No need to hurry, kitten. There's a festival in the town tonight."

So that's what it is. "I was wondering about the music." She straightened reluctantly, turning away from sea, moon, stars. Above the house of biscuit-colored stone more cliffs rose, olive-green vegetation hiding in deep vertical cracks, the top alive with trees older than Philadelphia. "Let me guess. You want to drag me away from the books to have a little fun, because I'm too young to be so serious."

"Something like that." His Italian was apparently very good, hers no more than passable though everyone was extremely polite with her attempts. The housekeeper, groundskeeper, and the kid Lukas paid to run small errands and fetch things for Signora Costa all apparently considered Bea to be slightly dim though well-meaning, a decorative bauble for the young husband Lukas played with relish. "I thought I could first drag you to bed and do something very pleasant, before we take the car downhill and spend a few hours drinking chianti in the square."

"Got it all planned out, do you?" Increasingly easy to forget just what he was, treating him just like a...well, a human being. A boyfriend, maybe.

It helped that he could hunt without killing anyone, and enough tourists passed through this picture-postcard place to make their own presence far less intrusive. Bea kept waiting for a shoe to drop, but nothing happened. All the restless studying couldn't get rid of the feeling, but sometimes it was easier to handle.

"I also have a gift for my lovely leman." His smile widened; relaxation looked good on him. There was something tucked under his arm; it looked like a rectangular box. "Would you like it now, or after I have you?"

She was suddenly very aware of the sundress, soft cotton against her skin. "Very sure of yourself, signor."

"Not at all, simply determined to keep my kitten in good humor. She has such interesting ideas, after all."

Good Lord. Her body, knowing what was inevitably going to happen, was already turning to liquid, and heat rose in her cheeks. "You're a nymphomaniac."

"I don't quite understand the term, perhaps you can explain it?" A wicked gleam in dark eyes, and he took a single step, the toes of his deck shoes resting just at the edge of an irregular patch of golden glow. "At length, while I—"

"You said something about a present?" Bea held out her hands. It felt greedy, but then again, he seemed to like this sort of thing. Little gifts—a pair of earrings she looked at too long in one of the overpriced tourist boutiques, a big floppy sunhat with a white ribbon though she wouldn't go walking in daylight for aeons, a new textbook. And bigger ones, like the funny boxy little car, or paperwork detailing repairs to the Noll Mountain house, all its contents shifted to climate-controlled freeport storage. And this villa, lit up like a big birthday cake the night they arrived.

"*Sì, signorina bella. Ecco.*" He produced a rectangular wooden container, even undid the small metal catch for her with solicitous care.

Bea pushed the lid up with a fingertip, curious almost despite herself. "Oh, wow."

Nestled on a bed of black velvet, a polished wooden stake gleamed, alive with silver filigree. The point looked extremely sharp despite the decoration, moonlight turned to metal.

"I take that to mean you are pleased." He tucked his chin slightly, looking down at the glitter. "Go ahead, pick it up."

She did, cautiously—silver could give her a rash, if it scraped skin too hard. Prickling-cool metal, warm wood, she turned it over in her hands, enjoying the different textures. "Is this some kind of comment on how we met?"

"Not quite." He set the empty box on the wide stone balustrade, then his hand closed over her wrist. Gentle pressure to turn her; she followed willingly, her back to his chest. "Claws are better, and in any case you must not try to strike through the ribs. Too much effort."

"I practiced a lot." She leaned into his warmth. He guided her hand and the stake in a circle, her wrist flipping to follow his direction.

His other hand skimmed down her ribs, halted just below the last bone-arch. "This is where you strike," he murmured in her ear. "Inward and upward, *so*." Very gentle, a mere indication of direction, just on the verge of tickling. "Even if you do not reach the heart you may still grasp a few large blood-channels and bleed your opponent to weakening."

"You're the soul of romance." Bea leaned back a little more; an insistent prodding against her lower back proved he was still interested. "Any particular reason why you're giving me this?"

"I thought you would like it." He nuzzled below her ear,

nipping gently, fangs scraping gently, infinitely controlled. "And reward me."

"That's a bribe, not a gift—" She gasped when he bit again, a little harder. Her hips moved restlessly; rising heat and swimming desire pooling low in her belly. *If I wore panties, they'd be soaked right now.*

"Hm." Maybe he wanted to say more, but he was too busy finding the most sensitive spot to kiss. His hands began to roam, her knees turned to warm butter, and she wasn't at all sure they would make to the bed.

They did not, but it hardly mattered. The moon rose higher, waves caressed the shore, and in the town below the music was joined by shouts of laughter as the dance began.

EXCERPT FROM ELDER'S PRIZE, BOOK TWO

The second installment of a scorching new dark vampire romance series by the New York Times bestselling author, Lilith Saintcrow.

Lookout duty was a necessity in any vampire hunting team, but Layla Cartland wished it didn't involve pretend kissyface...

Joining a vampire-hunting crew was not the first bad decision Layla ever made, but it's the one she stuck with. Her role is support and lookout; she wasn't supposed to get close to the action. But everything goes wrong one hot summer night—and she ends up kidnapped by a monster.

The demimonde calls him Nemesis, a soldier with centuries of faithful service, unswervingly loyal until the one prize every sanguinant longs for appears. Now he must use all his age and cunning to keep his new leman, even as the one he served for so long arrives to take her by force.

Caught between two immortals, drowning in desire, Layla's nights are about to get a lot more dangerous...

Chapter One

LOOKOUT DUTY WAS OF COURSE A NECESSITY IN ANY VAMPIRE hunting team, but Layla Cartland wished it didn't involve pretend kissyface with fellow soldiers.

"There's that grey Acura again," she murmured, shifting against warm, gritty bricks. A hot August night, still and soaking with humidity, had already plastered the pretty black sundress to her lower back. Even bare arms and legs offered no relief; the air was thick as cottage cheese and her toes were sweat-slippery inside cotton socks and combat boots. "Same license—and will you quit that? It tickles."

"I hate having my back to the street." At least Pete stopped rubbing his stubble on her hair. He was the only one short enough for her to see over his shoulder, and nobody would suspect a couple clearly making out between two separate night-club entrances of anything, much less surveillance. It was the second spot on their rotation, the only bare patch of wall in sight, and next they'd move to an alley-mouth half a block down.

She couldn't wait.

Layla could probably count the fact that stocky, snub-nosed Pete inevitably got a chubby as a compliment to her own mild attractiveness, though the cheap cologne he dabbed on for every operation involving decoy or lookout made her want to sneeze. The wall she was propped against thudded faintly with dueling bass beats, a giant's drowsy pulse. The bouncers were leaving them alone, more concerned with the lines of drunks and name-droppers trying to get in or out of the roughnecks' paradise known as Cactus YaYa or the slightly more expensive-drinking Blue Moon Spot; wall-humpers would be told to move along if the crowd got more restless, but until then they were in a golden zone, politely ignored.

"Pete and Layla sittin' in a tree…" Ackerman's voice came over the earpiece, a clear tenor singsong; he was perched on a rooftop wearing his goddamn cowboy hat, probably getting a breath of night breeze as well.

It was rare for him to unbend enough to tease anyone. Progress was being made, hopefully as a result of her own steady encouragement balancing out the rough teasing other males mistook for therapeutic instead of simple stupid hazing.

However, Pete now became even more tense—if that were possible. He was always amped on operations, even simple recon. "Fuck you," he snarled, the throat mic picking it up double and squealing slightly in her poor ear, and Layla had to repress a sigh.

"Cut the chatter." As usual, Dan's voice made her heart thump an extra beat. Unfortunately the leaps had been getting smaller lately. Especially when she wondered when this entire operation was *really* going to get off the ground. "Steve-o?"

"I got it, boss." Lanky laconic Steve, always professional, drawled over the invisible line. Group chat with vampire hunters, just the thing for a girl's night on the town. "Got three coming in from the west, big black Marias. Guessing that Acura's the lookout."

Or can't find a place to park. Layla didn't bother stating the obvious, but as usual, Ben just *had* to.

"Could be a civvie, looking for a place to squeeze in. Like Pete." Ben's slight wheeze said he was grinning like a jackal, his unplucked eyebrows waggling ferociously. "How's it looking down there, Petey? Nice and juicy?"

"For Chrissake," Pete muttered, thankfully too low for the mic to pick up.

Just ignore him; he does it because you respond. Bullies were the same everywhere. Layla patted her lookout partner's side, just over the hard hidden edge of Kevlar.

At least Ben did his job—sort of. Layla could even suppose his clowning might be a bonus, like the hair-trigger violence displayed at the least provocation. On the one hand, he'd been overwhelmingly on-target with the two biters they'd already put down.

On the other, it had taken both Dan and Ack to get Ben bundled out of the bar where they'd gathered intel about the Griskov bounty—plus all her own practice at soothing male tempers afterward to clean up the mess, with Steve glowering theatrically over her shoulder.

Finally the client agreed they were the team for the job—but no down payment, though, because Ben had fouled the waters almost past soothing. And Layla could be forgiven for thinking she was tired of cleaning messes, physical or emotional, all day every *damn* day.

Of course every squad member had reasons for this kind of work, and bad coping mechanisms to match. You didn't enter a fabulous career in vampire hunting unless you'd lost someone— or unless you had more psychological problems than a stick could shake at.

At least Dan was adamant about not taking on any more crazies, even if it meant a little less firepower. Small mercies, as her grandmother always said, were the only kind a woman ever got.

Not that it mattered at the moment. "I see them," Layla said softly, because she did. Three big glossy SUVs, black as midnight itself, trundling west along 21st Street. *Huh.* She inhaled sharply. "Three Marias coming in westbound, and two more just joined from Battery Road, heading east. Looks like same makes and models; I think we've got extra players tonight."

"Fuck me." Ack, grimly unsurprised—he never expected anything to go smoothly, even laundry. "I see 'em too. What we got tonight, friends and neighbors?"

"He could be leaving early, maybe upgraded his security detail." A crackle from Dan's mic—this time he'd drawn the squawker from the gear barrel, instead of Layla. "Eyes, hold your positions. Ben, Steve-O, stay loose. Ack, take your lock off."

A rash of *ten-fours*, including Pete's murmur. Layla's pulse began to pound, sweat greasy on her neck and arms. A crowded downtown street on a summer night, car horn blaring at the far end, shriek of drunken laughter from a group of college kids spilling out of a bar a block and a half up, faint thread of cigarette smoke on the unmoving air. Every salt-soaked inch of her shrank from the assault of noise, light, people.

It was only the adrenaline kicking her senses into high gear, but she still had to suppress a twitch.

"Pulling up now." She enunciated clearly, quashing the urge to yell. Her other hand rested at Pete's nape; he leaned protectively into her, torrid male sweat-smell now holding a metallic reek of the same stress-based cocktail pouring into her own bloodstream. "Both directions. They've got traffic corked, gentlemen."

Which meant five SUVs full of something bad against their small team. She waited for Dan to make the call. As usual, Suzy's face floated in front of her—not the awful butcher's ruin on the morgue table, but bubbly blonde Suze on her wedding day, smiling beatifically during the waltz, tiers of white lacy dress swaying around her legs. And Dan, his eyes closed, keeping his chin carefully near her piled curls. He'd looked so handsomely protective, and her best friend so peaceful, that Layla had gone right to the open bar and started in on the whiskey. Two fingers, neat, hold the ice.

At least she hadn't opened her mouth at the wrong time *that* day. No sir, she'd done the best thing possible, and been quiet ever since.

"Egg's cracked." She gazed steadily over Pete's shoulder as the SUVs popped their doors. "Looks like bodyguard details in standard... oh, *shit*."

"What? What shit?" Dan, as usual, didn't like it when she swore. "Give me something better, Eyes."

I've liked you for a long time, Danny, but sometimes you're a real prick. Layla buried the thought as far as it could go. "It's a biter," she muttered. "Just not ours. Repeat, *not* our target. It's another one; I think…" *Where have I seen that face before?*

"Fuck." Nobody yelled at Ackerman for uttering a blue word, no sir. "Angle's bad until a target gets closer to the door. Do you have an ID, Layla?"

I'm working on it. She mentally shuffled every laydown in the past few weeks—the face was familiar, and she *knew* he had to be a vampire. She just couldn't remember precisely which one; the most unsettling thing was that they all looked so goddamn normal until you got entirely too close.

Then the flawless matte skin, the slightly different texture to the hair, and most of all some indefinable, atavistic feeling of *predator, ohshit, run away* were all dead giveaways. It was terrifying how good the human-camouflage was, until you realized there were human monsters too.

Those were entirely out of Layla's control. At least you could feel a hundred percent good, moral, and American about killing a bloodsucking fiend.

"Man, let's just *go*," Ben muttered. Pitched right in the sweet spot for his mic to pick up, but not loudly enough for Dan to call him out for either cowardice or defeatism.

Layla pressed her bare shoulders against the bricks; this dress was pretty, kicky, and would be absolutely no use when the shooting started. She could remember the biter's face, the exact position of the grainy 8x10 photo, seeing it against a stack of manila files—worth their weight in gold, each the product of her own hard work, endless online arguing, and constant re-checking.

Her role was clerical, close logistics, and occasional surveillance, which was a pretty way of saying she was a glorified maid-plus-secretary. Still, that was necessary too. Without her, they wouldn't even *have* hardcopies of the files from O'Shaughnassey's crew, all verified sightings and intel.

Poor Shawn. God.

"Layla?" Dan, warningly. If the operation was called off now they might never get another chance at the biter who owned the Blue Moon Spot, but this definitely wasn't the big blond sonofabitch Roger Griskov.

No, this guy had a mop of curly dark hair, slightly glistening under the streetlights, and a nose that outweighed the entire rest of his face. He unfolded from the backseat of the middle westbound SUV, glancing to either side as soldiers marking terrain always did, and the shape of his chin was even more familiar. She just couldn't remember the name, though she could smell the cold leftover pizza she'd downed while doing what Ack called *homework*.

She was only certain of one thing. "He's a red-stripe." *Let that be enough.* "Skull and crossbones. Do not engage. Repeat, do not engage."

The biter wore a black sweater with leather elbow patches, far too heavy for a sticky summer night, and loose workman's pants—looked like Carhartts, plus heavy boots like Pete's, like Ack's, like her own, no doubt steel-toed as well. The beefy bodyguards moving with him had to be human employees, in dark suits tailored almost well enough to hide the shoulder holsters.

Naturally the biter wasn't carrying. He didn't need to, even a young biter was dangerous enough—and if civilians noticed him at all they would assume *bigwig*, maybe *mob boss*, and hurriedly look away.

But she knew what he was. Once you glimpsed what lay under the human-looking shells of a few demimonde inhabitants, nothing was ever the same again. She could swear the strange things all but announced themselves into a microphone; the guys, claiming they didn't see the details, called it 'women's intuition'.

When they weren't mocking her for vivid imagination, that was.

Pete shifted, and something about the movement might have caught the vampire's peripheral vision. The curly-headed monster glanced in their direction, and for a moment his gaze met Layla's squarely. She hurriedly glanced away—sometimes they could hypnotize, and skull-and-crossbones on any file meant serious bad news.

Her small movement did the trick. She finally remembered the name typed on the manila tab, written on the back of the 8x10 glossy.

Oh, no. No. Fucking hell. "It's the one they—" she began, but it was too late.

A high hard *ratatat*, Ben moving in from the alley across the street and spraying the two eastbound SUVs with a short burst. Which meant Steve-o had to back him up, because once the tango started you did your job, hell or high water. Ack no doubt took his shot too, but the crack of his rifle was lost under the sudden, closer noise.

Pete flinched, an instinctive movement jamming her hard against the wall. She didn't blame him a bit—very little was worse than hearing gunfire behind you, except maybe knowing a biter was there as well. Their earpieces howled with feedback, Dan shouting something; it had to be ignored.

Now the lookouts had only one job.

Run, and maybe save their own sorry hides.

Their escape route was a good one—an alley mouth lurked just on the other side of Cactus YaYa's entrance; they'd counted off the steps during daylight and on several other nights during recon. Pete's fingers sank brutally hard into her upper arm; he set his feet and hauled, trying to yank her against a sudden eddy in the crowd.

His grip was torn away and Layla was swept away on a tide of frightened human animals seeking any cover they could, which meant through an open nightclub door barred only by a single red velvet rope. The heavy, polished brass stand it was attached to fell with a clang lost in gun-chatter, pops, and screaming ricochets; it sounded like the biter's bodyguards were returning fire with a vengeance.

Layla's feet dangled a good six inches off the ground; if she went down she'd be trampled to paste. She grabbed blindly, getting a fistful of someone's fishnet shirt plus sweat-slick skin, and was dragged past overturned tables as the human wave crested. The screams almost managed to drown out a high-decibel assault of throbbing line-dancing music. Lights flashed, a migraine attack of whirling red-and-purple sparkles, and the poison of panic flooding through the front door spread through the dance space and packed galleries like ink in trapped water. A burst of stench—restrooms down a long hall to the right—and a puff of skunky weed-smell hit her, receded.

No use looking around for Pete, she was on her own. Fire alarms brayed; someone with incredible presence of mind or simply a modicum of drunken mischief must have pulled a lever, because piercing white strobes were now lighting up over back exits. Two of them, if she remembered the Cactus's layout, and now she blessed Ackerman's dogged insistence that she be the one laboriously going over social-media photos, building a layout of both clubs.

Just to be sure.

Owe you a drink, Ackie. Her bootsoles hit the floor; Layla staggered, yanked free of whoever she'd been clutching. Swept onward again, but she'd managed to aim herself in the right direction; now she just had to pray the fire exits really were in working order—and that she wouldn't be crushed or pummeled within sight of escape.

There was a moment of being squeezed between a woman in a fantastic silver wig and tiny bedazzled cowboy hat matched by a beaded dress clinging to her every Amazonian curve, and a person with a high pink-tipped mohawk and heavy brown beer bottle clutched in one beringed hand, the goddess's breast smashed against the side of Layla's face and the mohawk's hand blindly crawling across her ass—not to grope, but desperately seeking any purchase—before she was spat through a pair of flung-wide fire doors and into the back alley running parallel to 21st, propelled with such force she almost bounced off a bank of dumpsters across the way. The air was only slightly cooler outside, and screams spilling from the club's depths sounded like lost souls in a particularly cinematic hell.

Layla reeled at the edge of the crowd, realized she was going the wrong way to make any planned post-incident rendezvous, and decided to just keep running.

Chapter Two

He almost overlooked her, though Iuppiter's thunderbolt does not miss when a soldier has made his sacrifices and endured long enough. Or perhaps the gods were indeed dead, and it was only blind luck.

A flash like lightning—pale eyes peering shyly over a heavily padded shoulder, like a dryad in deep woods amazed at the woodcutter's intrusion. The soldier's gaze moved on, the rest of him already aware of wrongness in the night—heightened mortal pulses, a faint squeal of static from a certain type of short-range communication device, the subtle sensation at his nape meaning prey had noticed a predator.

Not danger, precisely, merely unfriendly attention.

The soldier almost thought his prey had hired mortal catspaws to distract Father's chosen sword; a silly measure, but ossification often made older sanguinant stupid just as it rendered the young prone to bloodcraze and glut.

Then a stray thread of scent brushed past, sound hurrying after light, storm-roar capable of paralyzing if the flash did not. Electricity was partly tamed nowadays, trapped in switches and wires; still, even in confusing modern times, mortals feared great weather events.

He might have scented her in any case, especially on a

simmering midnight when every exhalation collected in the bowl of concrete called a city street. Yet it was not certain—her kind was, after all, so very rare.

Priceless, in fact. A single breath halted the soldier midstride, images cascading through his skull as he sought to identify the tantalizing odor. Roses, crushed coffee beans, an exquisite stainless musk, all coalescing into those wide grey eyes and straight dark hair pulled ruthlessly back, a glimpse of high-arched cheekbone. There was a mortal male looming before her, leaning close, his hands no doubt roaming over soft curves.

A sudden vengeful snarl contorted the soldier's face, true teeth sliding free as the ever-chained beast roused within his bones. Blinding, utter rage stripped away centuries' worth of dust accreted upon his perceptions, falling like scales from a certain mad prophet's eyes, plummeting like a boy with melting waxen wings.

The assault of fresh colour, sound, other sensation very nearly undid the soldier, an ancient pulse pausing its steady march inside his bone-armored chest. Then a clatter of gunfire began, bullets humming like bees, and mortals began to scream.

For the first time in his long strange existence, the soldier put aside his orders and lawful prey. A new, overriding imperative sank claws into flesh and brain both; he blurred into a light variety of mistform, streaking after something he had never truly believed existed.

There were rumors, of course—*leman*, those fantastical creatures capable of warding aside the slow Gorgon-gaze of accumulating years, a prize every bearer of the Blood longed for. The soldier had never given such tales much credence, despite honouring their telling. After all, if gods and emperors could die, what else might be possible in a wide world teeming with prey?

The challenge was to face Hades with *dignitas*. He had fallen on his sword once, as a mortal. It wasn't so difficult.

She was borne upon the stampede, a jewel amid flotsam. The soldier arrowed overhead, buffeted by noise and various smoky substances, pushing against air-currents, ready at any moment to dive and tear through fragile mortal flesh if his new prize foundered. The sudden, overwhelming acuity of every sense was akin to a fledgling's first nights after full transition, drunk with the wonder of the Blood—yet far, far deeper.

He had not realized how close he trod to true-death. Ossification had stalked him with infinite cat-quiet patience. Even the control and discipline of his work was a trap, though he had sought to remain flexible by engaging with mortal catspaws and dogsbodies far more than one of his age normally did. Of course his duties as Father's head general necessarily had contact with security troops, but few pursued it so actively.

That was also part of the game, each interaction with brief ever-changing mortal creatures an attempt at insurance against the inevitable while longing for the unbelievable. Which had now occurred, albeit not quite in the way he'd ever imagined.

She spilled through a pair of wide-open doors, flung hard enough to clip a corner of the metal refuse-boxes standing sentinel in a spacious, well-brushed alley. He had to restrain a sudden urge to plunge, slip out of mistform, and shield her from the blow, but it was already too late. She was off and running again, quite fast for a mortal. Modern streets were as a rule much cleaner than those of his long-ago youth, yet for a moment he was at the sack of Karthago again, or Korinth, or any of a thousand other cities he had led warriors through.

Screams and wailing rose to foul a night's uncertain peace, though unaccompanied by smoke or cries of murderous joy. The gunfire was fading—his own squad would be withdrawing in good order, knowing well enough to avoid whatever sudden event had necessitated their commander's vanishment. Anything requiring the behavior he had exhibited was above or beyond their own concerns.

They would return to the outpost near the oilfield bearing news, though. And that was concerning. The soldier did not wish to think beyond the current moment, since there was quite enough to do keeping a fleeing leman in sight *and* dealing with the flood of luxurious, unwonted sensation.

He could lose through sheer inattention or mischance what he had just found, unless great care were exercised.

Entirely sumptuous, the layers of deadened emotional callus peeling away as he floated behind her. He could watch while glorying in the freshness, the sheer *newness* of every detail. A clinging black dress with straps over her tender shoulders, the full skirt fluttering as she ran, lovely bare lithe legs and heavy boots, a dark braid swaying as she fled—quite the picture, and he dipped lower as she flagged.

No creature, even a nymph, could run forever.

She turned aside, plunging into a small passageway connecting to yet another alley. Was she familiar with this place? Curiosity was another new hunger, burning all through him. How best to introduce himself? The old rumors were clear upon at least one point—a leman was to be taken at the moment of discovery, or swiftly as possible afterward.

Taken, and bitten. Then claimed.

He dove, slipping out of mistform, booted feet cat-soft meeting cracked pavement. Gliding after her, wholly intent, he wondered if he should pray.

Save that for when she is safe. And have you forgotten him?

The soldier had not begun this night thinking he would find himself at once disloyal *and* possessed of divine good luck, but he was now committed. The thrall had risen, a crimson burst in old, almost-dry veins, and he found not only was he awash in magnificent sensation but also—for the first time in centuries— incredibly physically aroused.

Stiff as a gladius, in fact. The need was pleasant in its sharpness; how long had he been an unthinking automaton?

Now he was awake, aware, *alive*. But just as he decided he had followed long enough, that his new prize must indeed be grasped, she put on another burst of speed.

Her pulse sang—every mortal's heartbeat was unique,

certainly, but hers was music engineered specifically for *his* hearing. He quickened as well, a hawk preparing for the dive, a giant swan ready to descend upon a staggering girl.

I long to know your name, pretty one. So glorious to *feel* again after centuries spent watching the waters of Lethe rise inch by inch upon his frame, trapped in a slowly calcifying body and mind.

Engine-noise, nearby and slowing. A mortal yell.

"Leila! Leila, come on!"

Like a young doe was she, running flat-out as if sensing the predator in her wake. Fists curled, arms pumping, the braid swinging to tap her back, she bolted from the alley and dove into the rear passenger side of a nondescript sedan, quick as a wink. The vehicle barely slowed enough for her to perform the maneuver, yet she did so with grace. One last skirt-flutter, and she was gone.

The soldier paused, struck by unfamiliar astonishment. He recognized another heartbeat within the car, one he had catalogued from sheer habit—the mortal male who had held her against the wall.

Lover? Husband? What true man would let such a beauty wander alone? But mortals were unaware of the rare flowers in their midst—and a good thing, too, lest they make leman even scarcer. Hunting the strange or different was not solely a sanguinant trait, or even confined to the wider demimonde.

Now that he had found such a rare, impossible miracle, everything he had ever heard concerning leman swirled inside him, a collage of tactical responses jostling for selection. It was traditional to remove all encumbrances from a new *aima-glyza,* in order to discourage panicked attempts at escape—and to make their transition to fledgling easier, for the moment she was bitten and claimed the Gift would begin to rise in her flesh.

At least his new objective was almost painfully clear. Father was a problem best solved in due course; the soldier could even anticipate the event with some pleasure.

His chains were now broken, an event any servant longed for, any master feared.

The soldier took to mistform again, and followed the fleeing vehicle.

Order Elder's Prize from your retailer of choice!

ABOUT THE AUTHOR

Lili Saintcrow currently resides in the rainy Pacific Northwest with her children, dog, cat, a half-feral library, and assorted other strays.

https://www.lilithsaintcrow.com

ALSO BY LILITH SAINTCROW

PARANORMAL ROMANCE

Tales of the Sanguinant

Daywalker's Leman

Elder's Prize

Fledgling & Archon

The Watchers

Dark Watcher

Storm Watcher

Fire Watcher

Cloud Watcher

Mindhealer

Finder

The Society

The Society

Hunter, Healer

Sons of Ymre

Erik

Jake

Nigel

SINGLE TITLE PARANORMAL ROMANCE

The Demon's Librarian

Desires, Known

Taken

Incorruptible

Rose & Thunder

SCIENCE FICTION & FANTASY

Roadtrip Z

Cotton Crossing

In the Ruins

Pocalypse Road

Atlanta Bound

Gallow & Ragged

Trailer Park Fae

Roadside Magic

The Wasteland King

HOOD

Season One

Season Two

Season Three

The Dante Valentine Series

Working For the Devil

Dead Man Rising

The Devil's Right Hand

Saint City Sinners

To Hell & Back

Selene

The Jill Kismet Series

Night Shift

Hunter's Prayer

Redemption Alley

Heaven's Spite

Angel Town

The Dead God's Heart

Spring's Arcana

The Salt-Black Tree

The Black Land's Bane

A Flame in the North

The Fall of Waterstone

Steelflower

Steelflower

Steelflower at Sea

Steelflower in Snow

Romances of Arquitaine

The Hedgewitch Queen

The Bandit King

Single Title Sci-Fi & Fantasy

Moon's Knight

Chained Knight

Rattlesnake Wind

She Wolf & Cub

Coyote Run

Harmony

Blood Call

The Marked

Afterwar

ROMANTIC SUSPENSE

Viral Agents

Agent Zero

Agent Gemini

Ghost Squad

Damage

Duty

Gamble

ALT-HISTORICAL FANTASY

Hell's Acre

Hell's Acre

Rook's Rose

The Bannon and Clare Affairs

The Iron Wyrm Affair

The Red Plague Affair

The Ripper Affair

The Damnation Affair

COLLECTED STORIES

Human Tales

More Human Tales

NONFICTION

The Quill & The Crow Vol. 1

HUMOR

SquirrelTerror

Jozzie & Sugar Belle

WRITING AS S.C. EMMETT

Hostage to Empire

Throne of the Five Winds

The Poison Prince

The Bloody Throne

WRITING AS LILI ST. CROW (young adult)

The Strange Angels Series

Strange Angels

Betrayals

Jealousy

Defiance

Reckoning

Tales of Beauty and Madness

Nameless

Wayfarer

Kin